PART OF YOUR WORLD

PART OF YOUR WORLD

ONCE UPON A TIME
IN TEXAS
BOOK TWO

KAREN WITEMEYER

HOPE & LIGHT
PUBLISHING

Scripture quotations are from the King James Version of the Bible.

Paperback ISBN: 979-8-9924205-3-1
eBook ISBN: 979-8-9924205-4-8
Large Print ISBN: 979-8-9924205-5-5

Library of Congress Control Number: 2026904686

This is a work of historical fiction; the appearances of certain historical figures are therefore inevitable. All other characters, however, are products of the author's imagination, and any resemblance to actual persons, living or dead, is coincidental.

Cover by Carpe Librum Book Design.

Books by Karen Witemeyer

Novels

A Tailor-Made Bride
Head in the Clouds
To Win Her Heart
Short-Straw Bride
Stealing the Preacher
Full Steam Ahead
A Worthy Pursuit
No Other Will Do
Heart on the Line
More Than Meets the Eye
More Than Words Can Say
At Love's Command
The Heart's Charge
In Honor's Defense
Fairest of Heart
If the Boot Fits
Cloaked in Beauty
To Love a Beast
Taming Lady Temperance
Part of Your World

<u>Novellas</u>

A Cowboy Unmatched
Love on the Mend
The Husband Maneuver
Worth the Wait
The Love Knot
More Than a Pretty Face
An Old-Fashioned Texas Christmas
Inn for a Surprise
A Texas Christmas Carol
In Her Sights
Star in the West

To Wes.

You took me to see *The Little Mermaid* when we were dating then courted me with a letter filled with the lyrics to "Kiss the Girl" after rewinding a cassette recording about a hundred times. Is it any wonder I wanted to be part of your world? Thirty-four years together, and our love is still growing. You are my happily ever after.

He that trusteth in his own heart is a fool:
But whoso walketh wisely, he shall be delivered.
Proverbs 28:26

Chapter 1

Galveston, Texas
June 1886

"Look, Mama! A mermaid!"

The child's excited call snapped Muriel Quinn out of the mist of her daydreams like cannon fire from a pirate ship. In a blink, she quit treading water and performed a surface dive to hide from the family standing on the pier by the Pagoda Bath House.

Daft girl. Gettin' swept up in dreams and forgettin' where ye be. If Da hears ye been swimmin' near the rich folk's beach agin, he'll lock ye away fer good. Or worse. He'd spear her with one of his disappointed looks. The ones that came with a heavy exhale and sagging shoulders.

It took a lot to make the powerful shoulders of Patrick Quinn sag, and each time she accomplished the feat, it left her soul a little bruised. She hated disappointing her da. Unfortunately, she'd developed a special knack for it. Ever since her eighteenth birthday, when her da decided it was time for her to start acting like a proper lady instead of an amphibious female who spent more time with fish than humans. She'd tried to be more ladylike over the last year and a half, even let her older sisters take her in hand. Well, until they tried to take away her swimming costume. They'd have been more successful asking her to chop off her hair and dye what was left of her red tresses squid-ink black.

Muriel continued her underwater swim in a path parallel to the shore and away from the Pagoda Bath House. Her well-conditioned legs propelled her through the Gulf currents as her arms pulled in perfect harmony. The water hugged her on all sides, offering the cool comfort of a dear friend. No blame resided under the sea. No embarrassment. The fish didn't consider her inferior because her dresses had been handed down from her sisters and rehemmed to hide the wear. The oysters didn't snicker behind their shells at her Irish brogue, and the crabs didn't look at her sideways because her father worked at the docks instead of owning the ships he unloaded. She could be at peace under the sea.

At least until she ran out of air.

Pushing for the surface, she kicked and surged upward, thrusting her head and shoulders into warm daylight as she drew in a deep, gasping breath. A grin stretched her cheeks as she closed her eyes and lifted her face to the sun. Could anything be finer than a long swim on a sunny afternoon?

Muriel rolled to her side and settled into an easy scissor kick with an occasional arm stroke that would draw her west at a leisurely pace that would keep her from tiring on her way to the small, natural cove that served as her private entrance to the Gulf. The cove sat nestled within a secluded inlet on a section of shoreline that possessed more rocks than sand. A place neither locals nor tourists bothered to explore. The perfect location for a would-be mermaid to venture ashore unseen. A necessity if she hoped to avoid scandal.

The high-pitched cry of a seagull echoed overhead, drawing a smile from Muriel. She interrupted her stroke to wave. "Good day to ye, Gulliver. Fancy a fish supper, do ye?"

As if he'd been waiting for her signal, the bird dove toward the water a few yards from where she floated. Wings fluttered against the water's surface, sprinkling water across her face as his beak snatched a fish. In three chomps, the guppy disappeared down the gull's throat.

Muriel laughed. "Such paltry manners. Did yer ma ne'er teach ye 'tis rude to eat in front o' company without sharin'?"

The bird ignored her and paddled several inches to the left before grabbing another fish.

"I s'pose not." Muriel chuckled. "O' course, I'm not verra keen on raw fish, meself. 'Specially morsels with the scales and bones still attached. So 'tis fine fer ye to keep it to yerself." Her legs gave a scissor kick. "I'll leave ye to yer supper. See meself to shore."

The seagull dove again then flapped his wings and launched into the sky. A few seconds later, half a fish fell from above and slapped the water in front of her face. Muriel flinched then burst out laughing.

"So ye *do* have manners!" She rolled onto her back. "Thank ye, kindly, Gulliver," she called. "Ye're a true friend."

Resuming her swim, Muriel added an alternating overarm motion to her sidestroke, in the style named after the English swimmer John Arthur Trudgeon. It would allow her to pick up speed. The sun's position warned that she'd been in the water longer than planned. If she showed up late to choir practice again, there'd be no pacifyin' Da.

Honor and responsibility go hand in hand, me girl. Respect yer obligations. Show that ye can be counted upon. 'Tis how trust is built and maturity is gained. The Lord himself said that the one who is faithful with small things will also be faithful with much. Ye dream of a big life, Muriel, but ye must prove that ye can be a good steward of the humble life ye live now before ye can be trusted with more.

Her father's most recent lecture resonated like a vibrating gong in her mind as she cut through the water. He told her she needed to grow up. Take on the responsibilities of a woman instead of flittin' about like a child. But she had, hadn't she? After the last of her three sisters married nine months ago, Muriel had taken over the chores of running her father's household. Cooking, cleaning, laundry. Did it really matter if dinner was a little late or the table linens not perfectly pressed?

Well, perhaps it mattered when Da invited his supervisor to supper as he had last week. She'd lost track of time while beachcombing with her nephew Fletcher that day. But it wasn't as if she'd been off stirrin' up trouble or anythin' of that ilk. She'd had the house tidied before their arrival and served a tasty meal thirty minutes later. Mr. Barstow even complimented her on her fine cookin'. Course, he'd had to skedaddle after only a few bites. Apparently, he'd had another appointment. Which wasn't her fault. She couldn't be expected to be privy to the man's schedule. Da hadn't seen it that way, though. 'Tis why he'd lectured her so thoroughly afterward. She'd withstood the bluster well enough, but when his shoulders sagged at the end of it, and he'd let her see his disappointment . . . well, her defiance had crumpled, leaving her with stinging eyes and a renewed determination not to let him down again.

But here she was, lettin' her fancies steal her time and slow her progress. She'd merely intended to use the Beach Hotel as a landmark to signal when to turn around and head back to her cove. But the hotel windows had glimmered in the sunlight and set dreams to dancin' in her head like music-box ballerinas. Spinning and twirling in elegant circles.

How she longed to be part of that world. A world of pretty dresses and handsome gentlemen callers. A place filled with servants to tend the chores so a lady could be at her leisure. A leisure she could spend however she chose. Swimming. Singing. Conversing with seagulls. When one had money, one was allowed eccentricities. At least that's what her sister Alana said whenever she told tales on the more unconventional ladies staying at the Beach Hotel where her husband worked.

Muriel understood unconventional. It might as well be her middle name. Yet, being unconventional wasn't a bad thing. Just look at Agnes Beckwith. The woman was a sensation. All the papers carried stories of her remarkable swimming feats. A regular performer at the Royal Aquarium in London, she'd swum five miles in the Thames from London Bridge to Greenwich in a little over an hour at the age of fourteen. The next year she doubled that achievement, swimming ten miles from Chelsea to Greenwich. Two years after that, she swam twenty miles. The woman was incredible, and only six years older than Muriel.

Da estimated the swimming distance to the Beach Hotel and back totaled about six miles. Muriel was no Agnes Beckwith, but if she had more time to train, she might be able to swim the entire length of Galveston Island one day. Maybe then, *her* name would be in the papers. Wouldn't that be grand?

Spotting the outcropping that marked the edge of her cove, she turned toward shore. Unexpected movement caught her attention, and she lifted her head farther out of the water. A small figure stood on the rocks, waving with large, sweeping arm motions. Was that Fletcher?

Her stomach clenched. Had something happened to Alana or one of the wee ones? Kicking her legs at a frenzied pace, she raced for the inlet. As soon as the water shallowed enough, she rose to her feet and waded forward, her tired limbs fighting gravity as well as the tide.

"What's wrong, lad? Has somethin' happened to yer ma?"

Her ten-year-old nephew wagged his head, but the movement brought little reassurance. He continued to urge her to shore with frantic gestures as he cast glances back toward the path that led into town.

"It's old Miss Seward. She's had one of her spells. Told me not to fetch the doctor. Said she'd be fine. But she didn't look fine. She was wheezin' somethin' awful, Muriel."

"Ye did the right thing fetching me." Muriel scrambled up the small beach and pointed to the rock where she'd left her sack of clothes. "Hand over me towel, would ye?"

Fletcher grabbed it and tossed it to her. She snatched it out of the air before it could hit the wet sand and immediately wiped it down her body. The swimming costume she wore had been patterned after the ones she'd seen in artists' renditions of Agnes Beckwith in the papers. Made of dark blue woolen knit, the one-piece garment sported short sleeves and drawers that stopped above her knees.

Da only permitted her to wear it because he knew the current sea bathing fashion for ladies required so many layers and flounces of fabric it would drag a woman down should she do more than play in the waves along the shoreline. He'd given her a boy's suit to repurpose for her use on the condition that she never let anyone outside of family see her wearing it. She'd be dubbed a trollop should anyone catch her in such attire. Alana had pleaded with her to give up swimming once she gained a marriageable age, but seawater ran through Muriel's veins. If Agnes Beckwith could swim in such a costume in front of crowds at the Royal Aquarium, Muriel could wear one in the privacy of the Gulf waters.

What she *wouldn't* do was strip out of said costume in the open, no matter how secluded her cove might be. So she toweled off and squeezed as much water from her hair as possible, then pulled a loose-fitting housedress over her head and fastened the buttons. It would be wet by the time she made it to Miss Seward's home, but it would keep her decently covered until she could change into something more appropriate.

After shoving her feet into stockings and sturdy half boots, Muriel hurried up the rocky path in Fletcher's wake, then ran alongside him down the back roads that led to their friend's house.

Laraline Seward had worked as the head cook in one of the estates on the east end of the island for nigh on thirty years until her health took a turn for the worse. Her doctor called it dropsy of the chest. She'd never married and had no family in the area, so when she lost her position, she moved into a small house around the corner from where Muriel and her da lived. Many in the neighborhood scorned her because of her tendency to brag about her life among the upper crust. Accused her of putting on airs. In truth, the old lady was just lonely and out of her element. A state Muriel understood quite well. Yet she told amazing stories and knew more details about the lives of the fancy folk than anyone else of Muriel's acquaintance, so it hadn't taken long for the two of them to strike up a friendship, one that soon included Fletcher as well. The dear lady might be a bit of a flibbertigibbet, but her heart was pure gold.

Keeping to the less affluent streets on the west side of the city, Muriel and Fletcher wove their way through homes and small shops, moving north toward the wharves. They turned east on Avenue I, ran past Muriel's home on the corner of Thirty-Fifth, and didn't slow until they reached Laraline's small house two-and-a-half blocks later.

Muriel didn't bother knocking. She barged right in and called her friend's name between heaving breaths. "Laraline? Where are you?"

"In . . . here."

Muriel pivoted to the right at the quiet squeak of an answer. After hesitating a heartbeat at the door to Laraline's bedchamber, she passed it by and headed to the kitchen instead. Laraline lived in her kitchen. Sure enough, she found the elderly woman sprawled in a wooden chair at the table, her hand pressed to her chest as if trying to restrain the rattling wheeze leaking from her mouth.

"Ah, Miss Laraline. What a sorry song ye're singin'." Muriel paused long enough to squeeze the lady's hand before heading to the cabinets. 'Twasn't the first time she'd found her friend in such a state. "Don't be fretting now, dear heart. I'll get the kettle on and steam some eucalyptus. You'll be right as rain in a trice."

It took a bit longer than a trice, but once Laraline started breathing the steam, her lungs seemed to relax. Fletcher helped her count out her inhales and exhales, stretching them until the ragged pattern finally smoothed into normalcy.

"Muriel. You're a godsend, child." The pink returned to Laraline's face, a combination of the warm steam and improved breathing. She eased away from the bowl of eucalyptus water and offered a shaky smile as she pushed back a tress of salt-and-pepper hair with a hand gnarled by years of bread kneading. "What would I do without you?"

"Fletcher's the true hero." Muriel tipped her head toward her nephew, who stood a little taller at the commendation. "I wouldn't have known anythin' was amiss without him."

"Sounds like a deed worthy of a reward." Laraline winked at the boy. "Fetch me that thingamajig on the counter, Mr. Fletcher."

Fletcher turned to the counter, his eyes widening at all the possibilities before him. Canisters, jars, bowls, a cabbage, a loaf of bread, a battered tea tin, and something that looked like a fancy butter mold.

"Which . . . ah . . . thingamajig, Miss Seward?"

Laraline waved her hand dismissively. "You know. The one with the whatsit on the side."

Used to deciphering the lady's odd terminology, Muriel moved toward the counter and extracted a large metal tin with pink roses painted on the side. Knowing she wanted to offer Fletcher a reward of some kind narrowed the options. No boy would consider a cabbage prize-worthy. The flour, sugar, and spices could be eliminated as well, leaving the bread, the tea tin, and a jar of strawberry jam as the most likely candidates. However, the old tea tin was the only option with a design on the side—the whatsit. And knowing that Laraline often kept candy inside the box sealed the deal.

Fletcher took the tin from Muriel and set it on the table in front of Laraline. "Is this what you wanted?"

"Of course. Silly boy. Do you see any other thingamajigs on the counter?"

Muriel bit back a laugh and gave Fletcher a small shake of her head, cueing him not to answer. Laraline might not remember the names of things very well, but she sure knew how to use them. Her cooking skills hadn't dulled a whit.

The older woman wrested the tin open and revealed a collection of pralines. "Go on," she urged. "Help yourself."

"Thank you!" Fletcher popped one into his mouth immediately then went back for a second as he chewed.

Laraline laughed. "I've never met a boy yet that could resist my pralines." She glanced up at Muriel and extended the box in her direction. "No girls, either."

Murial smiled and accepted the confection. After her long swim, she could eat half the box, but that wouldn't be ladylike, and she *was* trying to improve in that area.

"Now, Mr. Fletcher. I do believe you stopped by my house for a reason this afternoon, did you not? Do you have some new treasures for me to sort?"

"Yes, ma'am." Fletcher reached into his trouser pocket and dropped a handful of random objects onto the table. He sorted through the items he'd brought, moving aside the hairpin, seashells, and pennies before pushing a round item that looked like a fancy button and a strange metal clip toward Laraline.

She reached for the clip first. "This! Oh, this is quite wonderful. I used to have one just like it."

"What is it?" Fletcher asked.

Anything of value would need to be turned in to the Beach Hotel in case a guest wished to claim it, but Fletcher had amassed quite an assortment of odds and ends since he started combing the beach last year. His collection would soon rival Muriel's.

"This, my boy, is a *chatelaine clip*."

The name rolled off her tongue in a French accent that immediately captured Muriel's imagination.

"Sha-till-ane?" Muriel slid into the chair next to her friend and reached out a finger to touch the silver piece that looked a bit like a spoon that had been bent in half. "What does it do?"

"A lady uses it to keep necessary items near at hand. This flat part is tucked inside the lady's waistband and then delicate chains are attached at the edge of the ornamental piece here. A lady might carry a miniature notebook, a watch, or a vial of smelling salts. Mrs. Trimble wore a sewing chatelaine with a needle case, thimble, and a pair of miniature scissors. Housekeepers use them to carry their keys. I carried one with keys as well—keys to the pantry, spice cabinet, and the hutch where the silver was stored. Mrs. Trimble trusted me implicitly, you see."

"That's brilliant! But how does it work?" Muriel picked up the clip and flipped it over to the back.

"It looks like the chains have broken off of this one. Pity. But see here?" Laraline pointed to a set of tiny metal loops on the sides and bottom. "The chains would hang from those loops, each with a small hook on the end so a lady could attach whatever items she might wish to keep at hand."

Fletcher tapped the pearly circle, drawing their attention to the second item. "What about this one?"

Laraline picked it up and squinted as she turned the bauble over in her hand. "Well, this is a stumper. It's too small for a brooch.

Too big for an earbob. It looks like jewelry of some sort, though. Hmm . . ." All at once her eyes lit. "I've got it! A cuff latch. No . . . link. Cufflink."

Muriel dipped her chin and fingered the buttons running down her midsection. "Do ladies call these bodice links?"

Laraline chuckled. "No, child. Even socialites call those *buttons*."

Muriel's cheeks warmed.

"In fact," Laraline continued, "ladies don't wear these at all. Gentlemen, like Mr. Fletcher here, are the ones who wear cufflinks."

Fletcher frowned at his sleeve. "Why wear something fancy on your sleeve if you're just gonna hide it with your jacket?"

"Good question, young man." Laraline tapped Fletcher's hand. "Shows you have a sensible mind. You know those starched collars that men wear to church on Sundays when they're trying to look their best?"

Fletcher nodded.

"Well, fine gentlemen take that practice a step further and wear starched cuffs as well. They use a cufflink to hold them together at their wrist. You're right about their jacket sleeves covering them up most of the time, but some fellows tailor their shirts to have longer sleeves so just a glimpse of the cufflinks show while they're moving their arms about. I guess it's like a lady sewing lace onto her petticoats and gart—"

"I don't think Fletcher needs to hear about ladies' underthings," Muriel interrupted, wishing she could reach across the table and cover her nephew's ears. Gracious. The things that popped out of Miss Laraline's mouth. Alana would be appalled. She already thought the lady was quite—

"Cuckoo." The little bird poked his head out of Laraline's clock and announced the top of the hour. "Cuckoo. Cuckoo. . ."

Muriel jumped to her feet. It couldn't be five o'clock already. Surely not. Yet as her gaze latched onto the tiny white bird launching out of its little house over and over to announce the time, the truth dawned in horrifying clarity.

Choir practice.

Da was going to kill her.

Chapter 2

Muriel dashed home, changed clothes, and dragged a comb through her sea-snaggled hair before hying off to Grace Church. She slowed to a walk as she neared the front of the building, not wanting to burst into rehearsal completely out of breath. Yet it appeared she'd not be bursting into anything, for a familiar, stone-faced man stood sentry at the church entrance. Arms crossed. Legs braced apart. All that was missing was an iron spear in his hand.

"Da? I'm late fer choir practice. Would ye mind steppin' aside?"

There was no steppin' to be had. Her da offered plenty of glowering, though, as he blocked her path. So immovable was he that not even his long, white beard dared waver in the afternoon breeze.

"There *is* no choir practice, Muriel. Everyone left when their soloist failed to show up."

Muriel's throat tightened. "Everyone's gone?"

Her attention slunk away from her father's angry eyes and stared at the door behind him, wishing she could see through the wood and discover her da was mistaken. That her fellow choir members had just taken a break and were even now gathering near the pulpit to resume their rehearsal.

"Brother Crabtree ran through the piece fer twenty minutes, ever hopeful that ye'd honor yer responsibilities and make an appearance. But after half an hour, the poor man's optimism waned, and he dismissed the crew." Da uncrossed his arms and waved them about as if a strap wound tight inside him had snapped. "Do ye have no care for anyone but yerself, Muriel? Can ye not heed a clock when others are relyin' on ye, girl? People sacrificed their time to come to this rehearsal. To support *you*. And how do ye repay their gift? With irresponsibility and selfishness!"

Muriel winced at the shout, and her chin began to quiver. Da rarely raised his voice to her, and never in public.

His hand balled into a fist as he fought to control his temper. Inhaling a slow breath, he steadied himself before continuing. "An hour ago, I bragged to all the men at the docks that my daughter would be singing a solo on Sunday. Men slapped me on the back and said they'd cover the end of my shift so I could come to the final rehearsal and hear me wee girl sing. But did me darlin' girl bother to show up? Nay. She took a swim instead." His gaze focused on her hair, still wet beneath her hat. "She flitted about in the sea, ignoring her commitments, assumin' all would be forgiven."

"That's not fair, Da! Laraline Seward had one o' her spells. She needed help. *That's* why I'm late." Well, that and the fascinating discussion afterward about cufflinks and chatelaine clips. She hadn't *meant* to get so distracted. It just . . . happened. "Fletcher was waitin' fer me at the cove when I finished me swim. He told me of her trouble, and we hurried to Miss Seward's house straightaway."

Her father's bushy brows arched in surprise. "Is she well?"

"Aye. Her breathing settled after I made some eucalyptus steam for her."

"Glad I am to hear it." Da relaxed his stance. "And how's young Fletcher?"

The knots inside Muriel's belly loosened as her daddy's sympathetic nature exerted itself. "Ah, he's fine as frog hair. Eager to show his latest discoveries to his friends, no doubt."

Da's eyes lit with a smile. "What has the scamp uncovered this time?"

"The most amazing things! Did ye know that wealthy ladies sometimes wear a special clip tucked into their waistbands to carry keys and sewing things around with them? Fletcher found one. The little chain pieces had broken off, but the clip was in fair shape. It had a fancy design in the center like a piece of jewelry. Just think, instead o' carryin' necessities in yer pocket, ye could let them dangle on the outside in tiny silver cases. Wouldn't that be grand?"

"Not so grand if it falls off at the beach and gets lost in the sand."

Muriel patted the waist of her practical, navy-blue skirt and imagined it was made of fine, white linen. "Miss Seward said that ladies rarely wear them outside their homes. 'Twas surprisin' that Fletcher found one."

Da raised a brow. "What's surprisin' is that ye and Fletcher would pester Miss Seward with questions while she was feelin' poorly."

"Oh, she was feelin' much better by the time Fletcher brought out his treasures."

"So you had yerself a nice visit with Miss Seward then?"

"Oh, yes. It was quite..." Muriel didn't realize she'd stepped into a trap until her da's eyes narrowed into angry slits. She wagged her head from side to side. "I'm sorry, Da. I didn't mean to lose track o' time. Honest. I just got swept up in Miss Seward's stories and—"

"No more excuses, Muriel." Da sighed, and his shoulders fell in the dreaded sag of disappointment.

Muriel grew a little queasy.

"I've indulged yer whims far too freely. I don't doubt yer good intentions, daughter, but good intentions alone are as worthless as a leaky dinghy. Ye need self-discipline. Restraint. The sailor who fails to keep his lifeboat in good repair during fair weather will be left to sink when the storm hits. I don't want that for ye."

Her heart pounded in her chest. "I'll do better, Da. I promise."

He laid a hand on her shoulder, and she felt the heaviness of it all the way to her toes. "I know you will, Muriel, because there'll be no more daily swims until you prove to me that you can be responsible."

No swimming? He couldn't . . .

Mist covered her eyes. "No, Da. Please." She blinked, praying for him to reconsider. "Ye can't take the sea away from me. *Please*!"

His eyes glowed with regret, but his jaw held firm. "It's not forever, darlin'. Just until ye learn to be a woman others can rely upon."

His words wounded her heart nearly as much as his punishment. Did he really think her flighty and irresponsible? Tears pooled in her eyes, making her vision blur. She kept his house, cooked his food, did his washing. Did that count for nothing?

"Muriel . . ."

She turned to him, begging him with her eyes to relent. To be reasonable.

Torture etched his face, and hope kindled within her breast. Until he spoke.

"The sea's not goin' anywhere, dear heart. It'll wait for ye to get this figured out."

He reached out to touch her arm, but she jerked away.

"How can ye do this?" The accusation fell from her lips in a broken whisper. "The sea is my life."

"That's the problem, Muriel. Ye live in the sea and in yer dreams. Not in the place that matters most."

Choking on a sob, Muriel ran from the church, the ache in her heart so big, not even her beloved sea could fill it.

"Is it seaworthy?" Zane Erickson's father eyed the small sailboat the servants had just wheeled out of the shed with skepticism.

Zane ignored his father's dour mood and ran his hands over the weathered hull with reverence. "It will be when we get done with it. Right, Grandpa?"

"Yep." Grandpa Clem chuckled. "Happy twenty-fourth birthday, my boy."

Zane turned from the boat and embraced his grandpa. "Thank you!" He pounded the old man's back then retreated a step, his grin stretching so far his cheeks ached. "This is amazing! How long until we can launch her, do you think?"

"I bet we can have her shipshape in a week or two. Johnny down at the boatyard assured me the planks were solid. No woodworm or rot. She just needs a good sanding, a bit of caulking, and a nice coat of varnish before you take her out."

Horace Erickson shook his head. "I don't understand why you didn't just buy him a new one, Pops. For pity's sake. We can afford an entire fleet of catboats. This . . ." He waved a dismissive hand in direction of the single-mast vessel. ". . . pitiful excuse for a sailboat will make Zane a laughingstock among his peers."

Grandpa Clem raised a brow at Zane's father. "Maybe among *your* peers, but not among mine. Not among Zane's either. Besides, you know how much the boy loves to build things. Who am I to deny him that pleasure?"

"Who are *you*? You're the father of the most successful trader at the Galveston Cotton Exchange. As patriarch of this family, you have an example to set and a position to uphold."

Zane looked from his father to his grandfather, strains of an old and unresolved argument vibrating through the air between them. Grandpa Clem had grown up on a cotton farm, inherited the land, then expanded his holdings until he could afford to buy his own cotton gin. The expansions continued until he owned seven gins throughout south Texas. Zane's father sold the gins and invested in cotton shipping, tripling their profits. But like his father before him, he wasn't content to stop there. He campaigned his way into a position at the Exchange, one that earned the Ericksons a place among the wealthiest families in Galveston. He'd worked hard cultivating relationships until he possessed the political clout to run the cotton market, giving him the prestige and power to look down on those who worked with their hands instead of their heads.

Men like Grandpa Clem. Men like Zane.

Thankfully, Grandpa Clem had long ago decided not to play Father's verbal games. So, he thumped his son on the shoulder and shot Zane a wink. "You're the patriarch, son. Not me. I'm just the eccentric old man who likes to dig in the dirt and buy his grandson odd birthday presents."

Grandpa Clem retreated then, collecting a glass of lemonade from a servant before taking a seat on the iron bench near the base of the large magnolia tree at the heart of Mother's perfectly arranged garden.

Father blew out a heavy breath but didn't argue, a blessing Zane appreciated.

"I love the set of drafting tools you and Mother gave me, too, you know." Zane grinned at his father, just in case his excitement over the catboat had pricked his sire's pride. "Not even Mr. Clayton's case is as fine. The tooled leather is exquisite."

"Yes, well, it was your mother's idea. She, too, knows how much you like to build things." A note of sourness colored his voice, but Zane chose to ignore it.

"Perhaps, but if it weren't for your connections, I never would have had the chance to apprentice with Mr. Clayton. The man is one of the greatest architects of our age. You've given me an opportunity I never could have manufactured on my own."

His father stood a little taller and gave one of the haughty sniffs he'd perfected to keep others, including Zane, in their place. "I still wish you had the sense to follow me into the commodities business—so much more lucrative, you know—but if you are bound and determined to eschew my advice and follow your own path, I'm glad I could ensure that path winds through exalted territory."

Exalted territory? Good grief. How did Father manage not to choke on such oversized pomposity? Zane bit his tongue, not wanting to ruin the day by starting an argument. He'd learned long ago it was best not to challenge his sire directly. The man's mind couldn't be changed, anyhow. At least not by Zane.

"I *am* grateful to you, Father." Zane forced a half-smile to his lips before turning away and seeking less stuffy air.

He *was* grateful. His father's wealth had afforded him opportunities and privileges most people never experienced. Education. Connections. Money to indulge his passions. Had he not traveled with his family through Europe during his teen years, he might never have fallen in love with architecture. The Classical columns of Greece and Rome. The vaulted spires of Gothic cathedrals. The symmetry of Renaissance designs. The lavish opulence of the Baroque period. His heart came alive when gazing upon such wonders. He marveled at the engineering, lost his breath at the beauty, and longed to bring a design of his own to life one day.

Nicholas J. Clayton had already designed dozens of buildings and established himself as a master. One had only to look at his extravagant work with Galveston's Beach Hotel to see his genius. Wealthy men engaged him to design their homes, yet he also took on work for churches and school buildings. These were the projects that most stirred Zane's interest. Buildings intended to serve the public, not just a single family. Buildings designed to draw a person's attention toward something bigger than himself. Toward a purpose. Toward the holy God.

"Zane, darling. Are you having a good time?" His mother floated toward him, looking splendid in a gauzy white dress perfectly suited to the summer weather. She smiled as she handed him a glass of lemonade. "I wish you had allowed me to invite a few guests. I worry you'll grow bored at your own celebration with only ancient family members as company. You should have more young people about."

More young *women* about, she meant. She'd been on a mission to find him a bride ever since she turned fifty last fall, as if she were afraid she'd die before seeing her grandchildren.

"You and Father are far from ancient, Mother." Zane accepted the lemonade then leaned in and bussed her cheek. "Besides, I thought it would be nice to have a quiet family gathering this evening. Max is getting a group together to take me skating down at the Beach Rink tomorrow night. His father rented out the entire place for us."

"How lovely! I do hope Max is inviting several young ladies to attend as well. I'm not sure I trust you boys not to get into trouble if left to your own devices."

Zane chuckled softly. When Mother dropped hints, they landed with all the subtlety of bricks squashing his toes. "There will be plenty of young ladies there, Mother. Don't you worry. Mrs. Trimble is as anxious to find a match for Max as you are for me."

"I have a great deal of esteem for Catherine Trimble. In fact, she recommended a professional to me who has promised to assist us in our search."

Assist in their search? Their *bride* search? Zane's throat constricted as he took in his mother's gleeful expression.

"What *kind* of professional, Mother?"

Please let it be a tailor or a dance instructor or even a French linguist. Anything but . . .

"A matchmaker, of course."

Chapter 3

Octavia Underhill selected a blush pink rose in full bloom from the basket of flowers her maid had brought in from the garden and slid it into the center of her arrangement. She adjusted the greenery, the other roses, and the smaller clusters of white cosmos and lavender verbena until she found the perfect balance. Stepping back from the vase, she examined it from all angles, refusing to be satisfied until every petal and frond complied with her wishes. Octavia demanded perfection—from her students, her staff, and most of all, from herself.

One didn't amass a small fortune by being careless. Controlling one's fate required controlling one's environment and the people populating it. A talent Octavia always had possessed. At least when it came to servants, young schoolgirls, and society mothers eager to make advantageous matches for their children. Powerful men presented more of a challenge. Hence her preference to avoid conducting business with them. All the posturing and condescension affected her digestion. Yet an entrepreneurial woman must endure certain unpleasantries from time to time if she wished to ensure the success of her business. And Octavia craved success above all else.

She frowned at the stubborn rose leaf that refused to submit to her will. Taking up her pruning shears, she snipped the leaf off at the stem and discarded it. Disobedience could not be tolerated. Satisfied with the result, she set aside the shears, clasped the cut crystal vase with care, and carried it to the small parlor table her maid had set for tea.

"Vanessa." Octavia called to her maid without looking away from the vase. "Clean up the rest of the flowers then check that Cook has the canapés and madeleines ready. Our guest will be here in twenty minutes."

"Yes, ma'am." The young woman turned her face toward Octavia and nodded, her hands already busy tidying the side table littered with stems and unused flowers.

Vanessa had trained with her since she was fifteen. Now twenty-one, she'd had ample experience anticipating her mistress's needs. Not only that, but she'd become quite adept at collecting gossip and hints of scandal from the households of potential clients. Servants always knew far more than their employers realized. And when properly compensated, they often found the motivation to learn even more. Desk drawers just happened to fall open while being dusted, and extra polish was applied in rooms where nearby conversations could be overheard. Vanessa had developed keen insights for determining which servants could be bribed and which should be avoided. A skill that allowed Octavia's matchmaking business to flourish and kept Vanessa's family out of the poorhouse. Octavia paid her a commission for each secret that successfully hooked a client, and with a widowed mother and four younger brothers and sisters at home, Vanessa unearthed scandals faster than the tide unearthed seashells.

"Use the small silver platter with the delicate scrollwork, and arrange the treats in an alternating pattern."

"Yes, ma'am." The dark-haired maid bobbed in understanding. "I'll use the measuring stick for precise placement."

Octavia smiled. "Excellent. I'll inspect your work after I take a short respite."

Passing through the parlor doorway into the hall, Octavia allowed herself a small sigh. Perfection was exhausting. Yet necessary. She would have been penniless by now had she not learned to monetize her position in society.

Her late husband had provided her with status and a fine home, but little else. Certainly not affection. Clive Underhill had been forty years her senior when she'd married him at eighteen. Thankfully, he'd had the decency to die early. She'd only had to endure his attentions for a decade before his heart weakened enough to give out. Unfortunately, his bank account gave out with similar speed. In less than ten years after his passing, her inheritance had dwindled to dangerously low levels.

She could have married again. Most women in her position would have. Heaven knew, her ample curves drew enough masculine attention even now at the advanced age of fifty-five that she could have had her choice of partners in her prime. But Octavia had no wish to submit to the control of another man. So much better to captain her own ship.

As much as she adored the power and prestige she'd carefully cultivated over the last decade and a half, the path she walked was a lonely one. Hard to establish friendships when one's existence relied on carefully guarded secrets and manipulative maneuvering. Thankfully, humans weren't the only option when it came to companionship.

Octavia reached the conservatory at the end of the hall and eased the door open, careful to watch for escapees. Spying none, she slid into the room and closed the door behind her.

"Poopsies," she called in a sing-song voice. "Mommy's here."

A smock hung on a hook by the door, and Octavia slipped it on over her lavender batiste gown. Reaching into the smock's oversized pocket, she fingered a couple scraps of dried meat and extracted them. Vanessa made sure to replenish her supply when she cleaned the sand box in the corner and repaired any damage her pets might have done to the room.

Pursing her lips, Octavia made kissing sounds as she hunted for her little darlings. "Machi. Velli. Mommy has treats for you."

Potted ferns and draping ivy had transformed the ordinary sunroom into an adventuresome habitat, complete with rolled carpet tunnels and plush sleeping cushions. Cabinets with doors purposely left open and a sideboard with every other drawer exposed created stair steps as well as the hiding places her pets adored.

She reached into her other pocket and pulled out a bell wheel. Crouching on the wooden floor, she set the cast-iron toy on the boards and rolled it into the middle of the room. The bell housed in the metal ball between the two wheels jingled a merry tune.

"Come out and play, my little bandits," she sang.

Velli shot out of her carpet tunnel, her brown and white elongated body navigating the narrow space with ease. She launched herself at the bell toy, making guttural squeaking sounds as she hopped and pounced. Not to be outdone, her brother Machi scampered out of the sideboard drawer where he kept his hoard of stolen stockings, feathers, thimbles, ribbons, and buttons. His black overtones and larger size gave him the advantage as he tackled Velli and playfully nipped at her neck, but his sister had a few tricks up her ferret sleeves. She pushed the wheeled bell with her head and sent it rolling in the opposite direction then outraced her brother to reach it first.

Octavia chuckled softly. "Well done, Velli. I applaud females who use their heads to best a man. Or a hob, in this case."

She extended her right hand toward Machi, holding the meat where he could see it. His little black nose twitched before he forfeited the bell contest and moved in for a different prize.

"There's Mommy's good boy."

Velli had the most energy and offered the most entertainment value, but Machi was the best cuddler. And at this moment, Octavia required soothing more than levity. Machi accepted the dried meat from her fingers and munched on the treat. While he was distracted, Octavia scooped him up and carried him to the cushioned chair in the center of the room. The floral-patterned upholstery was in embarrassingly poor shape. Small tears and dozens of puncture wounds from ferret claws marred the fabric while scratches and teeth marks scarred the wood. Yet the padding conformed to Octavia's hips and back in a way that provided sufficient comfort, making it the ideal choice for this room.

Rubbing Machi's sable-soft fur against her cheek, Octavia lowered herself into the chair and exhaled a long breath. Clearing her mind of all the details surrounding her afternoon appointment, she focused instead on the silky texture of Machi's fur. Arranging him in her lap, she offered him another scrap of dried meat to munch on while she stroked his pelt, keeping one hand tucked beneath his belly to keep him from bounding away without permission.

She slowed her breathing and turned her attention inward. Calm. Soft. Easy. Smooth. Worries slid away with each rub of Machi's fur. She stroked her pet just as she planned to stroke her guest's ego. Soothing him. Letting him think he was in control, while she secretly orchestrated things behind the scenes. He'd be putty in her hands, just like Machi. Wooed into doing her bidding by a few tasty treats and a bit of petting. Everything would be—

Velli pounced from the arm of Octavia's chair into her lap, her slender masked face aglow with mischievous delight. Machi squirmed out of Octavia's hold, unable to resist the lure of playtime. The two ferrets scampered down her smock then dashed about the conservatory like a pair of overzealous circus performers.

Ah, well. Ferrets would be ferrets, she supposed. She'd return after tea with Velli's favorite peacock plume. Perhaps the rambunctious lady would settle enough for a cuddle session of her own after a game of snatch-the-feather. The furry imps tended to enjoy a late afternoon nap before perking up around dinnertime.

Octavia rose from her chair, pulled her arms from the smock's sleeves, then returned the protective garment to its hook by the door.

"You two behave yourselves in here. Mommy has a meeting to attend."

Octavia left the conservatory and climbed the grand staircase to the second floor then glided down the hall to her bedchamber. Once there, she tugged upward on the gold chain around her neck—a chain she never removed. Not because of something so maudlin as sentiment. Heaven knew, she felt no lingering attachment to Clive. Her parents, either, for that matter. After all, they were the ones who bartered her to a man more than twice her age in exchange for access to his steamboat line. No, she wore no locket or jewel at the end of this chain. She wore something of far greater worth. A key.

As the chain pulled free of the modest neckline of her bodice, she clasped the small brass key, enjoying the rush of power that swept through her at its touch. She crossed to the rolltop desk in the corner of the room, bent over its cover, and fit the key into the lock. A quiet click met her ears, bringing a smile of satisfaction to her face. Straightening, she opened the desk and retrieved her most prized possession. A journal. Ordinary on the surface. Plain, brown leather. Unadorned. Innocuous. Yet inside, it brimmed with secrets. Secrets people paid her very well to keep. Whispers of scandal. Corruption. Even criminal activity. The currency of her enterprise.

And the reason Mr. Horace Erickson was coming to tea.

"Let's get down to business, shall we, Mrs. Underhill?" Mr. Erickson moved his crumb-filled plate to the side, braced his elbows on his chair arms, then laced his fingers in front of him. His eyes gleamed in a predatory fashion that would have intimidated a less-experienced woman.

Octavia, however, had cultivated an immunity to such posturing. "Gladly." She offered him a pleasant smile as she met his gaze with confidence. A flash of annoyance lit his eyes, and it was all Octavia could do not to preen. "I assume you wish to discuss the terms of the matchmaking agreement your wife and I arranged yesterday."

"I do." He leaned forward, his gaze narrowing. "I wish to nullify the agreement and cancel your services."

Octavia clicked her tongue as she gave her head a gentle shake. "I'm afraid that won't be possible. Your wife signed the contract. It cannot be undone. Not without significant penalty." She widened her gaze and blinked in a parody of guilelessness. "Did she not show you the document? I would expect an experienced businessman like yourself to understand the nature of contracts. They are rather binding, you see."

"Do not condescend to me, madam. I am quite aware of the nature of contracts." His posture stiffened to such an extreme that even the hair in his sideburns seemed to stand at attention. "I'm also aware of the nature of blackmail. No court will uphold a contract such as yours. Extortion is illegal."

Octavia patted the table between them in a conciliatory fashion. "We both know you'll not be taking me to court, Mr. Erickson. Not if you want your secret to stay between us. Sure, you might ruin me by taking such action, but you'll ruin yourself in the process. Do you really think you'll be able to keep your seat at the Cotton Exchange when word gets out that you've been manipulating the market to line your own pockets? I'm not the only criminal sitting at this table, am I?"

The flat of his hand came down with enough force to rattle the silver tea service. "You go too far."

"My reputation as a matchmaker is impeccable, Mr. Erickson. I've access to girls from some of the wealthiest families in the south. Even as far north as Chicago. I can match your son to a young woman with a pedigree that will elevate the Erickson name to equal standing with George Sealy or W.L. Moody."

There it was. The glint of ambition. The aspiration for greatness.

Octavia smoothed a wrinkle from the tablecloth. "I'm a broker, not so different from you. Instead of connecting cotton suppliers with European textile mills, I connect young men of good standing with daughters of the socially elite. And like you, I take a commission. Each client is given the opportunity to pay my full fee upfront, though most choose to pay in installments. Understandable since there is no guarantee that a marriage will take place. As much as I would like to, I cannot force two young people to marry. That is the parents' responsibility. What I *can* do is provide opportunities for them to spend time together and form an attachment. All of which requires considerable effort on my part. Hence my need for insurance. What's to stop a mother from reneging on our bargain and refusing to pay the remainder of my fee once the introductions have been made? That is why the secrets are necessary. They guarantee that all payments will be made in a timely fashion. And once the full amount is satisfied, I *never* ask for more. I'm a reputable businesswoman. Do you really think that people would continue to recommend my services to their friends if that was not the case?"

"What about the Gladstones? They left the island in disgrace after an article appeared in the paper detailing Robert's involvement with a smuggling operation. You ruined him."

Octavia shrugged. "He ruined himself. He was the smuggler, not I. He also chose not to adhere to our agreement. I gave him several opportunities to pay what he owed. He opted to ignore my reminders. Decided to gamble and call my bluff." She locked eyes with Mr. Erickson. "I don't bluff."

She expected him to squirm at least a little, but he surprised her by hardening his expression. "Neither do I."

What did he mean by that?

"I don't know where you ferreted out your information about my business dealings, but I assure you, it is a pack of lies based on nothing more than rumor and slanderous speculation from those who wish to unseat me. My wife has no intimate knowledge of my work at the Exchange and, frankly, wouldn't understand it even if she did."

Octavia stroked a flawlessly manicured fingernail around the edge of her saucer. "I find that men often underestimate the intelligence of the women around them. Perhaps you should give your wife more credit. She might not be privy to the business conducted within the walls of the Exchange, but she hosts your business dinners, cultivates relationships with the wives of your partners, and notices when you come home with new, diamond cufflinks." She aimed a pointed glare at her guest's wrist where something rather glittery peeked out from beneath his coat sleeve.

"She obviously thought you capable of such practices or she never would have signed the contract."

Mr. Erickson's mouth tightened. "She would have signed anything to find our son a bride. She's obsessed with the idea." He shook his head. "Thankfully, she's also loyal and told me everything. Including that you had her write this so-called secret into a journal and sign her name to it."

"That is correct. Having the secret in the owner's handwriting allows for confirmation. I wouldn't want anyone to accuse me of slander."

One of his eyebrows twitched. From nerves? Guilt? Or the impulse to reach across the table and strangle her where she sat? Hard to tell. But one thing was for certain, she was under his skin. Exactly where she wanted to be.

"My wife also informed me that once the final payment is made, you will tear the page from the journal and burn it."

Octavia dipped her chin. "Yes. Once the contract is fulfilled, the evidence is destroyed. The owner is invited to bear witness to the burning."

Mr. Erickson rose to his feet and stalked toward her. Octavia's throat tightened as if his fingers had already closed around her throat. She forced herself to remain seated, however, her features smooth and unconcerned. The chances of him actually accosting her were quite small. Not in her home with servants to bear witness.

"I want you to burn it," he demanded as he stormed over to her chair. "Now."

Did he think she would give in to his wishes simply because he loomed over her? Octavia shot him a scathing glare as she slowly gained her feet. "I already explained that wouldn't be possible. The only way to dispose of that page is for you to pay the full amount up front."

"I'm prepared to do that. Five hundred dollars, isn't it?" He pulled an envelope from inside his coat pocket. It bulged in a quite delicious fashion.

"Five hundred fifty," she corrected.

"Right." He looked far too cocky for her peace of mind.

She tipped her head and studied him, suddenly wary. "I'll need to count it." She extended her palm.

He moved the envelope toward her then jerked it back. "Not until I see the journal."

"You don't trust me?" She batted her lashes.

He raised a brow. "Not even a little."

She sashayed around him toward the bookshelf that lined the wall behind where he'd been sitting, a location always within her field of view. Feeling his gaze burning a hole in her back, she crouched down to reach the shelf second from the bottom. She slid the journal from between two outdated copies of *The Farmer's Almanac* and returned to the table.

"Show me the page," he demanded, waving the envelope between them.

Standing well out of his reach, she opened the journal to his wife's page then turned it outward for him to see. She pressed the back of the journal against her breast, keeping it close as she tightened her hold.

She gestured with her chin toward the table. "Count the money where I can see it. When you're done, I'll remove the page, and we can trade."

He opened the envelope, held up a fifty-dollar bank note for her inspection, then counted out ten more upon the table.

Her heart raced faster with each one.

"Now, the page."

Octavia raised her voice. "Rogers. Come in here, please."

Her butler entered the room a moment later, a burly former sea captain who wasn't adverse to using his fists when called upon to protect his mistress.

"Yes, madam?"

"Keep an eye on our guest while I prepare his documentation, would you?"

He gave a nod then planted himself between her and Mr. Erickson.

She crossed to the small desk in the corner and removed a penknife from the drawer. She laid the journal on the desktop, extended Mrs. Erickson's page upward, then carefully cut it free of the binding. After tucking the penknife back into the desk drawer, she held out the removed page.

"Rogers, you may make the exchange." She still didn't want to get too close to Mr. Erickson. Not while her instincts continued to fire warning signals.

Her butler approached and collected the page. Then, before she realized what had happened, he snatched the journal from the desk with his other hand.

"What are you doing?" She jumped from her chair and grabbed for the journal, but he tossed it to Mr. Erickson with a flick of his wrist before she could reach it.

"No!" She chased the flying volume. That journal was her life! But she made it only two steps before her butler captured her arm and wrenched it behind her back. "Ow! You oaf. Let go of me!"

She kicked at his shins, but he ignored her paltry efforts to inflict pain and inflicted more of his own when he clasped her second arm and forced it behind her back to join the first. Holding both of her wrists with one meaty hand, he pulled something from his pocket. A cord. One he used to bind her wrists before forcing her into a chair.

"Vanessa! Help!"

"She and Cook are a bit tied up at the moment." Rogers stood above her, arms crossed.

Octavia kicked his shins again on principle. "You mutinous pirate. How could betray me like this?"

Horace Erickson strutted forward. "For money, of course. Isn't that what drives us all?" He took two of the fifty-dollar bills and handed them to Rogers along with something that looked to be a train ticket.

Next, he retrieved the page containing proof of his misdeeds that had fallen to the carpet while her butler had been busy manhandling her. He folded it into a tidy square, slipped it into his pocket, then returned to gloat with a smugness that turned her stomach.

"I'm renegotiating our deal, Mrs. Underhill. You will still find a suitable match for my son, only instead of the price you arranged with my wife, your payment will be the return of your journal." He opened the leather book and flipped through her carefully organized pages. "Oh, and just to make sure you are properly motivated, I will grant you four weeks to find a promising match. Every week that passes after the deadline, I will contact one person from your extortion list and inform them that their debt has been canceled. I imagine they'll consider me quite the hero."

The man turned from her and whistled as he exited her house. Whistled! Horrid man. A scream of frustration welled within her, but Octavia refused to give it voice. She'd not succumb to such weakness. Victims surrendered to hopelessness, and she refused to be anyone's victim. *She* controlled her destiny. No one else.

Besides, Erickson had made a grave error. He'd given her four weeks to plot. He might as well have handed his demise to her on a silver platter.

Chapter 4

Muriel sat on one of the large rocks that sheltered her secret cove and gazed out over the Gulf of Mexico. The salty tang of the ocean air filled her lungs and the breeze whipping her hair from its pins made her eyes water. It was the wind causing her tears, not self-pity. Not a soul-deep craving for what remained out of reach.

The cry of a seagull overhead called her bluff as the first tear rolled down her cheek.

Fine. It *was* more than the wind. She scrubbed at her eyes impatiently with the heel of her hand and sniffed in a decisive fashion. Feeling sorry for herself wouldn't help her situation. Her da had given her a challenge, and she aimed to meet it. To prove herself so dependable that he'd have no choice but to reinstate her swimming privileges.

She'd apologized to Mr. Crabtree and arrived early to services last week for a replacement rehearsal with the choir. She'd poured her heart into the gentle strains of "In the Sweet By and By," engaging with the words in a way she hadn't before. Mr. Crabtree had even dabbed his eyes at the end of her solo.

Singing had always been as natural to her as breathing or swimming, and without realizing it, she had taken it for granted. The notes came easily, requiring little effort on her part. Everyone complimented her vocal range and purity of sound. They called her voice angelic. Heavenly. A beautiful instrument. A rather apt description, seeing as how she approached making music much like an instrumentalist. Her voice became a trilling flute, a belting cornet, or a soaring organ. Lyrics served as a vessel for the melody. They were not *part* of the music. Not until her da's reprimand had brought her some perspective.

Heart full of grief and contrition, she'd been susceptible to the words of the hymn she performed in a way that had never penetrated her more carefree self. Words about the sweet perfection of heaven drew her inward-focused gaze upward to a loving Father and his promise of rest. A place of music and no sorrow. A place likened to a beautiful shore.

Her favorite verse rose in her mind as she gazed upon the ocean, and she sang it softly, just loud enough to be heard over the wind. Emotion clogged her voice, but she sang through it, her soul needing the balm of the words.

> "We shall sing on that beautiful shore
> The melodious songs of the blest;
> And our spirits shall sorrow no more-
> Not a sigh for the blessing of rest."

She *was* blessed. Blessed with music. With family. With a home by the sea. Blessed with a heavenly Father who exhibited endless patience and an earthly da who loved her enough to expect more from her than she expected of herself.

These last two weeks had been excruciating. Two weeks without the sea. No swimming. No boating. She'd not even dipped her toes in for a quick wade. Not that her da would have forbidden such a harmless escapade, but because she didn't trust herself to withstand the temptation of having a taste without diving in for the full experience. Two weeks of battling envy as tourists and sea bathers swarmed the beaches and pavilions. Two weeks of tedious clock watching and responsibility. Two weeks of beating down the resentment that flared whenever her da praised her efforts yet refused to reunite her with the water she loved.

I know I've let ye down, Lord. Let Da down. I've been selfish. Seekin' me own pleasure with little care for how me choices impact others. I know there be more to life than swimmin' and better uses of me time than dreamin' up fairy stories 'bout livin' in a fancy house with a handsome prince I'm not likely to meet. Yet . . . ye made me with a hankerin' for the sea and a body shaped for swimmin'. Surely ye formed me this way for a reason. Ye don't seem the type to make mistakes. So what am I supposed to do? Be who ye made me to be, or be what Da wants me to be? 'Tis a puzzle, fer certain. One that leaves me in a muddle. Is there a way to be both? If so, I'm gonna need ye to show me. I haven't had much luck findin' it on me own."

One of the hymns the choir had been rehearsing this week sprang to mind, and a chord struck in her spirit, demanding she give it voice. With no one around to hear, outside of God and the gulls, Muriel rose to her feet and sang from the heart, holding nothing back as she sought the Lord's guidance.

"Jesus, Savior, pilot me,
Over life's tempestuous sea:
Unknown waves before me roll,

Hiding rock and treach'rous shoal;
Chart and compass come from Thee-
Jesus, Savior, pilot me!"

Zane piloted his newly refurbished catboat through slightly choppy waters, grinning as the mainsheet swelled with the wind and sped him along the Galveston coast. Manning the tiller from a bench in the stern of the boat, he laughed aloud at the thrill of racing across the Gulf at speeds rivaling a galloping horse. Better than a horse, for a boat didn't tire. As long as the wind blew, the boat ran. And how he loved it!

Freedom. Complete and utter freedom. No matchmaking mama trying to tie him down, no father glaring in thinly veiled disappointment, no meticulous mentor evaluating his every measurement. Just a man and the sea.

And a song?

A woman's voice carried on the wind. A sweet, pleading call. Heartfelt and beautiful. Zane adjusted the tiller to steer the bow more into the wind, feathering the sail to forfeit power and slow the boat. He scanned the shoreline, seeking the source of the song, like a sailor falling prey to a mythical siren. Something about that voice stirred his soul and set his heart to pounding an irregular rhythm.

"Wondrous Sov'reign of the sea,
Jesus, Savior, pilot me!"

A hymn? Even more intrigued, Zane urged his boat nearer the shore. There. She stood on a rocky outcropping. A woman dressed in dark blue, arms open and raised, hair whipping about in the wind. Red hair? It was hard to tell from this distance, but it seemed to absorb the sunlight and catch fire.

His hand grew lax on the tiller, his attention riveted not only by the music but by the passionate woman in the throes of worship. In a low voice, he joined her song for the third verse, the words familiar yet somehow new as he softly blended his tenor to her soprano.

> "When at last I near the shore,
> And the fearful breakers roar
> 'Twixt me and the peaceful rest-
> Then, while leaning on Thy breast,
> May I hear Thee say to me,
> 'Fear not – I will pilot thee.'"

She repeated the final phrase, taking liberties with the notes like an opera diva, elongating some, trilling others, rising in a crescendo as she turned the music skyward, climbing up instead of down the scale until she hit a note of such purity, he rose from his seat, wanting to climb with her. The climactic tone rang through the air, raising gooseflesh on his arms. Slowly her arms lowered, and a change came over her. A stillness. Like a startled rabbit. She'd seen him. He felt the connection between them, even though he couldn't make out her features from this distance.

He stood there, watching her as she watched him, neither of them moving, the moment fraught with meaning too heavy to set aside. Then the wind gusted from a different direction, rocking the boat and whipping the long, horizontal pole supporting the bottom of the sail violently over the cockpit. Zane tried to duck, but it was too late. The wooden boom crashed into the side of his skull and launched him overboard.

A gasp tore from Muriel's throat as she witnessed the young man topple over the side of his boat. A knock on the head of that strength would surely render him unconscious. Without aid, he'd drown. A vice tightened across her heart.

Scrambling down the rocks to her cove, she tore at the buttons of her bodice. If she was to get to him, she couldn't be hindered by heavy fabric. She stripped down to her chemise and drawers as quickly as possible then ran into the surf.

Please let me reach him in time.

God had made her a strong swimmer. *For such a time as this.* Just like Esther in the Bible. She could do this. She *had* to do this.

Muriel cut through the water at top speed, pulling her arms, kicking her legs, ducking her face into the sea. Each time she took a breath, she sighted the boat, but she stayed on her original course, trusting her training to keep her on a straight line. The wind would draw the boat off course, moving away from its submerged captain.

Lead me to 'im, God. Don't let him drown. Please.

Coming even with the boat, she ceased swimming and scanned the water for signs of the white shirt he'd been wearing. A wink of something white tickled the edge of her periphery. She whirled to her right just in time to see a shoulder sink out of view.

No!

Muriel dove underwater. She had to find him. Save him. The salt stung her open eyes, but she pressed on. A glimmer of white caught her attention. She surged downward and clasped the man's arm. Thank the Lord! Hauling him to her, she positioned his back against her chest, wrapped an arm across his torso beneath his arms, then kicked for the surface. He offered no assistance, but the ocean gave them added buoyancy, and after a final, powerful kick, Muriel broke through and drew in a deep breath. No such breath echoed from the man in her arms.

Get him to shore. Ye can get him breathin' again if ye get him to shore.

Refusing to consider any other outcome, she lay backward, rolling him with her. She positioned his head to ensure his chin remained above the water line, then aimed them for shore, modifying her sidestroke to accommodate a passenger. Urgency added power to her kicks, and as they neared the shoreline, the tide gave them an extra push. Muriel adjusted their trajectory west of her rocky cove, knowing she'd need a flat, sandy area for him to lie upon.

Her feet touched sand, and a prayer of gratitude seeped from her soul. Keeping his head and shoulders supported, she dragged him out of the surf, using a wave to propel him as far up the small beach as possible. Hurrying around to his head, she hooked her hands under his arms and dragged him a few more inches away from the water before plopping down on her rear. It would have to be far enough.

Not only had Da insisted all his girls learn to swim, he'd taught them the basics of resuscitation. A skill she'd never thought to need. Five years of rust fell away in an instant, as memories of practicing the Sylvester Method on her sister Alana rushed to the forefront of her mind.

Muriel positioned herself on her knees at the young man's head and leaned over him to grab hold of his wrists. She lifted his arms over his head, stretching backward to expand his lungs as she brought his arms down along the outside of her knees. Then she leaned forward, using his arms like a giant lever. As she neared his chest, she encouraged his elbows to bend, and pressed his wrists into his ribs to compress the lungs as if he were exhaling.

She repeated the motion over and over, to the point of fatigue. Tears pooled in her eyes as hope faded.

"Ye can't die. Ye hear me?" Her voice choked. "I won't let ye."

As if she had any say in the matter. Only God could save him. All she could do was keep pumping his lungs, and she would. Until she collapsed.

Please, God. Help him breathe. He's too young to die.

He looked to be only a few years older than her. Slender. Arms well-muscled but alarmingly limp. Thick black hair cut short and dusted with sand framed a face with a straight nose and strong jaw.

She stared at him as she folded his arms and pressed against his ribs, her movements slowing as her muscles burned.

"Breathe," she pleaded.

She leaned backward and pulled his arms back over his head. She couldn't stop. No matter how exhaustion tempted her to succumb. He could be someone's husband. A father to wee ones. A beloved son. If someone had rescued her da or young Fletcher, she'd want them to persevere. Not to give in to weariness. Not to forfeit hope.

But he lay so still and pale. And his full lips carried a bluish tint. *Please, God.*

Her stomach twisted, but she kept on. Stretch and squeeze. Stretch and squeeze.

A muscle in his neck twitched. His eyelids fluttered.

Muriel sucked in a breath as a spurt of energy surged through her, renewing her vigor as she manipulated his arms. "Come on," she murmured. "Ye can do it. I *know* ye can. Breathe, mister. Breathe."

A gurgle sounded, so startling her, she dropped his arms. They fell into the sand at his sides, but as she reached to reclaim them, his chest rose of its own accord. Her heart pounded in her breast as hope gained traction. He began to cough and sputter, his chin wobbling.

Muriel jumped to his side, grabbed the shoulder farthest from her, and rolled him toward her, turning his face to the sand. The water he'd swallowed would need a place to go.

His coughs worsened into choking, but the sound was a heavenly music to Muriel's ears as water heaved out of him. He inhaled a gasping breath as shudders shook his body. She leaned over him, rubbing his arm and back, doing anything she could think of to warm and soothe him.

He sputtered and coughed, but he breathed too. Raspy, ragged, beautiful breaths.

Thank the Lord!

"That's it," she praised as she rubbed circles into his back. "Easy now. In. Out. Ye can do it."

As desperation gave way to relief, Muriel slowly became more aware of her situation. The wind chilled her damp skin. Skin clothed in naught but wet underclothes. Underclothes that had plastered themselves to her body, likely hiding nothing of what lay beneath.

"Zane!" A masculine voice shouted above the wind.

Muriel's head jerked up, and she twisted her neck to scan the grassy knoll. An older man carrying what looked to be a pair of binoculars in one hand ran toward them. She glanced down at herself and groaned. She might as well be naked.

The man in her arms had yet to open his eyes, but that could change at any moment. His lashes were fluttering, and his color was starting to return. She bit her lip then looked back toward the man hurrying down the beach. He'd be upon them in moments. She had to go. Surely, he'd lend her mysterious boatman aid in her absence.

Out of time and options, Muriel launched to her feet and fled for her cove, praying the newcomer would be too concerned for the man he called Zane to pay her any mind.

Chapter 5

"Zane. Can you hear me, son?" A firm hand pounded Zane's back. "Please, God, let him be all right."

Grandpa Clem?

Awareness crept over Zane in tiny increments. He was lying on his left side, his neck at an awkward angle, as if he'd lost his pillow. A cough seized him, one that made him sputter and gasp. Alarm shooting through him, he struggled to open his eyes. Shivers wracked him. Why was he so cold? He tried to sit up, but he couldn't seem to find the required energy. Another cough came, bringing something slimy with it. He grimaced and spit it out. At least he could manage that much. Not without a protest from his throat muscles, though. They ached something fierce.

Wait. Hadn't there been a woman? A hazy recollection tickled his mind. A lilting voice. An urgent plea. And . . . a song? He furrowed his brow, trying to capture the memory. But like an unhooked fish, it wiggled out of his grasp and disappeared.

"Zane? Open your eyes, boy. Come on."

He obeyed, but the simple action proved remarkably difficult to accomplish. "Grandpa Clem?"

His body chose that moment to make him aware of a hundred different aches all at once. Ribs. Head. Calf. Big toe. He squinted against the sunlight and groaned. "What . . . happened?"

"Thank the Lord." Tremors laced his grandpa's voice, signaling the seriousness of the situation.

Zane finally managed to tighten his stomach muscles enough to lift his head and shoulders from the ground. His grandpa immediately wrapped an arm around his shoulders in support and helped him sit up.

As Zane found his balance and his bearings, details began to filter through the fog in his brain. He sat on a beach. Sand coated his trousers, forearms, and probably a dozen places outside his field of vision. The tide licked his boots as it moved in and out, making him aware of his soggy state. The wet sand beneath him. His soaked clothes. Dripping hair and skin. A breeze whooshed over him, worsening his shivers and invalidating the sun's warmth.

"Here."

Heavenly heat enveloped him as his grandpa's coat covered his back. But when Grandpa Clem tugged the flaps of the coat under Zane's chin, he jostled Zane's head. Pain erupted inside Zane's skull. He hissed and pulled away.

"Sorry." Grandpa Clem eased back, then frowned as he examined the side of Zane's head. "You've got a good-sized gash above your ear." He sat back on his haunches. "Stars and garters, Zane. I thought you were a goner when I saw that boom knock you overboard. What were you thinking, taking your eye off the sail? I taught you better than that."

"There was a woman standing on a knoll near the edge of the water . . . singing . . . I think. My memory's still a little fuzzy." Zane turned his head slowly and blinked to bring his grandpa's face into focus. "She had the most incredible voice. Like an opera singer, but more . . . down-to-earth. She sang a hymn." A smile tugged the edge of his mouth upward. "I joined in for a verse, not that she could hear me. But after the final note, our eyes met, and something powerful just . . . hit me."

"The boom's what hit you, you numbskull." Grandpa Clem shook his head at him, but his tone had lost its heat. "Since when have you ever let a woman distract you? To hear your mama talk, you're impervious to feminine charms. Even the musical ones."

Because music wasn't meant to be stiff and formal, a mere checkmark on the list of wifely qualities a man of standing should appreciate. Music was supposed to evoke emotion—joy and melancholy, peace and tension. What he'd heard on that knoll had been so raw it had riveted him.

"Hers was no drawing room recital. It was worship. Authentic, heart-wrenching worship. Private and powerful. She didn't sing to impress. She sang because her spirit overflowed. It was . . . mesmerizing." He turned to peer at the top of the nearby knoll, but if the woman had been there earlier, she was gone now. Zane sighed. "Either that, or I hallucinated the entire experience after getting knocked in the head." He reached up and gingerly prodded the bloody knot a couple of inches above and behind his left ear.

"She weren't no hallucination." Grandpa Clem turned his attention toward the knoll as well, only his gaze seemed focused on the rocky outcropping near the water. "I saw her, too."

Imaginary billiard balls ricocheted through Zane's chest. She was real! Which meant she could be found. An influx of energy zinged through his lethargic limbs.

"I'm pretty sure she's the one who pulled you out of the water."

"What?" Zane turned back to his grandpa. He hadn't even considered how he'd ended up on the beach. All his concentration had been centered on remembering how to breathe and cataloguing his injuries. His gaze swung to the Gulf and landed on the small white boat bobbing several hundred yards from shore.

"How could it have been her? She'd not been attired in a bathing costume. She'd worn a normal-looking blue dress, and, I assume, all the necessary layers beneath it. Even an accomplished swimmer would have sunk with all that sodden weight. She couldn't have rescued me. Could she?"

Even as he made the denial, a flash of memory returned. A feminine voice urging him to breathe. A gentle touch rubbing his back.

Grandpa Clem shrugged then moved around to Zane's back and grabbed him beneath his arms. "I can't say if the woman you saw on the ridge was the same one who rescued you or not, but there was definitely a woman next to you on the beach." He tightened his hold. "Let's get you up."

With a grunt to match Zane's groan, Grandpa Clem levered his grandson to his feet then slid to his side to provide support. He kept one arm wrapped firmly around Zane's torso. A good thing, since Zane was pretty sure he would have crumpled back to the sand if left on his own.

"What did she look like?" Zane asked, craving as many details as possible about the woman.

Grandpa Clem chuckled softly as he set Zane in motion toward the carriage that waited at the edge of the beach. "My eyes ain't what they used to be, but I'm sure she weren't wearin' no blue dress. If I had to hazard a guess, I'd say she was in her underthings. Probably why she scurried off the moment as she spotted me trottin' down the beach. I was more focused on you, truth be told, but I can tell you one thing. She had bright red hair."

"That's her! It has to be. The woman on the knoll had red hair, too."

"Maybe it was. Or maybe you've got a red-headed guardian angel watching over you. Either way, I'm right thankful she pulled you out of the drink. I ain't ready to lose my favorite grandson."

Zane smiled as they neared the buggy. "I'm your *only* grandson."

Grandpa Clem winked as he positioned himself to help Zane onto the carriage seat. "That you are. So no more near-fatal accidents, you hear? I don't have any grandsons to waste."

"Deal." Zane grabbed hold of the mounting handle near the bench, then twisted his face back toward the sea. "What about the boat?" He didn't want to lose it. He and Grandpa Clem had put too much work into it.

"I'll send some lads to fetch it. Right now, I'm more concerned with getting you home and fetching the doctor."

Zane couldn't argue with that logic. A warm bed and a headache powder sounded rather wonderful at the moment.

Yet as the buggy rolled down the road, it wasn't thoughts of home that filled him with longing. No, it was thoughts of the mysterious woman who had saved his life. He scoured the knoll for any sign of her as they drove past. The fact that he found none did nothing to dilute the desire building within him.

He wanted—no, needed—to thank her. And after that? Well, if she happened to be unattached, he just might make his mother's dearest wish come true. If the lady proved amenable.

I don't know how, he silently vowed, *but I am going to find you.*

Muriel peeked her head out from behind a rock and scanned the beach for any sign of the man she'd rescued or his Grandpa Clem.

Neither one was anywhere to be seen. Thank heaven. She'd worried the older man would try to find her once he'd confirmed his grandson's well-being, but it seemed he cared more about getting the young man named Zane to a doctor than searching out the woman who'd inadvertently caused his grandson's accident.

Zane. 'Twas a name she'd not heard before. She liked it, though. It seemed to fit the young man she'd pulled from the water. Strong and straightforward. Focused. On her.

How her breath had caught when she'd opened her eyes to see him standing in his boat, staring at her. Not in a leering way. She'd been on the receiving end of a few of those stares when she wandered along the docks, looking for her da. Zane's attention had been different. Curious and full of appreciation. For a single heartbeat, her soul had felt connected to his. And then the untended sail swung across the boat and whacked him in the head.

Muriel sent another prayer heavenward on the young man's behalf, pleading for healing.

She'd never quite understood how a person could pray without ceasing until today. Every breath she'd breathed over the last hour had carried a petition on its wings. Petitions the Good Lord, in his mercy, had seen fit to grant thus far.

As she made her way home, prayers for Zane continued to dominate her mind and heart. It felt strange to be so consumed with thoughts for a man she'd never met before today. She didn't even know his last name. Yet Zane didn't feel like a stranger. He felt like . . . a part of her. A part that had begun to ache after being separated from him.

'Tis just because ye shared a near-death experience with the fella. It'll fade with time.

That's what Alana would say. Sensible, level-headed Alana. Muriel had been trying to think more like her eldest sister of late. Seemed the easiest way to train herself to act in a responsible fashion. Alana excelled in responsible behavior. Of course, she also excelled in bossing and nagging and disappointed sigh heaving, but Muriel didn't plan to take things far enough to suffer from those unfortunate side effects. However, as she skirted behind buildings so as not to be caught with a bodice dampened by wet underclothes and a coiffure reminiscent of tangled seaweed, she couldn't make the Alana logic stick.

Yes, she'd been through a harrowing experience with a stranger, but something more than the rescue bonded her to him. Perhaps their connection stemmed from the admiration she'd heard in his voice as he'd explained his encounter with her to his grandfather. Or the fact that he'd witnessed her soul, exposed and raw, and had drawn nearer instead of turning away. Whatever it was, she doubted she'd be forgetting Mr. Zane any time soon.

As visions of a dark-haired young man swam through her mind, she failed to notice the scowling features of the older man standing in her kitchen until she nearly ran him down.

"Da!" She sucked in a startled breath and hopped backward. "What are ye doin' home?"

He raised a brow and shot a pointed glance at the salt pork sizzling in the skillet on the cookstove. "Makin' supper, since me daughter couldn't be bothered with the chore." He shoved the skillet to the back of the stove with a clatter and turned to face her fully, his head wagging in a sorrowful manner. "Why, Muriel? Ye'd been makin' such fine progress. Why'd ye disobey me?"

"I didn't!"

"Yer hair is drippin', me girl. Ye can't expect me to believe that ye weren't swimmin' in the sea."

"It wasn't like that, Da. I swear! There was an accident near the cove. A man in a small boat took his eyes off the mainsail. When the wind shifted, the boom walloped him in the head and knocked him overboard. No one else was around. I had to go in, Da. He would've died!"

Her da's eyes widened then narrowed as he took in her damp bodice and dry skirt. "Ye swam out to an unknown man in yer . . . yer . . . unmentionables? Heaven's breath, child. Have ye no sense?" His hand trembled as he reached for the back of a chair. "Ye coulda been . . ." His words trailed off as he rubbed a hand down his face and over his beard.

"Would ye have me leave the man to drown?"

"Yes! If it meant ensurin' yer safety."

Pierced by the quaver in his voice, Muriel stepped close and placed her hand atop his where it gripped the back of the chair.

"I'm safe, Da. God protected me. Ye need not fear."

He grabbed her about the waist and pulled her into a bearish hug. "I can't help meself from fearin' for ye, girl. Ye're me daughter. If anythin' were to happen to ye . . . I don't know what I'd do."

Tears stung her eyes as she burrowed her face into her da's chest and soaked in the love he squeezed into her. After a moment, he released her and leaned back.

He cleared his throat. "So . . . ah . . . what became of the young lad? He survived, I take it?"

A pride-filled grin stretched across her face. "He did. I remembered yer training. Pumped his lungs until he coughed out the water trapped inside. For a while, I didn't think he'd make it." Her chest clutched again at the memory, and unexpected tears moistened her eyes. "I didn't give up, though," she said, her voice cracking. "I kept on and on until he finally breathed on his own."

"Of course ye did." His tender smile loosened the last of the knots in her stomach. He smoothed her hair from her forehead. "I've heard tales of mermaids rescuing sailors at sea. I guess I should expect nothin' less from me own little mermaid. I'm proud of ye, Muriel."

His praise warmed her from the inside out. "Thanks, Da."

Then his expression sobered, and Muriel's stomach twisted anew.

"But ye can ne'er tell a soul about what ye did today. It would ruin ye. And if ye ever see that lad about town, ye're to turn away and walk in the opposite direction. Do ye hear me, daughter?"

She nodded. "Yes, Da."

I hear ye, but I can't promise to heed ye.

For if she ever saw Zane again, walking in the opposite direction was the last thing she intended to do.

Chapter 6

"Did you really almost *die*?" Wilhelmina Davis blinked at Zane from across the table at Forbes's Confectionary, her brown eyes rounded in fascinated horror as she blinked at him above the rim of her ice cream soda glass.

"Yep." Zane fit his mouth to the straw of his chocolate soda, hoping the young woman would take the hint and pursue a different avenue of conversation.

His brush with death had made him annoyingly popular. When Max had shown up at Zane's door with Miss Davis and Miss MacArthur in attendance, his mother couldn't shoo him out the door fast enough. *Go have some fun*, she said. *It'll be good for you*, she said. A rather odd turnaround in attitude since she'd sent Max away earlier that morning when he'd shown up on horseback to invite Zane for a ride along the beach. Mother had insisted Zane needed his rest. Yet when his friend returned with females in place of horseflesh, Mother suddenly pronounced him recovered.

To be fair, treating a pair of ladies to a trip to the soda shop required much less physical stamina than riding, though his mental stamina was draining with alarming speed. Probably due to the fact that Wilhemina and Constance were eyeing him with the same morbid fascination one entertained when beholding a sword swallower.

Constance MacArthur scooted her soda glass aside and bounced forward to the edge of her seat. It seemed she'd only been consuming her ice cream out of polite courtesy and was now ready to establish her true purpose in coming—interrogation.

"Did you see heaven? What was it like? Was it shiny? Were the streets really paved with gold?" Questions shot out of her like notes from a music box that had been wound too tight. "My mama says heaven is filled with pearls and all manner of gemstones. That's why she loves visiting the Shaw Jewelry Company. Says it makes her feel closer to heaven."

Zane blinked, his mouth growing lax over the straw. Had she really just compared heaven to a jewelry store?

He gave his head a little shake, thankful that the throbbing from his injury no longer plagued him after a full week of recovery. "I'm afraid I can't comment on the aesthetics of heaven, Miss MacArthur, as I didn't actually visit. While I came close to death's door, I failed to walk through it."

"Oh." Her shoulders slumped and her bottom lip protruded in a pout. "That's a shame."

"Constance!" Wilhemina's shocked gasp reverberated in the air like a Chinese gong.

"What?" Constance frowned then rolled her eyes as she realized her faux pas. "Oh, for pity's sake, Willie. I didn't mean anything by it. Obviously I'm glad Mr. Erickson didn't perish. I simply thought it a missed opportunity to learn about the afterlife.

There's no harm in wishing he'd crossed over to the great beyond before safely returning to the physical plane." She looked to Zane and batted her lashes in a flirtatious bid for amnesty. "You didn't take any offense, did you, Zane?" She reached across the table and touched his hand.

He ordered his fingers into a strategic retreat, tasking them with napkin retrieval to avoid prolonged capture. Ever the diplomat, however, he offered his encroacher a friendly smile. "No offense whatsoever, Miss MacArthur."

And his mother wondered why he'd never shown interest in any of the young ladies of his acquaintance. What could possibly go wrong with marrying a woman who had no qualms about a man visiting the great beyond if it meant appeasing her curiosity?

Zane caught the apology in Max's gaze a heartbeat before it turned to amusement. Zane had to look away from his friend as his own amusement ballooned in response. Laughter begged to erupt, but he doubted the ladies would take kindly to such a reaction.

"Well, *I* heard that you were saved by a mermaid." Wilhemina batted her lashes in a way that did nothing to help him squelch the laughter inside him. "I'm sure it's just the superstitious ramblings of a drunken sailor, but wouldn't it be remarkable if it were true? Max told us that you don't know who rescued you. Is that still true? Surely, as you've healed, some level of memory returned." She leaned closer and more eyelash batting ensued. "Tell me, Mr. Erickson. . . Have you remembered anything about your rescuer? Anything at all?"

So she could add whatever he revealed to the already churning rumor mill? The amusement he'd been battling died a swift death as the need to protect his mysterious rescuer rose with surprising ferocity.

Zane shook his head, hoping the ladies couldn't detect the clenching of his jaw. "Nothing substantial, I'm afraid." Which was true. All he had were hazy impressions. Strong hands. A lilting voice. A comforting touch. And the red hair. "By the time my grandfather arrived, my rescuer had disappeared."

Wilhemina giggled softly. "Perhaps it *was* a mermaid, and she swam away before—"

The rest of Wilhemina's sentence failed to register in Zane's mind, for at that moment a woman with striking red hair passed by their window. He shot to his feet. Glasses rattled and females squeaked, but he barely noticed.

It was her. Certainty resonated in his soul despite the fact he had not a shred of evidence to support his assumption.

He half-tripped over his chair in his hurry to extricate himself from the table.

"Zane?" Max tossed a curious look his way as he steadied the soda glasses in front of the ladies to ensure nothing spilled upon their summer-white gowns.

"Sorry," he mumbled. "I saw someone I need to speak to." And she was nearly out of his line of sight. "I'll be back in a moment."

He rushed to the door and out onto the boardwalk. Stretching his stride as much as he dared, he wove through the stylish folk meandering along Market Street, offering frequent apologies when he clipped an elbow or kicked the back of someone's shoe in his hurry.

There! She stood at the corner, her smiling profile visible as the woman at her side pointed to something across the street. Zane glanced in that direction. A music store. Of course that would make her smile. Because she was the siren from the shoreline.

He grinned as he hastened forward, his gaze fixed on the woman in the simple shirtwaist and dark blue skirt. He had no idea what he'd say to her but he'd figure it—*oomph.*

Something rammed into Zane, or rather, *he* rammed into something. A portly fellow exiting a cigar shop. The unsuspecting bystander teetered on his heels, a hairsbreadth away from toppling backward onto his rump. Zane grabbed his arm to steady him.

"Terribly sorry, sir. I'm afraid I didn't see you there." He tugged the middle-aged man forward until he caught his balance, the smell of pipe tobacco wafting up from the man's coat.

"Goodness me. That was a near miss." The fellow offered a good-natured smile as he straightened the hat that had collided with Zane's shoulder. At least that's what Zane suspected had happened, judging by the narrow, brim-shaped bruise that seemed to be forming along the top of his upper arm. "No harm done, though, thanks to your quick reflexes, young man." He clapped Zane's shoulder, directly atop the bruised area.

Zane winced slightly but quickly turned the grimace into a smile. "Glad you came out unscathed, sir."

He craned his neck to peer around the man, and his stomach clenched. Where was she?

"Yes, well, I should have looked before leaping, I suppose." He chuckled. "Reminds me of the time I nearly found myself flattened by a runaway wagon. The owner had failed to set the brake, you see, and it started rolling backward down the cobbled street . . . I say, you might want to slow down a bit." His voice rose as he realized Zane had darted around him mid-sentence. "There are women and children about, you know. Have a care!"

Zane *did* have a care—a care for finding his missing redhead. He reached the corner where he'd last seen her standing. He peered ahead to the next block but spied no one wearing a simple dark blue skirt. Most of the ladies wore ruffled pastels and carried parasols. He glanced to his right, down Twenty-First Street. No sign of her. He turned to his left. Nothing. His heart pounded a frantic rhythm. She must have gone into a shop. But which one?

"I tell ye, Muriel. These fancy folk get the strangest notions." Alana shook her head as she scoured the shelves of the third bookshop they'd visited that afternoon. She kept her voice low, but nothing could dim her exasperation. "Five copies. Five! Who on God's green earth needs five copies of a book called *The Haunted Hotel*?" Her finger halted on a spine bearing the name Wilkie Collins. "As if working at the Beach Hotel wasn't strange enough already, now Liam has to endure a gaggle of gothic, ghost-lovin' grannies. It's ridiculous!"

Muriel slapped a hand over her mouth to mute her guffaw. "Gothic, ghost-lovin' grannies? Oh, Alana. Yer too funny."

A reluctant smile twitched the corners of her sister's mouth as she pulled a thin volume from the shelf then reached for a second copy. "Well, next thing ye know, they'll be asking Liam to supply bedsheets to hang from the ceiling of the private parlor where they plan to discuss their—Ow. Muriel? What is it?"

Muriel's fingers dug into Alana's arm, all thoughts of gothic grannies evaporating the moment a dark-haired man with strikingly familiar features stepped in front of the shop window.

"'Tis him." The whispered words echoed like a shout in her mind.

"Him who?"

"*Him*." Muriel sighed her answer, which was really no answer at all. Yet her sister must have deduced her meaning, for Alana grew still and joined her in staring out the window.

Mercy, but he were a handsome lad. Lookin' far better than he had upon their last meeting. Fine color in his face now, black hair wavin' about in the breeze instead of plastered to his head, and his eyes . . . Ah, those eyes. They were captivatin'. Hard to tell the color from several feet away and through a pane of window glass, but they gleamed with life, a fact that stirred gratitude in her heart. And not a little longing. His gaze swept the area in search of someone.

Someone important to him, judging by the intensity etched into his features. How she wished she could be the one he sought.

His face turned her direction, and her heart leapt. She held her breath. Would he see her? More importantly, would he recognize her? If he did, what would he do? Muriel's breath shallowed as she imagined his eyes widening with delighted surprise. He'd hold up a hand, signaling her to stay where she was, then he'd charge into the bookshop and find her among the shelves. He'd take her hand and place a kiss of heartfelt gratitude upon her knuckles. Then he'd peer into her face and confess his undying—

"Ack!"

Alana yanked Muriel downward so hard, she lost her balance during her plummet and fell against the bookcase, bruising her hip. The unit wobbled precariously, and Muriel thought for sure the gothic grannies were about to gain two new ghosts for their collection—a pair of shelf-squashed sisters. But the bookcase steadied and spared them a ghastly demise.

Muriel shot Alana a scowl. "What'd ye do that for?"

"I was protectin' ye, ye gooseberry."

"Protectin' me? Ye nearly bludgeoned me w' a bookcase." Muriel rubbed the sore spot on her hip as she tried to rise, but her daft sister yanked her back down.

"Not yet. He might still be there."

She prayed he was. Muriel tugged her arm free of her sister's grasp and gained her feet. Giddy anticipation pushed a smile onto her face as she searched the boardwalk outside the shop window, but he was gone. Her smile fell. She ducked around the shoulder-high shelves, made her way to the window, and peered out in all directions. A triumphant shout nearly escaped her when she spotted the back of a dark-headed man in a pale gray suit crossing the street toward the music shop.

Perhaps he'd found who he'd been looking for. She should be happy for him. So why did instinct demand she give chase?

She stepped toward the door, but Alana blocked her way.

"Ye can't go after him, Muri." The sympathy in her sister's eyes did little to soothe Muriel's rising temper. "He could ruin ye."

"He wouldn't do that!"

"How do ye know? Ye know nothin' about him." Alana kept her voice pitched low, but fervency wove through every word she uttered. "Did ye see the suit he was wearin'? I see suits like that every day when I visit Liam at the hotel. He's from money, Muriel. Above our station. He might be a gentleman who would thank ye fer savin' his life, or he might be the type to take advantage of a girl with stars in her eyes and romantic fancies in her heart. I know ye've been spinning daydreams about the man, but ye need to let him go. Nothin' good can come from it."

"Ye don't know that." Muriel jutted her chin. "Ye think I'm silly and naïve, but I felt something when our gazes locked before he fell overboard. Something powerful. I can't explain it, but I can't ignore it, either. I won't."

Alana sighed. "I know that look. Ye'll not be talked out of this folly, will ye?"

Muriel shook her head.

"Be careful, pet. People aren't always what they seem."

"I know."

Alana clasped Muriel's palm and squeezed. "Hold tight to the Lord's hand, Muri, wherever this takes ye. And if ye need me, I'll be there. No matter what. Yer me sister, and I love ye."

Muriel squeezed her sister's hand in return, her voice thick with emotion. "I love ye, too, Alana. And I promise I'll keep my wits about me."

Alana smiled a gentle, motherly sort of smile. "See that ye do."

Muriel gave her sister's hand a final squeeze then dashed out of the bookshop and hurried across the street to the music store. She searched the entire store, even climbed to the second floor where the pianos were displayed, but her quarry had disappeared.

Undeterred, Murial exited the music shop and turned right on Market Street. She might have missed him today, but all was not lost. She'd learned something valuable about him, something to aid her search. Muriel might not possess the connections to find a gentleman living among the East End elite, but she knew someone who did.

Chapter 7

"Muriel? I didn't expect to see you today. Did I forget you were coming?" Laraline Seward's brow puckered, but she opened her door wide in welcome anyway.

"No, ma'am." Muriel gave the older lady's arm a soft squeeze as she stepped inside the cottage. "Ye forgot nothin'. And if it be a poor time for me to be payin' a call, just say so, and I'll skedaddle. I can seek yer advice on the morrow." Though she hoped it didn't come to that.

Her heart had swollen to painful proportions the moment she spotted Zane outside the bookshop, and the tightness had only grown worse the longer she went without finding him. She wasn't completely sure she'd make it to tomorrow without something in her chest springing a leak.

"You know you're always welcome here, child. I just wish I'd known you were a-comin' so I coulda thrown some cookies in the oven first."

"As tasty as yer cookies be, Miss Laraline, that's not why I came. I need yer help."

"Then you'll have it." Laraline lifted her chin like a soldier awaiting orders. "Whatever you need."

Something *did* spring a leak then, though it was in Muriel's eyes, not her chest. Of course, her chest felt pretty warm and mushy at the moment, so maybe there'd been a leak there too.

Muriel threw her arms around Laraline and hugged her tight. The retired cook sputtered a bit then patted Muriel's back with her gnarled hands, obviously unaccustomed to spontaneous displays of affection.

"Well, get in here and close the door before the chickens decide to move in."

Muriel chuckled as she gave her cheeks a quick swipe with the back of her hand. "Yes, ma'am."

As they often did, they found their way to the kitchen. Laraline had a small parlor, but she'd lived too long in a kitchen to feel comfortable elsewhere. She gestured for Muriel to sit, then lifted a cloth off a nearly new loaf of bread, cut two slices, and slathered both with butter before carrying them to the table.

Muriel forced her impatience into the bouncing leg she kept hidden beneath the table and smiled as she accepted the offering. It was a physical impossibility for Laraline to have someone in her house for more than five minutes without feeding them. Not that Muriel minded the ritual. She lifted her slice and took a generous bite, savoring the touch of honey baked into the loaf. Some might consider bread and butter humble fare but only because they'd never tasted Laraline's loaves. Muriel was fairly certain the woman had found God's manna recipe, because her bread was divine.

Laraline sat down at the head of the table, took her own bite of bread, then turned her attention to Muriel. "So what pickle brings you to my door?"

Muriel leaned forward in her chair. "I need to find someone. A young man. One who likely comes from the fancy side of the island."

Laraline frowned and shook her head. "Girl, I thought you had better sense than to go chasing after a rich fella." She blew out a disgruntled breath. "Young'uns," she muttered under her breath. "Thinkin' money solves every problem." She wagged an arthritic finger at Muriel. "Honey, listen up and listen good. Money ain't the key to happiness. Some of the unhappiest folk I've ever seen are those in the big houses on the East End. You'll be much better off findin' you an honorable man who loves God and loves you. *That's* the key to happiness."

Feeling as if Laraline had just overturned her egg basket, sending her fragile dreams rolling away in a dozen different directions, Muriel scrambled to gather them back together. "Ye don't understand. I'm not trying to find him because of his money. I want to find him because my heart is connected to his."

Laraline's eyebrows arched. It seemed she'd need more convincing. "How can your heart be attached to his if you don't even know who he is?"

A valid question, and one lacking a sensible answer. But not everything in life was sensible. Some things had to be taken on faith.

"I can't explain it, but my heart . . . recognized him." She told Laraline about the boat, the rescue, and seeing him again today outside the bookshop. "I know 'tis possible he's a married man. He could be an arrogant snob or an unscrupulous womanizer. But my heart insists he's none of those things. I have to find him, Laraline. 'Tis the only way to learn what kind of man he be. If I discover me heart is steerin' me astray, I'll let him go. But if he's the one

God means to pair me with, I can't turn me back just because he's from the fancy side o' town. All I'm askin' is fer a chance to test the waters, Laraline. Will ye help me? Please?"

Laraline stared at Muriel long and hard, making Muriel squirm a bit beneath the scrutiny. At last, the cook released her breath and gave a small nod. "Very well, but you gotta promise me that you'll keep your wits about you. I've seen too many girls end up with babes without fathers because some handsome fella charmed the sense right out of them. I don't want that life for you."

Muriel pressed a hand over her heart. "I'll be careful, I promise. I won't dishonor God or me da by playin' loose wi' me virtue."

"Good." Laraline smiled for the first time since this conversation began. "Then let's get to work. What do you know about your mystery man?"

"Not much. His name is Zane. He has black hair and enjoys sailing." Muriel scrunched her nose. How could that be all she knew about him? There seemed to be so much more. But how did one describe the intangible? "Oh, there was an older man at the beach. Maybe a grandfather? I think I heard Zane call him Grandpa Clem."

A low whistle filled the air as Laraline's eyes danced. "Girl, you don't do things halfway, do you?" She chuckled. "I think you snagged yourself an Erickson."

"Erickson?"

Laraline nodded. "Yep. Not too many Zanes around these parts. And only one Clem I can recall. Clement Erickson. Self-made man in the cotton industry. His son, Horace, is the real powerhouse in the family, though. Runs the Cotton Exchange and, with it, half the town. He's got a boy named Zane. Used to come over to Trimble House often. Young master Max and he were best friends. Still are, as far as I know. Fine lookin' gent, that Zane. Polite, too. Always ready with a kind word for the staff. You can tell a lot about a man by how he treats those beneath his notice."

Muriel's speeding pulse zinged her blood about at such a pace that she grew a little lightheaded. "Ye *met* Zane during yer time at Trimble House? Oh, Laraline! I *knew* ye'd be the right person to ask. Surely, this is a sign from heaven."

A chuckle warmed the air. "Easy, gal. Don't go shapin' your rolls before they've had a chance to rise. Take the time to see the job done right. Though, I gotta admit, I feel better about this fishing expedition now that I know who you're anglin' for. Mr. Zane's a gentleman. Takes after his grandpa, that one. His father, on the other hand, well, let's just say his apple fell a fair ways from the tree. And took on a few worms."

Zane Erickson. She had a name. Now all she needed was an introduction.

"Catching a man like Zane ain't gonna be easy," Laraline continued as if she'd read Muriel's mind. "Folks like the Ericksons look for matches among their own kind. They won't let a gal like you anywhere near their son without someone to vouch for you. There's only one person I can think of who could get you in the door."

"Who?"

"The Match Maven. Octavia Underhill."

The Match Maven? Muriel had heard whispers of such a person, but she'd assumed they'd been based more in myth than truth. Had she really brought a hundred couples together? How romantic! Surely she'd help Muriel connect with the man of her dreams.

"Where can I find her?"

Laraline tapped a finger on the tabletop. "St. Ursula's by the Sea."

Muriel frowned. "She's a nun?" Seemed a rather odd hobby for a woman of the cloth.

"A nun?" Laraline cackled. "Heavens no. She's a widow. Teaches at the Ursuline Academy, though. Music, I think. From what I've heard, she was one of the academy's first graduates back before the War Between the States. After her husband passed, she returned to the academy as a teacher. Never had any children of her own, so she devotes herself to her students and helps them find advantageous matches in her spare time. Apparently, she's quite good at it. Before I left Trimble House, I heard that the mistress was considering hiring Mrs. Underhill to find a match for the young master if he didn't see about the business himself." Laraline shrugged. "I don't know if Mrs. Underhill will take you on since you ain't one of her students, but I suppose it couldn't hurt to ask."

Then ask was precisely what Muriel would do.

A school of overactive minnows swam about in Muriel's stomach the following afternoon as she walked past the chapel on Avenue N and arrived at the academy. The iron gate creaked as she pushed it inward. The sound echoed loudly in Muriel's ears, doing nothing to calm the fish frenzy in her belly.

She pressed a hand to her midsection and practiced the breathing technique she used to expand her lungs for swimming longer distances underwater. After releasing her breath in a slow, controlled exhale, her pulse steadied enough for her to stroll up the walkway without mishap. She opened the door and stepped inside, her eyes taking a moment to adjust to the dimmer light.

"May I help you?" A nun rose from behind a desk, her black habit swishing quietly about her as she stepped forward.

She smiled at Muriel, her face sweet and remarkably young. Muriel had been expecting a glowering, wrinkled visage with eyes that saw every sin she'd ever committed, but this Ursuline sister looked to be around Alana's age and her gaze exuded nothing but kindness.

"I'm here to see Mrs. Underhill."

The young nun dipped her chin. "I see. Is she expecting you?"

Muriel swallowed and rubbed her quickly moistening palm along the edge of her best dress, a green muslin dotted with small yellow flowers. "Nay. I've come to seek her help with a personal matter. Mrs. Catherine Trimble recommended her services." Perhaps not to Muriel, personally, but a secondhand recommendation still counted.

The nun seemed to recognize the Trimble name, for her smile widened. "Ah. Celeste Trimble graduated from our academy last year. Lovely young woman. Mrs. Underhill should be finishing her music instruction in a few minutes, though things might run over. Our pupils will be giving a recital next week, and Mrs. Underhill strives for perfection." Had her smile become a tad strained at that observation? Perhaps not. Her expression seemed as gentle as ever as she regarded Muriel. "May I ask your name, miss?"

"Oh, yes. I'm Muriel Quinn, ma'am."

"A pleasure to meet you, Miss Quinn. I'm Sister Mary Vincent." A hand previously hidden within her black sleeve appeared and gestured toward a bench positioned along the side wall. "Please, have a seat. I will let Mrs. Underhill know that you are here."

But Mrs. Underhill had no reason to see her. Making matches for Galveston's elite would have acquainted her with all members of the wealthy set. The name Quinn held no prestige beyond the docks. What if she turned Muriel away without ever giving her the opportunity to plead her case? She couldn't take that risk. This might be her only chance to meet the Match Maven. She had to see her in person.

"Could I observe the end of her class?" Muriel blurted. She offered a smile in hopes of covering her desperation. "I'm a musician, myself. A soloist for the Grace Church choir."

Oh, dear. Muriel nibbled on the inside of her lip. In an effort to portray herself as both musical and religious, had she just committed the sin of pride? Right in front of a nun? Sister Mary Vincent might be young, but she probably still had supernatural nun knowledge, including the ability to spot heart impurities at twenty paces.

"I don't suppose there would be any harm in that." Her eyes warmed with humor that did little to ease Muriel's guilt.

She'd clearly detected Muriel's selfish motives, but like the God she served, she opted to bestow grace in place of condemnation. Muriel's heart sent a prayer of thanks heavenward.

"Follow me."

Sister Mary Vincent led her down a corridor, the muted tones of a piano filtering into the hall the farther they proceeded. The nun took hold of the door handle, then turned back to Muriel, a finger to her lips. Muriel nodded.

They slipped inside as quietly as possible and kept to the back of the room. A group of eight young ladies adorned in black dresses stood near the grand piano at the center of the room. In contrast, the silver-haired woman seated at the piano wore a stylish, flowing gown in a gorgeous shade of dark purple. The melody she played tugged on a memory of an Irish tune Muriel's mother had sung when Muriel had been a wee lass. The pupil singing of flowers in summer did her best to follow the piano's line, but the top notes fell a touch flat each time she reached for them.

"Support, Clarice. Don't stab the note, dear. Float above it and drop down gently. Like a flower petal, remember?" Mrs. Underhill spoke in a singsong voice that sounded encouraging on the surface, but Muriel sensed an undercurrent of steel.

The music swelled with a run of notes that begged for additional ornamentation.

"This is your time to shine, Clarice," the instructor urged. "More coloratura. Show what you can do."

Clarice tossed down her music and stamped her foot. "I can't do it, Mrs. Underhill. It's too hard. Why can't I have one of the simpler pieces?"

The other girls went so still, Muriel thought they might have forgotten to breathe.

Mrs. Underhill rose from the piano bench with awe-worthy elegance. Her brows, however, formed a sharp vee, the way Da's did before he blistered Muriel's hide. Then her gaze caught on Muriel and quickly shifted to Sister Mary Vincent. At once, her forehead smoothed and a tight smile curved her lips. "Clarice, dear. I've given you this piece because you are the most talented young lady in the class. We must show you off to best advantage. Why be like everyone else when you have the chance to be memorable?"

She turned to the rest of the class. "I expect all of you to practice before we meet again. Our recital is only a week away. We must not be satisfied with good enough when we have the ability to be great."

"Yes, Mrs. Underhill," the girls chorused.

"You are dismissed."

The girls filed out of the room as quickly as they could go without running, each of them casting a deferential glance toward Sister Mary Vincent as they left. All but Clarice. A pout firmly in place, she fisted her hands and deliberately left the music where it had fallen before marching out of the room with enough starch to crisp up an entire laundry basket of sheets.

Sister Mary Vincent stepped away from the wall. "Mrs. Underhill, this is Muriel Quinn. She wishes to speak to you regarding a personal manner."

Mrs. Underhill scanned Muriel from head to toe, apparently finding nothing favorable. She waved her hand in a shooing motion. "I'm sorry, Miss Quinn, but I don't take on charity cases."

Charity cases? Muriel stiffened, her Irish pride flaring. "I'm no charity case, Mrs. Underhill. I be prepared to pay whate'er fee may be required."

Her face scrunched as if the sound of Muriel's accent offended her musical sensibilities. "You cannot afford me, child. Do you think you're the first lovesick girl to come here seeking my matchmaking talents? You're not. I take clients by personal recommendation only, and no one has mentioned your name to me."

Raising her chin, Muriel met her gaze. Perhaps all those showdowns with Da had been a blessing after all. Standing up to a stranger wasn't near as frightening as standing up to her da. "Mrs. Catherine Trimble be one of yer clients, yes?" It was a guess, but one with a high probability of being right since, to Laraline's knowledge, Max Trimble remained unattached. "I received the recommendation from her."

Mrs. Underhill raised a brow. "You might have *heard* her mention me, but I very much doubt you received a personal recommendation." She looked down her nose at Muriel's dress. "You don't seem the type to run in Mrs. Trimble's circle."

Because she wasn't. And the Match Maven had seen right through her subterfuge. Drat. There had to be a way to earn an audience. If Mrs. Underhill would just give her a chance . . .

"Come, Miss Quinn." Sister Mary Vincent extended a hand toward her, regret shining in her eyes. "I'll show you out."

"Wait! I just need a moment." She turned back to Mrs. Underhill, her mind swirling. Her toe tapped against the fallen sheet music Clarice had left behind, and an idea burst like a rainbow through the clouds of her mind. She bent down, scooped up the music, then presented it like a gauntlet. "I'll sing ye for it."

The woman tilted her head, her scorn dulling slightly as curiosity made an appearance. "What does that even mean?"

"Why be ordinary, when ye can be memorable. Isn't that what ye said?"

"Yes, but—"

Muriel waved the music, the paper crinkling. "Let me earn yer time. If I can sing this song the way ye asked that it be sung, ye promise to hear me out. That's all I ask. Ye don't have to promise to take on me case. Just listen."

"I have to admit, your offer intrigues me, though I doubt you can do this piece justice. 'The Last Rose of Summer' is fit only for well-trained voices."

Muriel refused to flinch beneath the instructor's low expectations. "I assure ye, Mrs. Underhill. I'm up for the challenge."

Chapter 8

Octavia raised a brow at the chit's audacity. Young women of the middle class rarely showed such confidence in the presence of the socially superior. She had to give the girl credit. She had gumption. But did she have the talent to back it up?

"All right, Miss Quinn. I'll call your bluff. Impress me, and I'll grant you an audience. Though I warn you, I don't impress easily."

The girl beamed a smile of such joy, Octavia felt compelled to frown to keep the atmosphere balanced.

"Thank ye, ma'am." She moved to where Clarice had stood a moment ago and glanced through the sheet music.

Not one to give an opponent any advantage, Octavia slid onto the piano bench and began playing the introduction without waiting for the redheaded urchin to indicate her readiness. Her eyes widened a bit in surprise, but she shuffled the music back to the first page and made her entrance in perfect time.

"'Tis the last rose of summer left blooming alone."

Octavia nearly missed a key, so shocked was she by the purity of the sound coming from the ragamuffin before her. Miss Quinn didn't belt out the notes, trying to impress with the strength of her musical prowess. Instead, she sang with a gentleness and ease that befit her floral subject matter. Even in the second measure where the melody jumped a sixth from the A to the F, she floated up to the note like a butterfly catching a breeze. No pouncing upon it like most amateur sopranos.

"All her lovely companions are faded and gone."

She moved into the third line, swelling with the music. Octavia moved with her, the challenge fading from her awareness as the music took precedence. And when Miss Quinn slowed the tempo to add the turn of coloratura at the end of the third line? Octavia followed, slipping out of the role of instructor and into the role of accompanist.

"No flower of her kindred, no rosebud is nigh
To reflect back her blushes and give sigh for sigh."

They progressed through the second and third stanzas, each as effortless and beautiful as the last. Octavia's mind began to spin. She could make a fortune off this girl. Folk songs, not arias, would be the angle. Ballads like "Red River Valley," "Oh, Shenandoah," and "Barbara Allen." She'd make grown men weep. They'd likely have to start in dance halls, but it wouldn't take long to earn their way to the opera house circuit. She could take a year off from teaching at the academy, travel throughout Texas, maybe even to St. Louis or Chicago.

Her ambition had expanded to New York by the time the final note faded into the concluding measures of the accompaniment.

Applause rose from Sister Mary Vincent at the back of the room, and the sound startled Octavia out of her plotting. She'd forgotten the nun was there.

"Oh, Miss Quinn," Sister Mary Vincent enthused as she made her way down to the piano. "That was lovely. The Lord has truly blessed you with an amazing talent."

Pink colored the girl's cheeks as she dipped her chin. "Thank ye, sister. I be hopin' to honor him with me efforts. 'Tis why I sing with me church's choir."

Octavia rose with stately grace from the piano bench, carefully banking her enthusiasm. "A talent such as yours shouldn't languish in a single church, my dear. It should be shared with the masses. Just think of the lives you could touch. With my training and connections, we could make you the toast of Texas."

The girl wagged her head, panic erupting in her gaze. "Oh, nay, ma'am. I can't be leavin' Galveston. 'Twould break me da's heart. Mine, too, if I'm bein' honest. I belong here. Near the sea." A new glitter entered her eyes. "In fact, 'tis the sea that introduced me to the man who captured me heart. The one I need yer help to win. His name is Zane Erickson. Do ye know him?"

The disappointment that had been rising like a wave in Octavia's chest receded with lightning speed. Zane Erickson? *That's* the suitor she sought? Her pulse zipped about like Machi and Velli in a pouncing frenzy. Perhaps working among the Ursuline nuns all these years had finally scored her some heavenly favor. What else could explain the miraculous appearance of the perfect solution to her ledger problem?

Keeping her expression carefully composed, Octavia turned to Sister Mary Vincent and dipped her chin. "Thank you, sister. You may leave us. Miss Quinn and I have business to discuss."

"Very well." The nun folded her hands into her sleeves, tipped her head in deference, then glided out of the classroom, closing the door behind her.

The lowborn schoolgirl with her unfashionably bright hair and cringe-worthy accent bounced forward and clasped Octavia's hand. "Oh, thank ye, ma'am. I can't tell ye how much this means to me."

"Yes, well . . ." She extricated her hand from the overeager girl's grip and took a step back. "I've not agreed to anything yet." Though the innocence shining in Miss Quinn's gaze proved quite encouraging. Naïveté made a subject so much easier to manipulate. Especially when the heart was involved. "Have a seat, child." She gestured to one of the student desks.

Miss Quinn hastily slid into the chair, her eyes nearly as large as her smile as she blinked up at Octavia.

Eager to please. An excellent start. Octavia grinned slightly as she pulled a chair from a neighboring desk and positioned it across the tabletop from her new client. Best to make the girl think of her as an ally. Although, she also needed to make it clear who was in charge.

"Now, dear, before we go any further, you need to understand that as much as I enjoy bringing lovebirds together, matchmaking is not a charitable pastime for me. It is a business. As such, payment will be required. And if I might speak plainly, I don't think someone in your *position* can afford my usual fee."

The girl's smile dimmed but determination flared in her eyes. "I know I ain't one o' yer wealthy clients, Mrs. Underhill, but I can pay in other ways. I can work for ye at yer home. Cleanin' and such. Or . . ." She straightened her posture and lifted her chin. "Or, if ye think people will pay to hear me sing, I'll give ye me voice for . . .

say, six months? Ye can keep all the profits I bring in to cover me fee."

Hmm. The girl had pluck and could think on her feet. Good. She'd need those qualities to pull off the scheme brewing in Octavia's mind.

"My dear girl, you must realize that winning Mr. Erickson's heart is not the only battle you face. If you hope to marry, you must also win the approval of his family. Should word reach the Ericksons that you are working as a servant in my household, not only would it destroy your chances of making a match, but it would destroy my reputation. Something I cannot allow. And as much as I would love to take you and your lovely voice on tour, I'm afraid that won't help your cause, either. As unfair as it may be, female performers are often assumed to be immoral. My chaperonage would protect your reputation in the eyes of most, but even a hint of scandal could taint you in the eyes of a family like the Ericksons. No, I'm afraid we'll have to come up with a different plan."

"Do ye have somethin' in mind?"

So hopeful. So desperate. So ripe for the picking.

Octavia manufactured a reluctant expression and sagged in her seat. "I do, but I fear it would be asking too much of you. You're so young. Too young, I think, to take on such a task. It could be dangerous."

Miss Quinn's shoulders straightened just as Octavia wagered they would. "I ain't afeared of danger. I wouldn't've jumped into the Gulf to save Zane from drowning if I cared about what might happen to me. Pullin' him from the sea and gettin' air in his lungs were all that mattered."

Well, *that* was certainly an interesting tidbit. She'd heard rumors of Zane Erickson's sailing accident from a week ago, but nothing about a young woman saving his life. Could the young man be as affected by the encounter as Miss Quinn obviously was? Sophie

Erickson had admitted that her son had shown little interest in courting the young ladies of his acquaintance, but a man had to be intrigued by the woman who rescued him.

"Me youth won't be a hindrance, Mrs. Underhill. Ye have me word. I'm strong. Whatever it is ye need me to do, I can do it."

Not with that horrible accent, she couldn't. The moment she opened her mouth around Sophie or Horace Erickson, she'd be shunned as a gold-digging fraud. No matter how intrigued Zane might be by his rescuer, it was the parents who must be convinced of the girl's suitability. Had Octavia possessed more time, she could teach the child proper elocution, but one week had already elapsed since Horace Erickson's ultimatum, and she couldn't afford any more delays. They had to pursue a more drastic plan.

"It is not the strength of your body that concerns me, Miss Quinn, but the strength of your mind. If you are to pass yourself off as a woman of good breeding, one suitable for marriage to a man like Zane Erickson, you'll have to be clever and willing to bend the truth." At the girl's frown, Octavia hurried to reassure her. "Just a few harmless prevarications. Half-truths, really." She waved a hand as if shooing invisible gnats. "Nothing of any importance. And completely temporary. As soon as you and Zane are wed, you can tell him everything. He's sure to understand. You did it for love, after all. He'll forgive your tiny misrepresentations, and the two of you will be adorably happy for the rest of your lives."

Or long enough for Octavia to get her ledger back, anyway.

Miss Quinn leaned back in her chair, hesitation radiating from her in waves. A hesitation Octavia could not afford. Yet she must be careful in her approach. The girl talked about singing for God's pleasure and apparently had a conscience when it came to deceit. Her faith might actually be authentic. An unfortunate affliction Octavia had thankfully avoided, despite her regular attendance at St. Mary's.

Octavia dipped her chin in a sympathetic manner. "You must do what you feel is right, of course. But I would hate to see Zane paired with a woman who doesn't care for him the way you do."

The girl blinked. "What do ye mean?"

Octavia widened her eyes in feigned innocence as she touched a hand to her chest. "My dear. You didn't think you were the only one vying for his attention, did you? His mother recently hired me to find him a suitable bride. I have several possibilities lined up, including the lovely Clarice, whom you met earlier."

Miss Quinn's nose crinkled at the mention of Octavia's spoiled pupil. *Perfect.*

"When you mentioned your connection with Zane, I knew at once that you would be the ideal candidate. The two of you were obviously meant to be together. But if you don't have the conviction to do what is required, I suppose Zane will have to settle for another young woman, one with the social standing that his parents expect."

"That's not right." The girl stiffened and leaned forward, her engagement restored. "Zane shouldn't have to pay such a price."

"I guess that's the real question, isn't it? Which is the bigger wrong—a few minor deceptions or letting the man you love marry a woman who will make him miserable for the rest of his life?"

"You're right. I can't let Zane suffer his whole life long." She raised her chin, a beautiful stubbornness glittering in her eyes. "I can bend the truth if it be needed, but only if absolutely necessary."

"Of course. I wouldn't dream of asking you to compromise anything truly important. In fact, we'll take steps to create the truths we need. For example, you can move into a spare room here at the Academy where I can give you some lessons on deportment. That way, when I introduce you to the Ericksons I can say with all honesty that you are one of my students from the Academy. And when young Mr. Erickson walks you home after a romantic

outing, he can bring you here instead of your father's house."
Which was likely some tiny plebeian cottage of no account.

"Yes. I can do that. As long as me da gives me permission."

Octavia smiled. "I'm sure you'll convince him. Deep down, all good fathers want to make their little girls happy. We can work out the rest of the details when you come to see me tomorrow, but first we need to discuss the subject of payment."

"Ye said ye had somethin' in mind?"

"I do. You see, Zane's father, Horace Erickson, is not the upstanding man that his son is. After his wife hired me, he caught wind of it and didn't want to pay my fee. So, he came to my home, bribed my butler, and stole a ledger that contains all my business records. He's using it to blackmail me into working for free. Horrid man."

Sometimes the truth really *was* the best weapon. Perhaps an edited version, but the truth all the same.

Miss Quinn gasped. "That's terrible! Did ye report him to the law?"

"No. I didn't want poor Zane to pay the price for his father's sins. His reputation and that of his sweet mother would be blackened if society learned about Horace's despicable actions. I don't wish the two of them any ill will. But perhaps there is another way to see justice done." She leaned forward and dropped her voice to a conspiratorial murmur, drawing Miss Quinn toward her. "If someone were to be invited into the Erickson home, someone who could search for this ledger without anyone suspecting . . . well, if she found it, she could return it to me, and righteousness would prevail."

Octavia touched the naïve girl's arm and employed her best pleading gaze. "What do you say, Miss Quinn? Will you help right this terrible wrong?"

Her mouth tightened, and she gave a nod. "I'll do it."

A triumphant cackle echoed loudly inside Octavia's head, but her exterior remained humbly serene. "Thank you, my dear. You truly are a godsend."

Not only would she get her ledger back, but she'd stick Horace Erickson with a lowborn daughter-in-law who would shame him at every turn. Glorious! Revenge was sweet indeed.

Chapter 9

"Da, ye don't understand!"

Patrick Quinn stood in the front room of their home, fists on hips and legs braced apart as if he were aboard a storm-tossed ship instead of a rag rug in the middle of their tiny parlor. He glowered at Muriel, the tendons in his neck standing at attention.

"What don't I understand? That ye think yerself in love with a rich man's son that ye've ne'er spoken to? Or that ye've promised to steal a book fer some strange woman in exchange for an introduction to the lad? A fella not even bright enough to get outta the way of a swingin' boom!" His face darkened to a deep, brick red. "Saints preserve us, Muriel. How could ye be so daft?"

Muriel mimicked his stance, not willing to back down an inch with something so important on the line.

"It's not foolish to love someone, Da. Even if we haven't had a proper conversation. How many times have ye told the tale of how ye knew Ma was the woman fer ye the first time ye spied her sellin' meat pies along the wharf? Ye didn't need a conversation to know yer heart, and neither do I."

He opened his mouth, shut it, then opened it again. "It's not the same."

"Why? Because I'm a female who can't possibly know her own minds?" Muriel jutted her chin.

Her da jutted his. "Nay, because ye're a female who doesn't know the evil that can lurk inside a man's mind." The hard lines around his eyes softened a little. "Ye're a trustin' soul, Muriel, but men—especially ones of the rich and spoiled variety—are not always what they appear. They shower a gal with pretty words and loving promises then take her innocence and discard her like an out-of-style waistcoat. Sometimes with a babe in her belly. I don't want that fer ye, dear heart. Ye're too precious to be some rich man's trash."

Muriel flinched at the ugly words her father flung. Never had he spoken so bluntly. He was trying to scare her, and she had to admit that her confidence felt more akin to a jellyfish than solid ground at the moment. Yet he was wrong about Zane and wrong about her. She might be trusting, but she wasn't naïve.

"Da. Ye know me. I'd never give meself to a man without marriage vows bein' spoken."

He wagged his head then reached out and stroked her hair. "Ah, me lamb. Some men don't wait on the givin'. They just take, no matter what the lady wishes."

"Zane's not like that." Of that she was certain. "Laraline knows him. She says he's kind and a true gentleman."

Her da raised a single brow. "Laraline's a sweet lady, but she's . . . ah . . . a few bricks short of a load, if ye know what I mean."

"She is not!" Muriel slapped lightly at her da's arm. "Just because she stumbles o'er her words sometimes, doesn't mean she's not clever. She knows more about the wealthy folk on this island than the two of us put together."

"That's not sayin' much," he grumbled under his breath. "Look, Muriel. Even if this Zane fella is the gentleman ye believe him to be, I still don't like the idea of you workin' for a woman I don't know. One who expects ye to *steal* somethin'."

"It's not stealin' if it's hers, Da."

His scowl returned. "So she says. People lie, Muriel. How do ye know she ain't peddlin' a fish story?"

Muriel heaved an exasperated sigh. "She works for the Ursuline Academy, Da. With nuns! What better references could she have?"

"I still don't like it." He wagged his head and crossed his well-muscled arms in front of his chest. "How can I protect ye if ye're not livin' in me house?"

Muriel's anger deflated. She drew alongside her da and nudged her hand against the tight crevice at his elbow. His muscles relaxed to allow her entry, and her fingers found their way around his bicep. No matter how frustrated he might be with her, he was still her da and would never shut her out.

"I'll be livin' in the academy with at least a dozen other girls. We'll have a gaggle of nuns and God himself guarding us. I'll be safe, Da. Ye don't havta fret."

"The day I stop frettin' about me girls is the day they put me in the ground." He groaned and tugged on his beard in a way that looked painful. "Ye shoulda talked to me first before makin' yer pledge, Muriel."

So he could talk her out of it? Or worse, put his foot down and forbid her?

"I'm a grown woman, Da. Old enough to make me own choices. Gettin' the chance to meet Zane Erickson all right and proper is important to me, and I can't do it without Mrs. Underhill's help. I'll do nothin' to shame ye, I promise."

"Ah, now." He opened his arms, wrapped one about her, and tugged her firmly against his side. "I could ne'er be ashamed of ye. I love ye too much fer that." He pressed a kiss to her forehead. "'Tis fear that has me riled. Fear that you'll be dragged under before ye realize the current's changed course. I'll be prayin' fer ye every day ye're away. Prayin' for that Erickson lad, too. That he treats me girl with respect, 'cause if he doesn't, he'll be answerin' to me."

Muriel's heart stopped for a moment then started up again at twice its previous speed. "Does that mean I have yer blessing?"

"Ack. I still don't like this harebrained scheme you've cooked up with this matchmakin' female, but 'tis yer choice to make, not mine. Besides, ye gave yer word, and Quinns honor their pledges."

Muriel squealed and threw herself fully into his arms, hugging him tight. "Oh, thank ye, Da. Thank ye!"

It was happening. Her dream was actually happening. First Mrs. Underhill and now her father. Two miracles in one day! No obstacle could possibly come her way that was more difficult to scale than what she'd just overcome.

Her da's arms relaxed, and she leaned back to smile up at him, but her brow crinkled at his stern expression.

"I need ye to promise me somethin', love."

The exuberant seafoam frothing through her midsection receded a bit. "All right."

He took her arms in his large, calloused hands. "If ye ever find yerself in trouble, no matter what kind, ye come home. And if ye can't come home, ye send word. I'll come to ye. Day or night." His grip tightened. "Promise me, Muriel."

A lump rose in her throat. How blessed she was to be so loved. Without condition. Without limit.

She dipped her chin. "I promise."

He tugged her back into a rough embrace, completely enveloping her within his hold. He squeezed her tight then set her away from him, blinking as if he had something stuck in his eye.

With an indecipherable grumble, he turned his back and strode straight out the front door.

Weren't tea parties supposed to be fun? Muriel rubbed the sore spot on her forearm where Mrs. Underhill had just slapped her with her fan. Again.

"Pinky down, Miss Quinn. How many times must I remind you?"

Several, apparently. She might find it easier to avoid the finger faux pas if there weren't so many other rules to remember. Keep the teacup handle at three o'clock. Don't swirl the tea when stirring, use a vertical motion, straight up and back. Don't clink the spoon, and don't let it touch the teacup when placed on the saucer. No slurping. No dunking. Tiny bites. Tiny sips. Whatever happened to giggling girls serving invisible tea to their rag dolls? Muriel bit back a sigh, tucked away her little finger, and focused on taking a dainty sip. Steam rose from the newly refilled cup, alerting her to the likelihood of scalding. Pursing her lips, she blew ever so gently across the surface of the—ow!

Mrs. Underhill's fan struck again. In precisely the same spot. All her piano playing had given the woman remarkably good aim. With all the abuse the middle C section of her arm had taken, she really hoped her mentor would seek out a different key to strike next time.

"Young ladies of good breeding do *not* blow on their tea, Miss Quinn. They wait patiently for it to cool to the proper temperature."

Ladies of good breeding obviously didn't have chores waiting for them.

Muriel straightened and set her cup back on the saucer sitting atop the lace-covered table Mrs. Underhill had set up in Muriel's chamber that afternoon. She'd been at the academy for nearly a week now, cramming a lifetime of deportment lessons into five days. Who knew etiquette could be so grueling? She'd been more exhausted each night this week than after a ten-mile swim.

Mrs. Underhill frowned and heaved a sigh of displeasure. "You'll never convince the Ericksons that you are a worthy match for their son if you can't even consume your tea properly."

"I'll do bet—"

"Silence!" She surged up from her chair, her deep purple skirt falling around her legs like a cloud of ink ejected from an angry octopus. "You cannot speak. Not to explain. Not to apologize. Not to ask a question. Nothing! We have no hope of success if you cannot follow this imperative."

She smacked her folded fan against the table hard enough to rattle the teacups in their saucers. Muriel flinched.

"Do you want to have a life with Mr. Erickson, or don't you?"

"Of course I—"

Mrs. Underhill shot her such a black look, words died on Muriel's tongue as if they'd been struck by the plague.

Another test, and she'd failed. But talking was as natural as breathing. It just . . . happened. Especially when she was nervous or defensive. And how in the world was she supposed to win Zane's favor if she couldn't speak to him?

Mrs. Underhill paced the small chamber, her fan smacking her palm over and over as she marched. "We've been over this, Miss Quinn. Silence is essential. If we had more time, I could give you elocution lessons, but I fear we'd need *months* to rid you of that low-born accent."

Muriel frowned at her mentor's snobbish attitude. She understood the necessity of hiding her lack of polish in order to gain acceptance among a station far above her own, but that Irish lilt Mrs. Underhill so despised was the song of her family. Her da, her sisters, they all spoke as she did. It was a cadence filled with love, with joy, with teasing, and with pride. Surely Zane wouldn't be so superficial as to turn away from her because of her accent. Yet, as Mrs. Underhill hammered home time and again, it wasn't Zane she had to impress. It was his parents. People on the rise in Galveston society, who longed to advance their standing and sought a daughter-in-law who would aid them in that endeavor.

"I can teach you the difference between a fish fork and a salad fork. I can correct your posture and curb your exuberance. I can dress you in the latest fashions and lend you a few pieces of jewelry to help you look like you belong." She swiveled and pierced Muriel with a pointed glare. "But the moment you open your mouth, the illusion dies! Along with your chance to snag the Erickson boy. You cannot afford to be an impulsive girl with biscuits for brains. You must be in control at all times. Focused. Purposeful. Intentional. This isn't a game. It's a war. One I intend to win."

War? Muriel shrank back in the chair, uncomfortable with the way Mrs. Underhill's eyes glittered. She was feeling more like a pawn and less like a partner in this endeavor. Perhaps Da had been right. Maybe she *had* been a wee bit hasty in tying her rowboat to the matchmaker's steamship. But how else was she to arrange an introduction to the man who held her heart?

Mrs. Underhill released a breath and collected her composure. Her face smoothed, the fan slapping ceased, and the fiery intensity of her gaze cooled to polite embers as she calmly strolled back to the table.

"Think of it this way, my dear. Great love requires great sacrifice. Think of our Lord Jesus remaining silent before his accusers. He did not defend himself or correct their misconceptions. He held tight to his purpose. His mission. That is what you must do. Put your girlish ways aside and adopt the mantle of a self-controlled, resolute woman. One with the maturity to focus her mind on her goal and make the sacrifices required to achieve it."

Muriel sat a little straighter. A mature woman. Focused. Determined. Willing to make sacrifices for love. Could she do it? Could she temper her emotions and swallow her words? She pulled her shoulders back. If it meant winning a place in Zane Erickson's world . . . yes.

A slow smile blossomed on Mrs. Underhill's face as she slid with genteel grace back into her chair at the table. "That's what I like to see. A woman setting her mind to the task at hand." She even went so far as to set her fan on the table. Muriel's bruised arm rejoiced. "It will get easier. You'll see. Besides, I've found that men quickly grow weary of women who blather on. A young lady who *listens* is much more attractive. The more I consider it, the more I believe this tactic will work to our advantage. We'll create an air of mystery around you." She winked as she lifted her teacup with perfect form. "Men love a good mystery. Almost as much as a pretty face. And you'll have both."

Muriel smiled at the compliment and carefully imitated her instructor's teacup handling, thankful the beverage had cooled enough to sip without scalding. The idea of Zane finding her attractive sent little bursts of pleasure zinging through her midsection, but she knew attraction wasn't enough. Not for an abiding love. They'd need to get to know one another. Connect on a deeper level. If she couldn't do that through conversation, she'd have to explore less conventional options. Perhaps write him letters. Or develop a private sign language that only the two of them shared.

Mrs. Underhill replaced her cup on its saucer with impressive clink-less-ness. "So, what plans are percolating in that head of yours?"

Muriel opened her mouth, then caught herself. She swallowed the answer waiting to be verbalized, and instead offered a tiny shrug and a playful glance that projected a response of *wouldn't you like to know.*

Her mentor chuckled softly, the sound resembling a purr of satisfaction. "There's hope for you, yet." She reached for a small cake and lifted it to her lips. "Remember, darling. She who holds her tongue, gets her man."

Chapter 10

Zane tilted his head and scrutinized the drawing he'd been working on for Mr. Clayton. A client wished to add an ironwork veranda to the front two stories of his Italianate villa and Clayton had tasked Zane with creating a design that would blend seamlessly with the existing architecture. A test of his readiness for larger projects.

Determined to prove himself, Zane had spent several days consulting design books, drawing the existing house, and making sketches of the ironwork fence surrounding the property. All added to his inspiration. A teardrop-shaped finial sat atop each fence post, adding a bit of softness to the angularity. The veranda would need to stay true to the rectangular shapes and flat roof dominating the house itself, but the corners could be softened in the same style as the fencing.

Rectangular shutters flanked each of the rectangular windows, but above each one, affixed to the red brick edifice, sat a rounded ornamental molding. One that curved at the outer edges and came to a point in the middle, as if someone had grabbed either side of a teardrop and stretched it wide enough to match the width of the window.

His design incorporated similar elements. The proposed veranda and its ceiling formed stark rectangles. Ironwork railings created a boxy border. Iron support posts stood tall and straight, placed in four pairs of two. Yet he'd softened the design with iron teardrops eighteen inches from the top of each slender pillar. Then he'd created an arch effect with lacy iron filigree reaching out from either side of the teardrops, like corner-hanging spiderwebs touching at the highest point in the center.

"I like what you've done with this project." Nicholas Clayton peered over Zane's shoulder. He reached past and planted a finger on the sketch of the porch corner. "I think we'll need to add a third pillar on each of the front two corners for added stability. Your design will still work. It just needs to be expanded. Make the adjustments tomorrow, and we'll take it to the client for approval next week."

"We?" Zane's breath caught.

Mr. Clayton's bushy mustache twitched as a smile stretched his face. "Only right that the designer meet with the client, don't you think? I'll want you on hand at the construction site as well. Calculating angles and load-bearing limits on paper is one thing, but seeing those calculations take shape in three dimensions is critical for broadening an architect's grasp of structural engineering."

Zane rose from the drafting table to face his mentor. "Thank you, sir. I'll make those revisions, and once you approve, I'll ink a fresh copy of the plans on drafting linen and have it ready by the end of the day tomorrow."

"Good." Clayton thumped him on the back. "Keep advancing like this, Mr. Erickson, and it won't be long before you're assisting me on larger projects."

Zane's breath caught in his lungs, making his chest ache in a most satisfying manner. "Like the Ursuline Academy?"

He'd seen some of Clayton's initial sketches. It rivaled the cathedrals of Europe in craftsmanship and Gothic styling.

Clayton chuckled. "That one's probably a few years away yet, lad. I have several residences in the works that will need more immediate attention."

"Of course." Zane fought off a wave of disappointment as practicality asserted itself. "I'd be delighted to assist on any company project."

"You're bright and capable, Mr. Erickson. Perhaps by the time the Ursuline Academy job is ready for us, you'll be ready for it."

Zane grinned. "I look forward to that day."

"As do I," Clayton said. "After finishing construction of the Ursuline Academy in Dallas three years ago, people have been wondering why I haven't yet designed a building equally grand for our dear sisters here in Galveston." He leaned in and winked. "What they don't know is that the one in Dallas was a trial run. I have even bigger plans for the one here in my backyard." He swept a hand out in front of him as if painting a picture. "It will be my crowning achievement. Towers, turrets, spires, and flying buttresses. All eyes will be drawn to the heavens, to the Master Architect, Designer of the universe." His hand lowered as he gave a small shrug. "The sisters haven't officially commissioned the work yet. I imagine it will take some time to raise sufficient funds for such an undertaking, but Mother St. Agnes has been dropping hints."

"I have no doubt that you will surpass all her expectations."

Clayton nodded, his expression growing serious. "I always give my best to each project, but there is something special about working on a building that is dedicated to the Lord's work. A feeling of higher purpose. A melding of pressure and privilege, responsibility and reverence. The striving for perfection is both exhausting and exhilarating."

"A study of contrasts," Zane observed. "Like the strength of stonework supporting an airy vaulted ceiling."

"Precisely." Clayton thumped his shoulder again then tipped his head toward the veranda sketch. "File your work. I've delayed you long enough."

"I will, sir. Thank you."

As Nicholas Clayton fetched his hat and departed the office, Zane cleaned his work area and made sure all the other draftsmen's work was properly stored. As an apprentice, the menial office work fell on his shoulders, but he didn't mind. Looking over the work of more experienced men served as an education all its own. Yet he dared not take the time to examine the drawings of George Sealy, the associate architect, or any of the other draftsmen tonight. Not if he wanted to escape his mother's wrath. She expected him to be home by five-thirty, and according to his pocket watch, it was already five-forty.

Zane fit his hat to his head then made sure to lock the office door behind him before he hurried home. In truth, he'd rather go out with Max tonight, tell his friend about his conversation with Mr. Clayton, and celebrate his good fortune with a game of billiards or a good gallop on the beach.

Instead, he'd be stuck inside, pretending not to be bored stiff while his mother introduced him to whichever female she'd scraped from the bottom of society's barrel to foist upon him in hopes of stirring his interest. Why did mothers think it their duty to find brides for their sons? Much more sensible for the sons to do their own choosing. Was she really so desperate for grandchildren that she must do all in her power to hurry things along? Or was it Father's ambition motivating her desire to pair him with an appropriately well-positioned society miss?

A sigh escaped him as he marched at a fast clip down Avenue J toward home. Father might prioritize him selecting a bride who came with advantageous business connections, but Mother simply wished for him to be settled and content. She wasn't so much trying to run his life as she was trying to help him find happiness. He couldn't blame her for good intentions even if he didn't care for her methods. It might rankle that she didn't trust him to take care of matters himself, but with his increased focus on building his career in architecture, he'd not exactly been seeking courtship opportunities.

Until a mysterious siren saved his life then disappeared all in a single afternoon.

He'd been seeking *her* every time he was out in public. Sometimes without even realizing it. Yet any time a flash of red hair crossed his periphery, his head swiveled and his feet diverted their path to follow, until she either vanished or he got a good enough look to recognize that she wasn't the lady he sought.

A few days ago, he'd come up with a scheme to seek her with purpose. Starting this Sunday, he planned to visit every church on the island until he found her. She'd been singing a hymn, so she likely attended church somewhere. He just had to figure out where. His mother wouldn't care for him not being beside her at their own services, but if his absence meant finding a bride, he doubted she would protest too vehemently.

Still, he needed to treat whatever young lady he found in his parlor with kindness and respect. She didn't deserve to bear the brunt of his frustration. So, as he jogged up the stone steps of the large Queen Anne style house he called home, he set his frustrations aside and prepared his mind for gentlemanly attentiveness.

The front door opened before his hand could reach the latch. Grandpa Clem waved him inside and relieved him of his leather drafting case.

"Best hurry yourself in there, boy, before the bees in your mama's bonnet start churning out honey. The situation's sticky enough already."

Zane removed his hat and hung it on the rack in the entry way. "How do you mean?"

"Your mama's not pleased with the little gal the matchmaker brought. Heard her whispered accusation to the woman about tryin' to pass off a defective miss as an acceptable bride when she's obviously not Erickson material. All because the lady don't talk. Ain't her fault her pipes don't work. The rest of her seems to be in good working order. She ain't dimwitted or nothin'. Walked straight over to the bookshelf and snagged a tome on shipbuilding to read while the hens pecked at each other on the other side of the room."

The lady couldn't speak? Good heavens. They really were scraping the bottom of the barrel.

Compassion, Zane. The poor girl can probably sense Mother's disapproval.

He knew what it was like to be scrutinized and found wanting. None of Clayton's staff had expected him to possess any actual talent or be willing to do the grunt work required to gain the required skills. They'd seen him as a pampered rich kid on an architectural lark. Their prejudice created barriers that had taken months to wear down. Least he could do was offer a bit of kindness to a young lady in an awkward situation. Though, he'd need to take care not to give her any reason to expect a future courtship. He'd never toyed with a woman's affections, but on one or two occasions in the past, young ladies had jumped to incorrectly optimistic conclusions that had made things rather unpleasant for all parties involved.

"Quit dawdlin' and get in there." Grandpa Clem planted a hand on Zane's back and shoved.

Zane chuckled as he stumbled forward. Grandpa had never been a big proponent of subtlety.

Smoothing out his gait, Zane ran a hand over his hair to make sure no stray pieces were standing at attention after removing his hat. Reaching the parlor door, he hesitated, needing a moment to breathe. If Mother was in a state, he'd need his wits about him.

"Don't worry," his grandpa murmured from behind him. "I think you're gonna like this one."

Zane's head swiveled in time to catch his grandpa's wink before the cagey codger darted past him on his way upstairs with Zane's satchel. Was the entire family plotting the demise of his bachelorhood? He'd thought Grandpa Clem his ally, but it seemed he'd turned mutineer.

He grabbed the door handle and yanked it open. The sooner he got this fiasco over with the better.

"Zane! *Finally.*" Mother stepped away from a striking older woman with silver hair wearing a dark violet walking suit.

The woman's attention suctioned onto Zane like a starfish latching onto a rock. Cool. Assessing. Calculating.

Slightly disturbing.

His mother grabbed his arm and dragged him deeper into the room and thankfully broke him free of the matchmaker's gaze.

"Where have you been?" she hissed. "You were supposed to have been here twenty minutes ago."

"I apologize. Mr. Clayton wanted to go over a few details with me."

Her grip tightened. "Far be it from me to compete with the almighty Mr. Clayton."

"Mother," he warned in a low voice.

She bit back whatever other complaint she'd been ready to fire at him and sighed instead. "Well, you can make it up to me by putting your best foot forward with Miss Quinn. She's a little unusual, but then, none of the *usual* ladies have captured your fancy, so perhaps Mrs. Underhill knows what she is doing."

Lifting her face and her voice, Mother crossed the red and gold Turkish carpet to the small sitting area in front of the hearth. "Miss Quinn, I apologize for my son's tardiness, but he has arrived at last."

He'd kept his gaze on his mother to this point, not comfortable searching the girl out in the room while his mother discussed her in less than flattering terms, but he marched a smile onto his face like a good little soldier and prepared his tongue for a gracious greeting. But the moment he spied the carefully coiffed red hair, his mind ceased functioning. As did his feet. His mother strode forward, but he remained rooted to the carpet.

Some part of his brain registered Mother's frown when she cast a confused glance over her shoulder. She was saying something, probably making introductions, though for the life of him he couldn't decipher the words. Not when his siren, dressed in an elegant sea-green day dress, rose from the sofa like a mermaid rising from the waves.

Her gaze met his with a shy eagerness that immediately tripled the speed of his pulse. A smile blossomed across her face, crinkling her hazel eyes in a way that made it impossible not to smile in return.

It was her. He had no proof, but he didn't need any. His heart recognized the truth.

Unfortunately, his brain failed to recognize the truth of his addled state and allowed his tongue to move when it should have remained firmly locked in place.

"I found you."

Chapter 11

"*You* found her?" Mother laughed. She turned to Miss Quinn. "Isn't that just like a man to take credit for the work we women have done?"

Zane's neck warmed.

"I'm sorry, my boy, but you can't claim credit simply because you opened a door and walked into a room. Mrs. Underhill did the finding. At my behest, I may add. So, if there are any finding fees to be awarded, the ladies will be the ones collecting. Won't we, Miss Quinn?"

A smile stretched across the young woman's face. Not a debutante's shy smile that barely curved the lips. Nor the coquettish smile of a lady set on making a conquest. No, this smile beamed with energy and delight. Full coral lips spread wide, exposing white teeth, while lovely hazel eyes twinkled with good humor. He found himself forgetting his embarrassment and smiling back.

"Forgive me, Mother. Miss Quinn." He bowed to each of them. "I would never dream of stealing the credit for an accomplishment not of my making. In truth, I had just been remembering a young lady that I met at the beach a couple weeks ago." Miss Quinn flushed a bit at his words, stirring hope that his assumptions about her had been correct. "A young lady I very much wished to meet again. Then I walked into the parlor and found her sitting beside my hearth. It quite took me off guard."

Mother looked from Zane to Miss Quinn and back again. "You've met Miss Quinn before?"

He didn't look away from his siren, just nodded his confirmation. "I believe so, yes. But only Miss Quinn can verify." He took a step closer to her. "You're her, aren't you? The lady who pulled me from the sea and saved my life."

Her lashes lowered as the pink in her cheeks deepened. Then she glanced up into his face and nodded.

He knew it! It *was* her.

"Good heavens!" Mother pressed a hand to her chest. "*This* is the woman who saved you? Surely not. No woman of good breeding could swim into the depths of the Gulf. Her bathing costume would drag her to the bottom."

Some of the light dimmed from Miss Quinn's eyes, and her chin dipped to her chest.

A muscle ticked in Zane's jaw. "Well, I, for one, am thankful for her swimming prowess. Had she been a helpless miss hobbled to the shore by antiquated social mores, I would have perished."

Her chin lifted, and she gazed at him as if his black trousers and frock coat had just transformed into a suit of shining armor. A rather invigorating yet terrifying prospect. He wouldn't last long on a pedestal. Then again, wasn't that precisely where he'd put her these past weeks?

"I didn't mean to imply . . ." Mother sputtered in an effort to smooth away her insult. "I had no idea . . . that is . . ." She ceased talking and took hold of Miss Quinn's hand, causing the young woman to startle and blink like a snared rabbit. "Forgive me, Miss Quinn. My son is correct. You are deserving of my most heartfelt gratitude. Had you not been there . . ." Her voice clogged. She cleared her throat and adjusted the set of her chin as if doing so would dam up her emotions. "Well, I dare not even imagine the outcome." She gave a sniff then gestured toward the Rococo-styled sofa and chairs situated around them. "Why don't we all have a seat. It seems we have much to learn about each other."

"Excellent notion, Mrs. Erickson." The matchmaker inserted herself into the conversation with practiced precision, commandeering Miss Quinn to ensure the young lady sat beside her on the sofa. Whether to support her or control her was hard to tell.

Miss Quinn seemed to pack away her personality and become a proper miss as she took her seat next to Mrs. Underhill. Her eyes lowered as she folded her hands in her lap and demonstrated admirable posture. As if he would be impressed with a straight backbone. Every girl in society had one of those. No, it was the impish sparkle in her gaze and the genuine delight in her smile that captured his interest. Yet he was denied both as she wrapped herself in the cocoon of social expectations.

Patience. He could bide his time. Endure the formalities. Besides, he wanted to learn everything he could about her. Might as well get the boring stuff out of the way first.

"Mr. Erickson. Mrs. Erickson." The matchmaker nodded to him and his mother in turn. "May I present Miss Muriel Quinn?"

Muriel. A beautiful name. Lyrical. So fitting for a sea siren.

"Miss Quinn is a new addition to the Ursuline Academy, but her pedigree is impeccable. Her father is in shipping."

Miss Quinn's brow twitched, almost as if her expressive features were trying to break free of the propriety subduing them. Did she object to Mrs. Underhill's characterization of her father? Or had the movement simply been a meaningless facial tic? He doubted his mother had caught the half-wince. Her attention remained riveted upon the matchmaker as she recited Miss Quinn's bridal résumé. Zane listened with half an ear. Social standing and familial connections had no bearing on his future happiness. He'd rather live a simple life in a small house with a woman he loved than in a mansion with a rich woman who cared more about appearances than affection.

He supposed it possible that Miss Quinn might care about money and social standing, like most others of their class, but somehow, he just couldn't believe it of her. The woman who had stood on that rocky outcropping and poured her heart into a song meant for God alone, was a woman of passion and deep faith. A woman who didn't prioritize the opinions of others, else why expose her soul in a public place? She cared more for the well-being of a stranger than herself. His identity hadn't been known to her when she'd jumped into the sea to save him. He could have been a dock worker or fisherman. His status hadn't mattered. Her actions spoke of bravery, of sacrifice, of noble intent. Not of ambition or the desire to climb the social ladder.

"And what of her ... mutism," Mother asked, breaking Zane out of his musings. "Was she born with this affliction? My husband will want to know if the condition could be ... hereditary."

Mrs. Underhill dipped her chin. "A reasonable concern, of course."

Zane blinked. He'd forgotten all about Miss Quinn's inability to speak. He'd been so overwhelmed by the discovery of her in his house that he'd given thought to little else. His siren had possessed a rapturous voice. One that ensnared his spirit. Had the woman who rescued him been a different woman from the one who'd been singing upon the shore? Surely there hadn't been two redheaded women in the deserted cove that day.

He searched Miss Quinn's face, but her gaze remained directed at her lap.

"I can assure you that the loss of Miss Quinn's voice is a recent development. One we are quite hopeful will be remedied with time. She sustained an injury to her throat two weeks ago."

Zane's attention snapped to the matchmaker, who eyed him in such a way that left no doubt in his mind as to what, or rather, *who* had caused this injury. A drowning man thrashing about insensibly. Concerned only with his own dire predicament. Giving no heed to who he might hurt in his desperate bid for salvation.

His breath caught in his throat and a leaden weight pressed upon his chest. *He'd* done this. He'd destroyed her voice. That passionate, glorious, God-given voice. Horror pulsed through his veins and threatened to drown him a second time.

Throwing himself out of his chair, he fell at Miss Quinn's feet and caught her hand between both of his as emotion choked him and made his own voice rasp with regret. "This is my fault, isn't it? I can't bear to think that my stupidity in the boat that day did this to you." He hung his head. "I'm so sorry, Miss Quinn. So wretchedly sorry. I should be the one to suffer. Not you."

"Zane." Mother's horrified whispered needled him in the back. "What do you think you're doing? Get off the floor this instant."

He ignored her. His need to atone overrode his need for propriety. Yet how could mere words atone for what he'd caused? What if she never sang again? Never spoke again? All because he'd failed to heed the position of the boom.

In his misery, it took a moment for him to realize that Miss Quinn was pulling her hand away from his grasp. Of course she was. He'd probably frightened her, making free with her person in such a manner. He dropped his arms, shrinking into himself. Why couldn't he act as a normal person around this woman? She must think him an emotional idiot.

He began to slink away, but before he could escape, she clapped his face between her hands and angled his chin upward. His eyes widened, and his gaze latched onto her face. Her ardently beautiful face. She didn't look at him with disgust or pity or even false politeness. Her hazel eyes sought his with desperation. She shook her head in a negative motion with such vigor, a tress of copper hair slid free to bounce beside her right ear.

She pounded her chest with her palm, as if trying to communicate that she was responsible. Which was utter rot. Then she raised a finger and dug around in the pocket of her skirt, squirming about on the sofa until she finally produced a small notebook and pencil. She opened it to a fresh page, scribbled a handful of words upon the paper, then handed it to him.

NOT your fault! She'd underlined *not* three times. *My choice.*

"You're an extraordinarily generous woman not to hold me responsible, Miss Quinn. Yet, there's no escaping the fact that had I been attending the sail as I ought, your injury never would have happened."

She returned pencil to paper. Silence filled the room as she wrote a longer note, the only sounds the scratch of the pencil and the ticking of the mantel clock. And Zane's heart. Though its pounding probably filled only his own ears. Finally, the scratching stopped, and she turned the notebook outward to face him.

If you hadn't fallen overboard, I never would have met you. Any temporary loss is worth that gain. Please don't worry about my voice. It <u>will</u> come back. I promise.

She promised? Zane wagged his head slightly as a smile found its way onto his face. He didn't know if that promise was based on a mighty faith or naive optimism, but he found he liked the positivity of it. Why not believe the best? He was starting to.

Did she really consider meeting him worth the price fate had forced her to pay? Rather extravagant in his estimation. He was no great prize. Yet he understood the sentiment, for nearly dying seemed to him quite a reasonable price to pay for meeting *her*. More bargain by the minute, as a matter of fact.

"Zane, please." Mother's pained tone pierced his conscience. "Retake your seat."

He pushed to his feet, his gaze holding Miss Quinn's as he stood. A smile brightened her eyes, stirring a tornadic whirl inside his chest that left him a tad lightheaded.

"May I call on you tomorrow evening? I know a great little ice cream shop."

She was nodding before he got more than half the invitation out.

He grinned, her overt eagerness delighting him more than any coy flirtation could have.

"Zane, really. We've barely learned anything about her."

His gaze remained locked on his siren. "I've learned plenty."

And he liked it all.

Chapter 12

Octavia practically purred as she settled onto the cushion inside her closed carriage. That couldn't have gone better had she scripted it herself. The Erickson heir had *groveled*. Right there on the carpet like a subservient whelp. How utterly glorious! The little urchin had performed better than Octavia had dared hope. She'd held her tongue for the entire meeting and had done an admirable job of enticing young Zane with her innocent enthusiasm.

An enthusiasm she might be laying on a bit thick. Octavia fought to keep her eyes from rolling as her charge thrust a hand through the lowered window on the far side of the carriage and waved at Mr. Erickson with all the subtlety of a foghorn.

The girl knew nothing of the delicate cat-and-mouse machinations required to lure men. She lacked sophistication, wore her every emotion on her sleeve, and couldn't even flirt properly. By all rules of engagement, she should have been politely dismissed. Yet she'd achieved the exact opposite. She'd finagled an invitation from one of the most sought-after bachelors on the island.

The carriage lurched forward, and Miss Quinn rocked in her seat, giving no indication that she planned to cease her ridiculous waving.

Octavia reached across and tugged the girl's arm inside the window. "That's enough, dear. Men appreciate encouragement, but they also like to be the ones to pursue. You might scare him off if you seem *too* eager."

She withdrew at once, flopping back against the padded seat as if to hide herself from view. Must the girl do everything with such . . . energy? Proper decorum was much less exhausting. Octavia sighed. Thankfully, Zane didn't seem to care much for proper decorum, so she supposed she would endure Muriel's penchant for exuberance. At least the girl had proven easy to manipulate, though she'd soon be operating outside of Octavia's supervision. Wild things could be unpredictable, and unpredictable could be dangerous to the one holding the strings.

"We have very little time together before we reach the academy," Octavia said as she moved her handbag to her lap and unfastened the clasp, "so I need you to pay careful attention to what I'm about to tell you."

The little twit had far too many stars in her eyes to focus.

"Muriel!"

The girl blinked and finally snapped out of her dreamy trance.

"Keep your wits about you, Miss Quinn. I have no patience for stupidity, whether naturally occurring or induced by lovesickness. Remember, if you cease to be of use to me, our agreement will be nullified. Not only will I reveal your lowborn status and complete lack of advantageous connections, but I will also leave Mrs. Erickson with the impression that you deceived me from the start. I will paint you as a morally bankrupt fortune hunter who cares nothing for her son and seeks only to gain his wealth and prestige by trapping him into marriage."

Her young companion's brows arched so high, they nearly reached her hairline. Impressively, though, she didn't give voice to her outrage. It seemed she had taken at least one of Octavia's lessons to heart. Maintaining silence one hundred percent of the time made her less likely to make a verbal slip in the Ericksons' presence, so Octavia had insisted she cease talking altogether.

The girl started digging in her pocket for that infernal notebook of hers, but Octavia didn't have time for a paper duel.

"Never mind that. I can hear your internal protests from here." She waved her hand through the air as if dispersing a swarm of irritating gnats. She raised the pitch of her voice in an imitation of girlish affront. "That's not fair. You'd be *lying*." Octavia pressed palm to breast and executed a wonderfully melodramatic gasp that any hapless damsel would be proud to have in her arsenal.

Then she narrowed her gaze and closed the space between herself and her charge with all the predatory grace of a lioness stalking her prey. "Let me make myself very clear. If you do not retrieve my ledger in two weeks' time, I will ruin you. And not *only* you. I'll ruin your entire family. My late husband had many connections in the shipping industry. I've maintained those since his passing. A few whispered accusations of misconduct in the right ears, and your father will soon find himself unemployed. I also happen to be good friends with the manager of the Beach Hotel. Your sister's husband works there, does he not? It would be a shame if he were to be caught with items stolen from guests' rooms in his possession. I doubt any establishment within a hundred miles would hire him after such a blemish on his record. Hard to provide for a wife and three young children whilst unemployed."

The girl paled and her wide eyes grew moist and shimmery. Good. Now that she was properly cowed, they could get down to business.

Octavia pulled a brown leather journal from her handbag and handed it to Muriel. "This book is identical to the one Horace Erickson stole from my home. Study it. The dimensions. The style. The color. You need to be able to recognize it immediately if you come across it. Once you find it, you can replace it with this empty one. That should keep Mr. Erickson from noticing that it is missing, at least for a while."

Muriel's hands trembled slightly as she took the book and laid it in her lap.

"What you need to do now is create opportunities to be inside the Ericksons' home. Use your wiles to get young Zane to invite you to dinner parties and soirees his parents are hosting. Search the house. Especially Horace's study. The journal might be hidden in plain sight or locked away in a desk drawer."

Hopefully, he hadn't taken it to his office at the Exchange. Horace didn't seem like a man who would leave valuables in a place accessible to the public, though. Better odds that he kept it at home with a wife and staff who'd been trained not to ask questions.

Muriel lifted her hands palm up, and Octavia read her concern as if it were a newsprint headline. "A pair of hairpins and a little finesse can open most any locked drawer or cabinet. I'll send my maid Vanessa to you at the academy later this week to give you some pointers. She's been cultivating a romantic entanglement with a footman who works at the Erickson home, so she'll be around. Keeping an eye on you. Reporting your progress back to me." Octavia narrowed her gaze to pinpoint precision and jabbed Murial right between the eyes. "You will do *whatever it takes* to secure my journal, Miss Quinn. Or your family will pay the price."

Muriel failed to join the other girls in the dining hall for the evening meal. How could she eat when her insides were swirlin' about like a whirlpool, thanks to the opposing currents colliding in her belly. Agony warred with ecstasy, leaving her confused and slightly dizzy from the back-and-forth of her thoughts.

What kind of cold-hearted villain had she gotten involved with? She'd been so certain God had directed her along this path. But what if she'd been led astray by her own desires? Da had been right to call her daft. Naïve too. Why else would she not consider that the consequences of her actions would impact more than herself? She'd seen the cold truth in Mrs. Underhill's eyes. Her threat was no empty bluff. She wouldn't hesitate to harm Muriel's family to get what she wanted. If Da, Alana, or any of the wee ones suffered for her impulsive choice . . .

Tears welled in Muriel's eyes as she sat on the edge of her bed. What had she been thinking? Blindly trustin' a stranger and her own flawed judgment instead of seeking wise counsel. From her da. From God. Instead, she'd donned a pair of thick, rose-colored glasses and seen precisely what she wanted to see. A way to Zane. Never once did she think to examine the water around her for sharks.

Don't let them suffer on account of me foolishness, Lord. She buried her face in her hands. *I'm sorry fer not seekin' ye first, like the Scriptures say. I was seekin' Zane. Seekin' me own desires. Now I'm in an awful tangle, and I don' know how to get meself free.*

Wiping her damp eyes on the cuff of her sleeve, she straightened. Moping wouldn't help her situation. Finding the missing journal would. It was the only way to protect her family. Until tonight, she'd considered the journal her secondary mission. Cultivating a relationship with Zane came first. Not anymore. If she had to risk her future with Zane to save her family, that's what she'd do. Even if it meant learning how to pick locks with hairpins and snooping through private rooms.

But, oh how she wanted Zane, too! Muriel pushed to her feet and paced the length of the small room she'd been given. Instead of joining the older students in one of the larger dormitories, she'd been cloistered in a spare cell in the convent wing. It only took about four strides to get from door to window, so she made several passes as she relived every moment of her second meeting with the man of her dreams.

Zane Erickson had been everything she'd hoped for and more. Much, *much* more. Mercy, but he was a broth of a lad. Thick black hair free of pomade had begged her fingers to take a wee ramble through the short strands. Eyes the color of the sea when kissed by the sun had sent her pulse into a thundering gallop. Then there'd been the small cleft in his chin beneath a well-formed mouth that smiled easily. And a tanned complexion that hinted at a love for the outdoors. Consciousness definitely became him.

Yet his handsome face hadn't melted her heart. His kind manner and vivid integrity had accomplished that feat. She paused her pacing at the outer wall, the fading light of the summer evening drifting through the high window that had been left open to allow a bit of a breeze. Muriel turned and leaned her back against the cool, whitewashed brick as a vision of Zane kneeling before her filled her memory. How distraught he'd been to think he'd caused her injury—an injury that wasn't even real. Just another of Mrs. Underhill's twisted half-truths. Half-truths that Muriel had done nothing to correct.

Pretending to have no voice had seemed harmless when Mrs. Underhill first proposed the scheme. How wrong she'd been. Harm had screamed at her from Zane's devastated gaze and passed through her skin as his hands clutched hers in agonized apology. Was he still blaming himself? She'd tried to relieve him of that burden without revealing a truth that would banish her from his home, but he hadn't seemed convinced. How could he be? Half-truths only beget confusion, not understanding.

Ah, to be sure, I've got meself into quite the pickle. What am I to do, Lord? If I confess the full truth, not only will I lose Zane before I've the chance to get to know 'im, but I'll bring the wrath of Mrs. Underhill upon me family. I don't see a way out.

Muriel turned her gaze to the crucifix on the wall near the washstand, the only decoration in the room. The church she attended used a simple, unadorned wooden cross to signify Christ's sacrifice, but seeing the suffering Jesus hanging there—the thorns cutting into his head, the nails piercing his hands, the way his head drooped in agony and exhaustion—sharpened the quills that jabbed her spirit.

She might not be lying outright, but she was participating in an act of deception. She doubted her Lord would approve.

A soft tapping at her door brought her out of her musings. After swiping away the moisture pooling in her eyes with the back of her hand, she crossed to the door.

Sister Mary Vincent stood in the hall, a small tray in her hands. Kindness radiated from her eyes. "I noticed you didn't come down for supper and thought you might be hungry."

Muriel opened her mouth to thank her then stopped herself as Mrs. Underhill's threats flashed through her mind. Apologizing with her gaze, Muriel dipped her chin and opened the door wide.

The young nun smiled as she stepped inside. "No need to fret, Miss Quinn. Mrs. Underhill explained about your vow of silence." She placed the tray of bread, fruit, and cheese atop the modest writing desk positioned against the wall at the foot of the bed. She retrieved a tin cup from within her pocket and moved to the washstand to fill it with water from the ewer. "Vows to the Lord are sacred things, and I commend your desire to quiet yourself in order to hear God's voice more clearly. After listening to you sing, I knew immediately that God had blessed you with an incredible gift. Yet great talent can also make one susceptible to pride. You are wise to guard against such attack."

Muriel shook her head, her conscience swelling to painful proportions in her chest. She couldn't allow this godly woman to be tainted by her deceit. And maybe, just maybe, Sister Mary Vincent could help.

Moving in front of the door to block the nun's retreat, Muriel pulled her notebook and pencil from her pocket and scribbled a handful of words on the page.

Vow given to Mrs. U, not God.

I'm trapped in a scheme.

No way out without good people getting hurt.

She thrust the notebook at Sister Mary Vincent. The young nun's brow furrowed as she read, but when she handed the tablet back to Muriel, no condemnation marred her expression.

"I cannot begin to guess what challenge you are facing, Miss Quinn, but I do know that our God can make a way where there is none. When the Israelites were trapped between the Egyptian army and an impassable sea, there seemed to be no way out . . . until God opened a path. He can do the same for you, if you have the courage to follow where he leads." She glanced meaningfully toward the Bible sitting on the corner of the desk. "Seek the Lord's guidance." After delivering that very nun-like and not particularly helpful advice, her mouth turned up at the corners. "You might start with Isaiah 42:16. I've found that courage is much easier to grasp when one has first been buoyed by hope."

Sister Mary Vincent stepped around Muriel, pulled open the door, then glanced back over her shoulder. "I shall pray for you, Miss Quinn."

Muriel dipped her chin, her heart brimming with a gratitude that couldn't be captured in words even if she'd been free to speak them.

After closing the door, she crossed to her desk and reached past the food to clasp her Bible. She thumbed through the pages to the book of Isaiah and found the recommended verse.

"And I will bring the blind by a way that they knew not; I will lead them in paths that they have not known; I will make darkness light before them, and crooked things straight. These things will I do unto them, and not forsake them."

The promise soaked into Muriel's spirit. The Lord would make a way. He would not forsake her. Yet she must be willing to let him straighten the crooked places in her. The bent truths and misshapen motives. She'd once watched a smith refashion a plow blade that had been damaged by a rock. It took a lot of heat and hammering to make the crooked blade straight again, but in the end, the plow had been restored.

I can't say that I'm lookin' forward to the heat and hammerin', Lord, but I'll do me best to submit.

And maybe in the process her honor would be restored.

Chapter 13

Zane stood outside the Ursuline Academy and checked the straightness of his tie before ringing the bell to announce his presence. *Breathe, man. Just breathe.*

Thank heaven he'd had the revisions of his veranda design to focus his mind at work today. The pressure of providing Mr. Clayton a quality sketch had been the only force strong enough to keep his mind from constantly drifting to a certain titian-haired mermaid. Not that visions of Muriel hadn't still found their way into his mind. They had. Often. Each time he wrenched his mind away from her, he did so with the promise that he'd be able to see her tonight. And now here he stood, all thought of ironwork and classical proportion systems stored away in mental drawers so he could give his full attention to the young woman his heart had been seeking for years.

The heavy door pulled inward and a middle-aged woman garbed in black with a frightfully stern countenance peered up at him, a question in her eyes.

"Zane Erickson, ma'am." He tugged off his hat and offered a smile. "I'm here to escort Miss Muriel Quinn to Forbes's Confectionary."

She looked him over from head to toe as if measuring his worthiness. Her raised brow seemed to indicate she lacked conviction that he met the standard, but she admitted him anyway.

"This way, sir."

Zane followed the nun through a dim corridor, his shoes tapping loudly against the stone floor. His heart tapped its own rhythm, doubling the tempo of his steps.

The nun assigned the duty of petrifying male callers drew to a halt and aimed a steely glance at him that promised the wrath of God would strike should Zane disregard her instructions. She stretched an arm toward an open doorway to his right. "You may wait in here, Mr. Erickson. Miss Quinn and her maid will be down shortly."

Her maid? He hadn't thought a public outing to an ice cream shop would require a chaperone. He went there all the time with his friends, including those of the female variety. But then, he'd not been paying court to any of those ladies, and they'd not been alone. He should have expected that a woman living in a school run by nuns would have a stricter code to follow. Not that he minded . . . too much. Though it might make the surprise he'd planned for the walk home a little awkward.

The sister left, and Zane paced the small receiving room, making an effort to distract himself by noting the elements of gothic styling, but not even the vaulted ceiling or the pointed arch design above the door managed to capture his attention for more than a moment. He'd gotten desperate enough to start counting the individual panes in the line of tall, narrow windows along the outer wall when the sound of footsteps had him abandoning his tally and pivoting to face the open doorway.

The stony-faced nun held him back with a stare as effective as being jabbed in the chest with a spear. Did she practice those *fear of God* injection glares, or was it a natural talent? Either way, she'd found her calling. No dishonorable intention could survive that withering glare. Even with completely *honorable* intentions, Zane still felt the pinch. He had to remind himself that he'd done nothing wrong.

Thankfully, he didn't have to endure the hostile stare of the guardian nun much longer, for a vision in dark green entered and offered an opportunity for escape.

"Miss Quinn." He stepped forward and sketched a bow, his hat tucked beneath his left arm. "I'm delighted to see you again."

Delighted was such a tepid word. Enraptured. Jubilant. Exultant. Those would be better descriptors for the swirling giddiness that attacked his abdomen at the sight of her. Yet, he doubted Sister Steel-Eye would approve, and he didn't want to do anything to sabotage this meeting.

Muriel tilted her head back and lifted her lashes. Her hazel eyes lit with a joy so genuine he didn't need the smile blooming upon her face to recognize her pleasure. Though her smile *was* a sight to behold. Straight, white teeth on full display, she held nothing back. Except her voice. But he'd prepared for that.

Sister Steel-Eye cleared her throat. "Mrs. Underhill has provided her maid, Vanessa, to accompany Miss Quinn this evening."

A fetching brunette he hadn't yet noticed nodded in his direction, her gaze rather direct for that of a servant. She quickly diverted her attention to the floor, but Zane couldn't escape the feeling that her matchmaking mistress had secured her services for more than propriety. She'd no doubt been tasked to spy on the couple and report her observations. As much as he disliked the idea of having his personal business bandied about, he had to admit that having a chaperone who favored his romantic success could be a boon. She'd likely not interfere with his attempted courtship. Unlike Sister Steel-Eye, who continued glaring at him as if he were a wolf making off with one of her lambs.

Warding off a shiver, Zane turned to Muriel and offered his arm. "Shall we go?"

She nodded with bountiful enthusiasm and fit her hand into the crook of his elbow, her cheeks pinkening slightly at the contact. He understood the feeling. A delicious warmth permeated his chest, and his pulse decided to take up the polka. Thankfully, the walk to Forbes's gave them time to adjust to each other. Since he couldn't ask her about her day or her opinions on current events, he prattled on about his studies, pointing out a few examples of architectural styles as they passed different buildings. Instead of simply inclining her head politely, Muriel quizzed him by squeezing his arm and pointing to additional structures. In fact, she went a step further and tugged him off Bath Street to turn down Avenue I. He suspected her intention and was proven correct when she stopped a couple blocks later in front of the First Baptist Church. She gestured to the unusual white building then turned to him with an expectant gaze.

Unused to having someone other than his professional colleagues demonstrate any true interest in his architectural knowledge, Zane grinned as he shared what he knew of the building.

"This church displays an unusual blend of Gothic and Eastern Orthodox styles. See the rounded vestibules? That circular style is reminiscent of the domes utilized in Eastern Orthodox churches, yet all the arches over the doorways and windows come together in a gothic point to draw your gaze upward."

She tilted her head as if following those arch points into the heavens. Then she lifted her hand and started counting. She tugged her hand away from his arm and held up seven fingers.

Zane chuckled softly. "Yes, seven steeples. Most churches are satisfied with one, but I suppose they were aiming for perfection."

Her brow scrunched slightly as if she didn't quite understand his comment.

"Seven is considered a number of completion or perfection. It harkens back to the seven days of creation."

Her face cleared, and she nodded right before snagging his arm again and tugging him around the corner toward the more Gothic side of the church. This section of the building sported a steep triangular roof, yet it boasted a circular window at the apex that indicated an Orthodox influence. It really was a fascinating study, but as much as he enjoyed sharing his observations on the subject, this evening was not about impressing her with his knowledge of building design. It was about building a relationship. Or at least laying a foundation for one.

However, Zane couldn't resist pointing out two of the buildings that bore his mentor's fingerprints as they continued their walk. After they'd crossed Avenue H, he drew her attention to Eaton Memorial Chapel with its more classic Gothic Revival lines.

"I'm apprenticing with Nicholas Clayton." He tried to keep that statement from sounding like a brag even though he was particularly proud of the connection. "He designed this chapel. It might not be as grand as Trinity Church on the corner or St. Mary's on the next street over, but I've always been rather fond of it. Its smaller scale might not inspire as much awe as its larger counterparts, but I like its unpretentious feel. As if everyone would be welcome, regardless of status or influence."

She leaned into his side and squeezed his arm in silent agreement.

A throat cleared somewhere behind them, reminding Zane they weren't alone. Score one for the chaperone. Muriel straightened away from him, and he immediately missed the feel of her nestled against his side. He'd not expected to find a woman who shared his appreciation for the simpler things in life. Not among the elite, anyway. It reinforced his conviction that Muriel Quinn was indeed the partner God intended for him.

Muriel stole a peek at Vanessa and winced at the girl's disdainful stare. The maid had not been shy with her opinions when she arrived at the academy that afternoon to dress Muriel's hair and give her a tutorial on lock picking. A lesson that proved challenging since very few locks existed in a school run by nuns. Mrs. Underhill had thought ahead, though, and instructed her maid to deliver a tea caddy and a jewelry box, each sporting a different type of lock—one called a warded lock, and the other a lever lock. Muriel had no success with either, probably because it felt sinful to learn the skills of a thief, especially with Jesus looking on from the crucifix on the wall. She was already walking a tightrope regarding the not bearing false witness commandment. She wasn't too keen about breaking the *Thou shalt not steal* one, even if it was for a good cause.

Until Vanessa had clutched her arm with a painful grip and jerked her out of her reticence. "Do you think this is a game? Mrs. Underhill is desperate to get that journal back. She's dangerous, and she doesn't make idle threats. If you want to survive, you've got to quit being a namby-pamby and get down to business. There's no room for lofty ideals or prudishness when dealing with the missus. She only cares about one thing—results. Fail to give them to her and you'll suffer for it."

Muriel had slunk back from the maid's vehemence. What horrible things had she witnessed in Mrs. Underhill's employ? There must have been many to create such a haunted look in her eyes. Perhaps she'd even felt the sting of that suffering herself.

"You have family?" Vanessa asked, her eyebrow raised in challenge.

Muriel nodded.

"Good. Use that. That's what I do." She pushed the tea caddy across the desk until it sat again in front of Muriel. "What if your mother or sister were trapped in a trunk with no fresh air to breathe and the key to open the lock was inside this box? Changes things, doesn't it?"

The horrible image of Alana or Fletcher suffocating inside a trunk ripped through her chest and spawned a new motivation.

"Don't think of what you're doing as stealing. Think of it as protecting those you love. Because that's what it is. The missus has no qualms about hurting folks who cross her, and nothing hurts more than knowing your actions, or *lack* of actions, caused someone you love to suffer."

By the time Vanessa had ceased the lock lesson and turned to hair duty, her disgust with Muriel had become quite evident. Not only for Muriel's lack of skill with the locks, but for her foolishness in getting tangled up with Mrs. Underhill in the first place. *Naive nitwit* and *starry-eyed stupidity* had been muttered under her breath more than once as she expertly molded Muriel's tresses into an elaborate braided masterpiece that Muriel could never hope to replicate. Not that she'd want to with all the hair pulling and scalp scraping involved in the procedure.

"Nicholas Clayton also designed Harmony Hall." Zane's voice pulled her back into the sunshine as he tipped his head toward an impressive building across the street, one covered in fancy arches and what seemed to be stone sentries keeping watch from the rooftops. Muriel's stomach tightened. She swore she could feel Vanessa's gaze searing her shoulder blades from behind. Must she be watched from above too?

Let it go, Muri. Ye'll have plenty o' time to fret about desk drawers and the like later. There be no locks waitin' fer ye at the confectionary. Just the man you've been cravin' to know.

Determined to let neither glaring chaperones nor statuary ruin her evening, Muriel gave her full attention to Zane as he pointed out different architectural features. She might not run in the same circles as the Ericksons, but she had heard of Nicholas Clayton. He was one of Galveston's most noted celebrities. Zane must truly be talented to work with such a skilled artisan. To think that Zane might design a church or town hall himself someday. Wouldn't that be something? She'd likely stop people on the street just to tell them that her husband had designed that building.

Husband. Oh, how she hoped Zane would fill that role one day. Her heart nearly burst from the strength of her wishing. But he might not want her once he learned of her deceit. That's why she'd written the letter weighing heavily in her skirt pocket. She couldn't afford to reveal everything. Not yet. Not until she knew she could trust him. But she had to open herself to him at least a little. How else could she hope to build something with him as beautiful and lasting as the hall standing before them?

More pedestrians filled the walkways as they neared Market Street. Most of the shops were closed at this hour, but the restaurants and coffee houses did a brisk business, and the Tremont Opera House stood less than a block away. Oh, how she'd love to see a production there someday. What would it be like to hear a true opera singer perform? Gooseflesh popped out on her arms at the thought. But she really needed to get her mind out of dreamy somedays and focus on the day she was walking in right now. The delight of Zane Erickson's company tangled with the darkness of Mrs. Underhill's looming shadow made the road before her rather treacherous. She needed to watch her step, lest she trip up and destroy everything she sought to build.

Thankfully, the pressure relented once they reached Forbes's Confectionary. Zane purchased a soda for Vanessa, and the maid settled at a small table in the corner and pulled out some knitting to keep herself busy while Muriel and Zane took a table near the front window. Once seated, Muriel pulled out her notepad, determined not to make Zane carry on a one-sided conversation for the entire evening. She'd even planned ahead. Turning to her first page, she passed it to him.

"Tell me about your family." Zane looked up from the page and smiled. "Well, you met my mother. She can be a little overwhelming at times, but she means well. She supports my studies, which I appreciate, and she runs the Ladies Auxiliary for our church. My father . . ." His smile flattened. "He works at the Cotton Exchange. Expected me to follow in his footsteps and wasn't too pleased when I opted for an architecture apprenticeship instead." He shrugged, but a lingering disappointment dulled his gaze. "He's not the warmest of men, but he's had to harden himself in order to succeed in the business world. I suppose I shouldn't judge him too harshly since his success has provided our family privileges we wouldn't have enjoyed otherwise." Yet the way he said it made Muriel suspect that Zane would have preferred a few less privileges and a few more evenings with his da.

His expression lightened as he leaned back and tapped the edge of the table with his thumbs. "Now Grandpa Clem. Oh, you'll like him."

He went on to tell several stories about the man he obviously adored. Grandpa Clem reminded her a bit of Laraline. A hard worker with plain-speaking ways and an appreciation for the simple pleasures in life. The more stories Zane told, the more his eyes gleamed, banishing the discomfort brought on by thoughts of his father.

The waiter arrived with their ice cream orders, interrupting their conversation. Muriel didn't mind, though. She'd never had ice cream served in such a fancy dish. Cut glass with a pedestal foot. And the ice cream itself was fancier than anything she'd ever seen. It had been molded into a scallop shape, like a delectable seashell topped with sugared strawberries. A wafer cookie jutted out from the side, begging to be devoured first.

Zane's quiet chuckle brought a blush to her cheeks. The woman of means she pretended to be surely wouldn't react in such a way. But she didn't want Zane to fall in love with a pretend woman of means. She wanted him to love *her*. So she did nothing to hide her excitement and was rewarded with a bright smile from the man across from her.

"Do you want to try mine?" He pushed his dish toward her, a rounded oval of chocolate ice cream looking absolutely decadent. She shook her head, but then on impulse, reached out and snatched one of the chocolate curls from the top and popped it into her mouth.

Zane laughed, the sound almost as delicious as the chocolate melting on her tongue. She offered him one of her sugared berries in exchange, and when he took one in his spoon then combined it with a bit of chocolate from his own dish, her heart did a little melting of its own.

After taking a bite—all right, several bites—of her ice cream, she recalled that she hadn't yet told him anything about her own family. She turned the page in her notebook and slid it toward him. She couldn't give many details thanks to the picture Mrs. Underhill had already painted, but she could share the things that really mattered. The way her ma had sung lullabies and rocked her in the big chair at bedtime before the Lord had called her home. How Alana had been both mother and sister to the three younger Quinn girls after Ma's passing. How two of her sisters moved away after marrying, and how thankful she was that Alana remained in Galveston. Not only because Alana was her best friend, but because her children were three of Muriel's favorite people in all the world. Her two adorable nieces were the perfect size for snuggling even if they were too young for adventuring with their Auntie Muriel just yet. Their big brother, however, loved to scamper all over the island and comb the shore for treasures. Then, of course, there was Da. The father who had always been her hero, especially when he found a way to nurture her love of the sea.

"That's how I feel about my Grandpa Clem." Zane dipped his spoon into his ice cream but made no move to lift the bite to his mouth. "He just seems to understand me. The way I like to build things, to create with my own two hands instead of paying someone else to do the crafting for me. He's such a man of abiding faith, too. There's no one I respect more."

Including his father, she imagined, though he didn't voice the words.

They returned to eating their ice cream, and the soft clinking of spoons on glass proved to be conversation enough for the moment. Still in possession of her notebook, Zane turned the page and read her next question. He winked at her then cheated and turned the page to read her answer. She nearly called him out on it, but the ice cream in her mouth stopped her from making that mistake.

She'd asked him about his hobbies and then went on to tell him about her swimming, while pleading with him to keep her secret. His mother had been right that it stretched the bounds of propriety. Her sisters had been telling her that for years. She told him of her admiration for Agnes Beckwith, the English swimmer who had set so many records and how she dreamed of swimming the length of Galveston Island someday. She also told him of how free she felt in the sea. Free from expectations, free from judgment, free to be herself.

"I feel the same when I sail . . . when I'm not getting knocked overboard, of course." He dipped his chin, a touch of color staining his cheeks as his dark hair fell across his forehead. He lifted his chin and grinned, the embarrassment banished in favor of happier memories. "The wind in my hair, the spray of the waves in my face, the boat running like a racing horse that never tires. But what you've done . . ." He lowered his voice as he leaned across the table. "That's incredible."

The admiration in his voice filled and stretched her heart. He didn't think her swimming shameful or unfeminine? If he did, he hid it well. But no. She believed him. He thought her incredible. And wasn't that the most delicious treat of all?

Their eyes held for a long moment before she darted her gaze down to her notebook and was reminded of his skipping the question. Although, sailing *did* count as a hobby. But surely he had more than one, and she wanted to learn about all of them.

Muriel pointed to the notebook and then pointed to him.

He held up his hands in surrender, though his crooked smile didn't seem very repentant. "I know. I know. My turn. But I'd rather show you than tell you, and this isn't the place. Will you walk down to the wharf with me? It's not far, and I promise to return you to the academy well before curfew."

He stood and held out his hand to her. Muriel didn't hesitate for a second.

Chapter 14

A tangy salt breeze blowing off the bay cooled the air as Zane and Muriel strolled past the iron works foundry toward a narrow wooden bridge that led to Lufkin's Wharf. Her da worked mainly on the Central Wharf, but at this time in the evening, he'd be home, so she needn't fear running into him. Though she'd not have minded catchin' a glimpse of him from a distance. It seemed an age since she'd seen him.

Halfway across the bridge, Zane stopped and leaned his back against the wooden railing. The breeze ruffled his hair as he reached into the pocket of his coat and pulled out a flute of some sort. Not a fife, like the ones played in the drum corps during parades, but one with a whistle-shaped mouthpiece and a body that pointed downward.

Zane set it to his lips and arranged his fingers over the holes. He inhaled, and then the sweetest music filled the air. Gentle, pure tones, clear and bright. It took only a measure or two of him playing for her to recognize the melody. "Jesus, Savior, Pilot Me." The hymn she'd been singing the day of his accident.

He remembered. More than that, he'd taken the time to learn the song. His fingers moved with confidence to shape the notes as he breathed through the instrument.

Her throat ached to join the song. To voice the lyrics running through her mind. To meld her voice to Zane's music. But she'd trapped herself in silence. Denied the gift the Lord had given. Yet the gift was not hers alone. Zane had it too. His music entreated and cajoled, bringing delight to her heart despite her vocal banishment. He played with a natural ease that had her closing her eyes and swaying with the gentle rhythm as the melody wrapped its sweet arms around her soul.

She sang the words in her mind until the first verse came to a close. He didn't start the second verse, just let the final note diminish into the evening air. Muriel opened her eyes and met Zane's gaze.

"It's called a recorder." He pulled a handkerchief from his pocket and wiped the mouthpiece then held it out for her inspection. "Some call it an English flute. My Grandpa Clem taught me to play. He learned from his father, who learned from his. We aren't sure how far back the tradition goes, but it seems to be a rite of passage for the Erickson men. My father even learned how to play, though I haven't heard him make music in years."

He wiggled the instrument in front of her, his smile growing. "Want to try it?"

A chance to make music? Oh, yes! Muriel bounced on her toes as she searched his face to ensure he wasn't teasing. He extended it closer to her, and she accepted, soda bubbles shooting geysers through her midsection.

The wood warmed in her hands, the polished maple finish gleaming in the low light of evening. She tried to replicate how he'd held the recorder, but she must not have done it correctly for Zane came alongside and helped her position her hands, the left covering the upper holes while the right covered those below. Heat flooded her face as he gently arranged her fingers, scooting close to her side as he did so.

Heavens, but her pulse was thumpin' like she'd just raced Fletcher to the end of the pier and back.

"There's a hole on the back side . . . here . . . for your thumb." He adjusted her grip, his cheek nearly touching hers in the process.

She really should be paying attention to what he was showing her, but all she could think about was how close he stood, and how wonderful it would be to lean ever so slightly to the left and brush her cheek against his.

Once her thumb found its place, Zane dutifully stepped back, allowing Muriel the space she really didn't want but probably needed. Her eyes followed him, though, as did her chin and entire face, twisting away from the instrument to maintain whatever connection she might finagle from his gaze.

His eyes crinkled in a smile, and her belly flipped like one of Alana's pancakes, dangling in midair for a heartbeat before finding its way to the platter.

"Give it a try."

Muriel smiled, set her mouth upon the whistle, and gave a mighty blow. A dreadful screech blasted from the recorder, startling a group of sleepy seagulls from the roof of a nearby warehouse.

Zane lurched backward, and his face contorted as he jiggled a finger against his ear. His good-humored laughter came next, though, and soothed her embarrassment.

"Sorry," he said. "I should have warned you. You don't need to blow hard. Just use a steady stream of air, like when you sing. Try covering the top two holes and thumb hole. That's an A. You can use the thumb on your right hand to balance the recorder while your other fingers hover loosely above the holes."

Determined not to imitate a tortured seabird this time, Muriel concentrated as she rested the mouthpiece against her lower lip and blew into the whistle. A note emerged! A little shaky and not terribly beautiful, but it was a note.

She released the mouthpiece and grinned up at Zane, exulting in the pleasure etching his face.

"Great job!" He reached into his pocket and pulled out a second flute then demonstrated some basic fingerings.

They practiced for a few minutes, and Muriel managed to pick up the first few bars of "Three Blind Mice." It helped that adding one finger at a time moved the notes down the scale. Of course, when they got to the trickier bit about the farmer's wife, Zane took off, adding intricate flourishes, until returning to the simplistic melody where she could join.

It was ridiculous how much she loved it. Making music with Zane. Even silly nursery songs about doomed rodents. She could have stood on that bridge serenading the gulls all night. They must have played that tune at least ten times before Vanessa called a halt to their concert.

"We really ought to be heading back, Miss Quinn."

Muriel enjoyed a fleeting pied piper fantasy, where a blow on her flute would mesmerize the gulls and send them squawking down upon Vanessa's head in protest. Imagining the young woman shrieking and dashing about as she tried to swat birds out of her hair made it a little easier to accept her unwelcome interruption, though disappointment still tugged hard on Muriel's heart as she handed the recorder back to Zane.

"Why don't you hold onto it for a while?"

Muriel shook her head, thinking she must have misheard. This was a family heirloom. She couldn't keep it. What if something happened to it? She thrust it toward him. He pressed it right back toward her, his gaze warm and kind and so heart-stoppingly tender that her will to fight evaporated.

"It's all right. That one's mine. I'll hold on to Grandpa Clem's." He held up the one he'd been playing. "I figured you might enjoy a different way to make music. Until you're able to sing again." He shrugged and his expression turned a bit sheepish. "But if you really don't want it, I'll take it home with me."

She hugged the recorder to her chest and twisted sideways to protect her prize. There was no way she would let him think she didn't want it. Not when the gift had been so thoughtfully given. She'd play it every day and think of him with every note.

His eyes brightened, and she couldn't help but smile in response. Until she considered his motive. He thought to restore music to her since he believed her voice lost. Such a beautiful gesture. And completely unnecessary. Her voice wasn't lost, merely trapped inside a box of her own making.

With the sun dipping low on the horizon, Zane escorted her back to the Ursuline Academy via the most direct route. He offered a few comments here and there, but one-sided conversations were hard to maintain when your partner was distracted, and Muriel could think of little more than the letter in her pocket, and the fear that once he read it, their time together would end.

When they reached the academy door, Zane turned to face her. "I enjoyed our time together this evening, Miss Quinn. Would you permit me to call on you again?"

Muriel nodded eagerly, praying he'd not change his mind.

His smile brightened the shadowy street and gave her the courage to reach into her skirt pocket.

"My mother would be honored to host you for dinner tomorrow evening. I could come get you around six?"

Dinner in his home? Muriel's stomach tightened. Mrs. Underhill would expect her to search for the journal. Maybe even pick a lock.

Muriel hid her worries behind a smile and another nod. Then before she could lose her nerve, she pulled the letter from her pocket and pressed it into his hand. His brows raised, but he took the note and slid it into his coat pocket. She dipped her chin to bid him good night then followed Vanessa inside the academy.

Zane whistled his way home, the tune of "Three Blind Mice" earning him more than one raised eyebrow from passersby. Not that he cared in the slightest. It was his new favorite song. When he reached his house, he skipped up the front porch steps.

"Went that well, did it?"

The creak of a rocking chair and a whiff of tobacco smoke drew Zane's attention to where Grandpa Clem sat in the shadows, enjoying his evening pipe.

"It was *perfect*." Zane sauntered over to his grandfather and leaned against the whitewashed railing. "Thanks for loaning me your recorder." He pulled the flute from his coat pocket and held it out. "She loved the music, by the way."

Grandpa Clem's eyes twinkled as he claimed the instrument. "I thought she might. A person with music in her soul needs an outlet. The way you talked about her singin', I knew she had more than just technical skill. She has the heart."

"Enthusiasm, too," Zane said with a chuckle. "She woke all the gulls with her first attempt."

"Did she, now?" Grandpa Clem stretched his legs out in front of him and crossed them at the ankles, a grin stretching his weathered cheeks.

"She doesn't do things by half measures."

Grandpa Clem's expression morphed into something more serious as he met Zane's gaze. "A fact I thank the Lord for every day. You'd not still be among the livin' if that little lady lacked gumption."

A sobering thought, yet one that only served to deepen his appreciation for Miss Quinn. "She was actually interested in my architecture babble, too." He wagged his head, still amazed at how well the evening had gone. "She pointed out different buildings and asked questions." With her eyes, at least. Such expressive eyes. Changing like the sea. Adventurous. Playful. Shy. Bold.

Secretive.

Zane's euphoria dimmed a bit as he recalled the odd look that had crossed her face when she handed him that letter outside the academy. Her mouth had been smiling, but her eyes had been rife with apologies.

"There's something special about her, Grandpa. About the way I feel when I'm with her. I can't explain it. It just feels . . . right."

Grandpa Clem took a drag on his pipe then blew out a line of smoke in a long, slow exhale. "It works like that sometimes. A fella recognizing his mate the first time he sees her. 'Course sometimes a man is swayed by a pretty face and all the hot blood that starts pumpin' through him so that he *thinks* she's the right one, when she ain't. That's why the Good Lord gave man a head as well as a heart. Be sure you're usin' both."

"Yes, sir." He'd never been one to be carried away by emotion, but then he'd never met a girl who tempted him to throw caution to the wind, either.

He couldn't imagine Muriel Quinn being anything other than what she appeared. Kind, genuine, joyful. She had such zest for life and a heart for family. Reading the little bits she'd shared with him at the ice cream shop had made that clear.

So why the shuttered look when she'd given him the letter?

Reaching into his coat pocket, Zane fingered the envelope, a sudden craving for privacy hitting him.

"Think I'll turn in." Zane pushed away from the railing.

"'Night," Grandpa Clem said around the stem of his pipe.

Zane thumped the man's shoulder and headed toward the door.

"Hey, Zane?"

He turned. "Yeah?"

Grandpa Clem leaned forward in his rocker, his gaze pensive and penetrating. "Just because a woman is perfect for you, don't mean she's perfect. Best not expect her to be."

Chapter 15

Zane headed for the staircase that would take him to his room, but his mother swept through the entryway and intercepted him before he'd ascended past the third step.

"Not so fast, young man." How she managed to scold and tease at the same time was a mystery Zane doubted he'd ever solve. "Did you really think you could escape upstairs without giving your mother a report?"

Biting back a groan, Zane turned to face the matriarch of Clan Erickson. Not quite ready to fully capitulate, however, he held his ground on the third stair. "Spying on me from your sitting room again?" He raised a brow but couldn't manage to hold the affronted expression for more than a couple of seconds before a grin took its place.

She waved off the accusation with a sweep of her hand through the air. "It's a lovely room. The perfect place to enjoy a good book and a cup of tea in the evening."

"It also happens to have a window providing a view of the front porch."

"Does it?" Her eyebrows arched in mock innocence. "I hadn't noticed."

Zane rolled his eyes. "You're a terrible liar."

"Thank you." She winked and sashayed closer. "*You're* a terrible escape artist."

"I don't know about that. I can outrun you."

"But you won't. You love me too much to leave me in suspense."

An impenetrable argument. Of which she was well aware. Her smile bloomed with triumph.

Zane trotted down the steps and offered his mother his arm. "One of these days, I'm going to have my own home, and you'll have to find new ways to ambush me."

"If this home of yours comes with a wife and children, I won't have to."

A reluctant chuckle rumbled from his chest. "Somehow, I think you'll still find a way to run me to ground."

She patted his arm. "Of course I will, dear. 'Tis a mother's duty to insert herself into the lives of her children. And *grandchildren*."

"Whoa, now. It's not time to start knitting baby booties just yet."

Mother shook her head and clucked her tongue. "Come now, Zane. You know me better than that. There's already a small trunk in my dressing room filled with booties, bonnets, and blankets just waiting for the next generation of Ericksons. Your father's not the only one who plans for this family's future."

Zane drew to a halt outside the sitting room door. "Speaking of Father, should I fetch him before making my report?"

His mother's smile dimmed slightly before brightening with a false cheer that made Zane's chest ache. "No. I'll fill him in later. He's out with Mr. Barnum at the lodge tonight."

The Masonic Lodge where all the men with power and influence in Galveston congregated. Father had once told him that he accomplished as much work there as he did at the Exchange. But what price was he paying for that success?

Zane's parents' relationship had been deteriorating for years. They put on a good show for neighbors and business associates, but they rarely spent any time together at home, apart from the dinner table. Father either closed himself in his office or went out with men from the Exchange. Mother spent her evenings reading, embroidering, or apparently knitting baby booties on the sly. Was it any wonder she was so invested in Zane's life? Her husband had cut her from all the meaningful parts of his.

Zane wanted so much more than a dutiful union. He longed to share his *life*, not just his bank account. A vision of Muriel playing the recorder with eager enthusiasm banished the shadows brought on by his father's neglect. While tonight had only been their first outing, and she'd likely been trying to impress him as much as he'd been trying to impress her, he'd noticed nothing artificial about her interest. He'd escorted enough young women to tell the difference between genuine enthusiasm and the feigned variety manufactured to win a man's favor.

Joy had radiated from Muriel this evening. Whether they'd been looking at architecture, eating ice cream, or playing music, her eyes had danced, and her smile had beamed. Her joy had fed his own and left him whistling on the way home. Whistling!

How he craved a home filled with love and laughter. A family that actually liked each other and spent time together because they enjoyed each other's company, not under the duress of dutiful obligation. The hints Muriel had revealed about her own family gave him the impression that the Quinns had captured some of that familial magic. Who better to help him establish the family of his dreams than a woman with insider knowledge of how such relationships worked?

Mother seated herself in her favorite chair and turned up the lamp on the table near her elbow, one she'd obviously turned down to aid her spying through the front window with the drawn curtains.

"So, tell me about your evening." She smoothed her skirts then leveled a probing gaze at him. "Are you still enamored with this young woman after spending time with her, or will she be joining the dozens of others who failed to hold your interest past the first outing?"

Zane removed his hat and sprawled on the sofa next to her chair. "There have hardly been *dozens*, Mother. And there would have been a lot less had you accepted my protests and not insisted that I escort certain ladies about town on a trial basis."

"Well, how else were you to know if any of the young ladies of our acquaintance might suit? I'm still not convinced you gave Elsie Dumore a fair assessment. She's a lovely girl from a good family. She's well educated, a skilled pianist, and possesses a keen appreciation for art. The two of you should be a perfect match."

Except she complained about the heat incessantly, belittled those she thought her inferiors, and declared Grandpa Clem to be an adorable country bumpkin. The addition of the word *adorable* had done nothing to soften the insult. Zane would never marry a woman who held his grandfather in contempt.

"Unfortunately, Miss Dunmore's disposition failed to shine as brightly as her accomplishments. Miss Quinn, on the other hand . . ." He smiled as he recalled the mischievous expression on Muriel's face as she stole a curl of shaved chocolate from atop his ice cream. ". . . was utterly delightful. Never have I enjoyed an evening more."

Mother leaned forward in her chair, hope glimmering in her gaze. "Do you plan to see her again, then?"

Zane sat up straighter and slapped his palms against his knees. "Yep. Invited her to our family dinner tomorrow night." Mostly just to spend time with her but also to see how she acted around Grandpa Clem. She didn't seem the type to put on airs, but he'd rather know now, before he fell for her any harder.

"Family dinner. *Tomorrow?* And you thought to sneak upstairs without telling me this vital piece of news?" Mother lurched to her feet and paced to the window. "Good heavens. I'll have to speak to Cook." She pivoted and targeted Zane with a pointed gaze. "Do you know what foods she likes? Or more importantly, what she dislikes?"

Zane rose to his feet and laid gentle hands upon his mother's shoulders. "Don't go to any special trouble, Mother. The queen isn't paying a call. Just a young woman who might one day be part of this family. Whatever you and Cook have already planned will be more than sufficient. I want her to experience a real Erickson family dinner. No frills. Just family. All right?"

"Fine. But I'm asking Cook to make her famous chocolate cake for dessert."

Zane grinned. "Good choice. I happen to know Miss Quinn is fond of chocolate."

Mother reached out a hand and smoothed back the section of hair that always flopped over his forehead, just like she used to do when he was a boy. Her expression softened. "You really like this girl, don't you?"

A swelling warmth climbed from his stomach up through his chest. "I do."

"Then I'll endeavor to like her, too. Even if she can't speak."

Zane bent his head and kissed his mother's hair. "Thank you." He stepped back. "Just think—tomorrow you won't have to ambush me at the door to know how the evening went. You'll already be privy to all the pertinent details."

Mischief lit her eyes. "I might ambush you anyway. Just to keep you on your toes."

Zane chuckled. "Thanks for the warning." He dropped his hands from her shoulders and edged backwards a pace. "Now, have I satisfied your curiosity enough to earn my freedom?"

"Yes, yes." She made shooing motions with her hands. "Run off and do whatever it is young men do these days to pass the time."

He didn't know what other young men did, but he intended to read a letter from a particularly fetching redhead. Muriel might not be able to speak with her voice, but she could speak through words penned upon paper, and he didn't want to wait a minute longer to hear what she had to say.

After collecting his hat, he took the stairs two at a time and closed himself in his room. He spared only enough time to remove his collar, tie, jacket, and shoes before slicing open the envelope and extracting the folded pages from their sheath.

Dear Zane,

Is it all right that I address you as Zane? I realize it's not proper on such short acquaintance, but that is how I think of you. How I've thought of you since the day I pulled you from the sea.

His pulse vibrated like a guitar string strummed by her words. Zane. She thought of him as Zane. Such a little thing on the surface, but it carried deep implications. Implications of intimacy. Of attraction. Of—dare he hope—affection?

Dropping the envelope onto the desk, he crossed to the upholstered chair next to his armoire, dropped into the seat, and propped his feet upon the matching ottoman. Tilting the page to catch the light from the gas sconce mounted on the wall above his head, he returned to her words.

You will probably think me foolish, heaven knows my father and sister thought me so, but I wish to explain my feelings so that perhaps you might not think too badly of me when you learn of my deception.

Deception? Zane's feet fell to the floor and braced his body as he straightened in his chair. The warmth that had been running through him cooled several degrees and caused his stomach to tighten.

That day on the beach, as I held you in my arms and prayed for the Lord to spare your life, something happened to me. I don't want to call it love, because how can a person fall in love with someone they've never met? But something shifted inside me. The best description I can offer is that it felt as if my heart recognized yours. Like combing through the sand and finding one of them fancy shatelanes with a key still attached and knowing without even trying that it fit the lock on the door of my heart.

Zane frowned. Her grammar had slipped, and she'd misspelled chatelaine. More than that, she talked about the waist chain as if it were a rare object, not something every housekeeper wore on her belt. Yet her analogy fit his experience. She, at least, had been conscious at their first meeting. He'd literally been half-dead, yet he'd still felt a pull to find her. Felt the mysterious connection binding them.

When I first saw you at your home, and you said that you had hoped to see me again, I thought . . . maybe you felt it, too. So perhaps you will understand why I did what I did.

Did what? Impatiently, he shoved the first page of her letter behind the others and poured over the second page.

I wanted so badly to find you, but I didn't know how. Until a friend of mine told me about the Matchmaker. This woman had connections all over town. She could help me find you. Better than that, she could convince your parents that I was a suitable candidate for your affection.

Mrs. Underhill did not wish to take me on as a client, however. I had to take extreme measures to convince her, and once she agreed, she made it clear that the only way she would help me would be if I helped her in return. I gave her my word that I would do so. Then she *made me promise that I would follow her instructions to the letter. Those instructions included me pretending to be temporarily mute. I cannot give you the reasons. Not yet, anyway. I shouldn't even be telling you this much, but after your reaction to the news of my false injury, I couldn't let you go on thinking that you were to blame. My voice is <u>not</u> impaired. It's probably coated with a thick layer of rust by now, but you caused me no harm.*

Zane – I'm in a tangle. I've involved myself with a spider, and now I'm caught in her web. You and I don't know each other well yet, and I understand that you have no reason to trust me, but I'm taking a chance by trusting you. Please keep my secret. Just for a few weeks. I'll explain everything after I fulfill my duty to Mrs. Underhill.

I pray that you and God both will forgive my role in this deception. As much as I would like to blame the entire scheme on Mrs. Underhill, I agreed to participate, and therefore bear equal responsibility.

I care for you, Zane. Honestly and truly. Please don't end our courtship before it begins. But if you feel you must, I will understand. If our positions were reversed, I would have a hard time trusting someone with my heart if he hadn't been trustworthy in other matters. I do promise that I will never lie to you from this point forward. Every word I write will be truth.

Forgive me.

Muriel

Zane's hand dropped like an anchor, the weight of her words suddenly too heavy for him to hold the letter aloft. He sank against the cushioned back of his chair, air expelling from his lungs on a quiet groan.

She'd deceived him. She'd come into his house and pretended to be something she wasn't. Why? To play on his sympathies? To trick him into offering for her? Was she like all the rest—more interested in the Erickson name and inheritance than in Zane himself? He felt as if he were drowning all over again. Lost and thrashing in dark waters, unable to determine up from down, truth from mirage.

Like a lifeline tossed into his murky sea, Grandpa Clem's words came back to him. *Just because a woman is perfect for you, don't mean she's perfect. Best not expect her to be.*

How had he known? Had he sensed something amiss about her? But wait. Why would he imply she was perfect for him?

Memories from their meeting in the parlor fed his gasping heart. Muriel's hands on his face, eyes imploring him to believe that her lost voice was *her* fault, not his. Her note insisting he wasn't to blame. Her insistence that her voice would return. She hadn't been completely forthright, but she'd not taken advantage of his distress either.

Recollections of Muriel singing to the Lord with all her heart, her spirit laid bare in every note, swirled through his mind. No one could worship like that without having an authentic relationship with the Father. She'd not been putting on a show. She'd been in a secluded place, singing only for the ears of heaven. He'd been the interloper.

Yet if she were devout, how could she also be a deceiver?

Mrs. Underhill.

There had definitely been something shifty about that woman. Yet his mother had employed her, so he'd assumed her to be respectable. Perhaps not. He shuffled from the third page back to the first and read the entire letter again, this time approaching the document like a blueprint—shelving his emotions and focusing on the details.

Fact number one. Muriel cared for him.

She could have lied about that, but it made no sense that she would admit to being dishonest about her ability to speak in that case. If she intended to manipulate his feelings for her, confessing her deception would jeopardize her agenda. Besides, every moment he'd spent in her company proved she genuinely enjoyed being with him. She was too young to be *that* accomplished an actress.

Fact number two. Mrs. Underhill was pressuring Muriel to do things she wasn't comfortable with.

Muriel had tiptoed around the details, but on closer examination, Zane deduced some troubling signs. Her conscience protested the deception. She wanted to be honest but didn't feel like she could. She felt trapped. Webs and spiders. And what of this mysterious task she'd promised to do for Mrs. Underhill? Perhaps Muriel was the one truly being manipulated, not him. Zane's jaw clenched.

Fact number three. Muriel believed his parents would not approve of her if she didn't hide parts of herself.

Why? He couldn't puzzle it out. Why would her voice be a detriment? She outshone most opera performers. Perhaps the trouble pertained to her speaking voice? But why would that matter? He turned back to the section in her letter about the chatelaine. A misspelling didn't mean much, but unfamiliarity with an item common in most households might. An item common in most *wealthy* households. Was that the issue? Was she not the lady of society the matchmaker had made her out to be? Her letter proved her to be literate and possessed of a basic education, but perhaps she was not of his class. Perhaps her way of speaking would make that disparity obvious. But if that were the case, how did she come to be a student at the Ursuline Academy? A school known to serve the daughters of the elite.

Zane pushed up from his chair and paced the length of his room, putting together a few facts from his side of the equation.

Fact number one. He cared for her.

That hadn't changed. The devastation he'd felt at the initial reading of her letter only confirmed the engagement of his heart.

Fact number two. He owed her his protection.

Whether anything came of their relationship or not, she was a young woman floundering in matters over her head. She'd saved him from drowning. It seemed only right that he repay her in kind.

Fact number three. He didn't care one iota about her social standing or lack thereof.

Grandpa Clem told stories all the time about how happy he and Grandma Iris had been in their small, one-room cabin when they first married. Money didn't equal happiness. Love did. If he were fortunate enough to find love with Muriel, he'd not let such a barrier stand in his way. Even if his father chose to disinherit him, which he might, Zane wouldn't think twice.

In the meantime, Muriel needed him, and he intended to be there for her. Though he planned to keep his eyes as open as his heart.

Chapter 16

The following evening, Muriel stood in the academy entry hall staring out the window, hoping to see a carriage stop in front of the school. Each time a buggy approached, she held her breath, and each time it turned down a side street or passed by, air leaked out of her and deflated her posture. Until the next conveyance rolled down the street. She'd decided to come down twenty minutes early instead of continuing the fruitless pacing of her too-small chamber, but being able to see the street only heightened the torture.

What she wouldn't give for a swim. To get out of her head and into the sea. Where she could stretch her muscles and work through this horrid anxiety. Would he come? Or did he despise her now?

Oh, Zane. Please come.

The rattle of wheels on packed dirt focused her eyes once again on the street outside the window. A piano-box buggy drawn by a sleek bay with black mane and tail approached. The top of the carriage had been folded down, making it easier to see the man driving. A man with dark hair visible beneath his black Homburg hat.

Her pulse surged like it did after a long swim. It could be him. *Please, let it be him.*

The buggy drew near, then drifted toward the side of the road. The side in front of the academy. The driver drew his horse to a halt and set the brake. As he turned to alight, his face became clear.

Zane!

He'd come. Muriel jumped back from the window, not wanting him to catch her peerin' out like an impatient eejit with no manners.

Sister Mary Vincent tucked her sewing project back into her basket then rose from the bench where she'd been darning a pair of stockings and bearing witness to Muriel's fretful vigil. "See now? I told you he would come." She smiled and crossed the entryway, her black robe swishing along the stone floor with a peaceful smoothness Muriel envied. "No gentleman would issue an invitation then fail to appear. It would reflect poorly on him and his family."

Muriel's stomach cramped. Was that why he'd come? Out of social obligation? The dreadful thought sat in her belly like undercooked fish, stirring up a nausea that brought the sting of bile to the back of her throat. Heaven help her. She might be facing the most excruciating dinner of her life. At least no one would be expectin' her to talk. Perhaps her silence was a mercy.

When the knock came, Muriel jumped again, about as easy in her skin as a sunburned sea lion. Thankfully, Sister Mary Vincent made no comment. She simply glided forward to answer the door.

"Evening, sister. I've come to escort Miss Quinn to dinner."

Muriel nibbled on her bottom lip. He sounded cordial. Too cordial?

Ah. Eno' with the frettin'. If his likin' fer ye has soured, ye'll know soon enough. No use makin' yerself ill tryin' to guess.

"Of course. She's been waiting for you." Sister Mary Vincent stepped aside and afforded Muriel a clear view of Zane, handsome as ever in a dark gray coat with black trousers and vest, his hat tucked under one arm.

His face lit when he saw her, and her heart latched onto hope with an iron grip. He strode inside and sketched a bow. "You look lovely, Miss Quinn."

She ducked her chin, pleased at his words yet feeling a bit like a fraud in the elegant silk gown Mrs. Underhill had arranged for her to borrow from one of her pupils. She'd been afraid the pale mauve fabric would clash with her hair, but the ivory lace trimming the scooped neckline and elbow-length sleeves struck a surprising harmony with her coloring. Vanessa had styled her hair in a complicated twisted chignon that Muriel would never be able to replicate, which was a shame because it did rather flatter her face.

He drew near, and she lifted her face, searching for clues in his expression about whether duty or desire had brought him here. His eyes crinkled as he smiled. That was a good sign, wasn't it?

"Are you ready?"

Hopeful more than ready, but she nodded and moved toward him. He offered his arm. She took it, her heart pounding against her ribs, more due to nerves than romantic flutterings. With a wave to Sister Mary Vincent, Muriel walked into the early evening sunlight and allowed Zane to help her up into the open carriage. Thankful that a meal with family didn't require Vanessa's chaperonage, Muriel settled herself on the padded bench and placed her handbag on her lap, its odd contents increasing her unease. Zane circled the buggy then climbed in the other side. The seat shifted with his weight, and his leg brushed against hers as he sat.

Before he could take up the reins, she touched his arm to get his attention. He looked her way, and she reached into her bag to retrieve the first item. His recorder.

She'd played the small flute all morning, its pure tones lifting her spirits even as she fumbled with fingerings. Eventually, she got the hang of proper air flow, and trial-and-error taught her enough notes to play several simple songs by ear. Remembering the joy of playing with Zane the evening before had banished her worries until Vanessa showed up and lectured her on how to hunt the Ericksons' home for the missing journal. Hence the second odd object in her bag.

Knowing the meaning the flute held for Zane, and *not* knowing if she would see him again after tonight, she held it out to him. 'Twas a treasured family tradition. He shouldn't be forced to see her again just to reclaim it.

Zane didn't take the flute from her, however. He circled his fingers around hers and pushed the instrument back toward her. "Keep it a while longer." His gaze met hers, a message glowing in their blue depths she really wanted to interpret as forgiveness but wasn't sure if that might be her own wishful thinking reflecting back at her.

She raised her brows in question.

"I'm sure," he said, reading her mind. "I hope we might play another duet one day soon."

Her heart pounded again, but this time the cause was definitely romantic flutterings. His hand on hers, his lopsided smile, his hint that they might make beautiful music together one day. Her own smile found its way out of the clouds and radiated a bit of light in his direction.

Zane withdrew his hand, cleared his throat, and turned his attention to driving while she tucked the flute into her bag. Her knuckles brushed against the leather of the replacement journal Vanessa had insisted she bring. The chances of finding the stolen journal tonight were slim. The chances of her being alone long enough to make the switch if she did find it? Thinner than the nearly transparent pages of her Bible.

Despite the low odds, Mrs. Underhill expected a report on her findings in the morning. A meeting Muriel dreaded but couldn't escape. Not if she wanted to protect her family.

After rounding the block, Zane turned the buggy down 25th Street and relaxed into the seat as they traveled the straightaway. She watched the houses grow larger, and her stomach pinched. As many times as she'd entertained the dreamy notion of living in a castle with a handsome prince, the elegance of Zane's house had intimidated more than excited her during her first visit, and the grandeur of the neighborhood surrounding it now pressed a heavy realization upon her—she didn't belong here. Would never belong here.

"I read your letter."

Zane's quiet words whipped Muriel's head around. She searched his profile for clues and sagged a bit in relief when he glanced her way long enough to offer a small smile.

"I'm not ready to end our courtship just yet," he said.

Muriel gripped the metal handrail near her hip to keep from melting straight off the seat. He wasn't turning her away. Thank heaven. She hadn't ruined everything, after all.

"I've decided to keep your secret for the time being, though I hope you'll come to trust me enough to tell me more of your story." He glanced her way again, and this time his gaze lingered on hers. "I want to help you, Muriel. Whatever trouble you are mixed up in, I'll help you sort it. If you'll let me."

Tears misted her eyes as she mouthed the words *Thank you*. The loneliness that had been plaguing her since she left her da's house lifted with the gift of Zane's promise. He wanted to court her. To help her.

Well, at least until he learned that helping her meant crossing his father.

Muriel sat back against the seat and blinked the remaining moisture from her eyes. She never should have made that accursed bargain. She should have been patient. Sought help from people she knew. People she trusted. But she'd let her impatience goad her into leapin' before she looked, and she'd landed square in the middle of a marshy lagoon full of slimy algae and venomous water snakes.

They pulled up in front of the mansion Zane called home, and Muriel prayed for calm. Oh, how she wanted his family to like her. Just as she wanted her family to like Zane. When they were finally allowed to meet him. At least she'd already met his mother. And while the lady hadn't been particularly warm when they'd first met, she'd softened somewhat when her son took a liking to the strange girl without a voice. Hopefully, she cared more about Zane's happiness than the pedigree of her future daughter-in-law.

Muriel had only met Zane's grandfather briefly, but the twinkle in his eye when he'd passed her on his way out of the parlor had lifted her spirits. He'd been dressed in much simpler garb than the rest of the Ericksons, and looked as if he'd be right at home sittin' in a pew at Grace Church or eating supper in her da's kitchen. She hoped he'd be joining them tonight. She sensed he'd be an ally, and heaven knew she needed all the friends she could get.

Zane drove the buggy around to the carriage house where a groom came out to tend the horse. After climbing down, Zane came around to her side and took her hand as he helped her down. A little tingle ran up her arm as she slid her fingers into his palm. So strong and steady. Dependable. And the way his eyes latched onto hers? She didn't want to look away. But she did. It wouldn't do for her to misjudge the step and take a tumble in the dirt before dinner.

Zane tucked her hand into the crook of his arm and led her up the stone steps to the front porch. The butler opened the door as they approached, and Zane nodded his thanks to the man. Muriel exhaled a nervous breath as the door closed behind them, but Zane turned one of his adorable smiles on her, and she couldn't help but smile back.

"It'll be fine." He leaned close and whispered in her ear as they made their way to the parlor. "Grandpa Clem is salt-of-the-earth, and Mother is as worried about making a good impression on you as you likely are of her."

Muriel seriously doubted that, but it was sweet of him to say so.

"Father might seem intimidating, but disapproval is his natural temperament, so don't let him get under your skin. He's more concerned with work than entertaining anyway, so he'll likely disappear into his office after dinner."

Muriel heard the pain behind the words and ached for him. She and Da might not always agree, but they *always* loved and supported each other. 'Twas what family was all about.

Zane led her into the parlor. Mrs. Erickson smiled and welcomed her into their home. Mr. Erickson *didn't* smile but dipped his head in a perfunctory bow that would have been mannerly if not for his scowl. Grandpa Clem had dressed up a bit for the occasion, adding a jacket and string tie to the plain shirt and trousers she'd seen him in last time. His eyes twinkled just as much as she remembered, though, and this time he added a wink for good measure.

"You play checkers, Miss Quinn?"

Not the usual greeting, but his grin was so infectious she couldn't help but nod enthusiastically.

"Excellent!" He clapped his hands then rubbed them together. "I'll challenge ya to a game after supper."

She raised a brow, and he cackled.

"Ah ha! Think you can beat me, do ya? We'll see about that. I ain't gonna take it easy on ya just because you're a guest."

Oh, she and Grandpa Clem were going to get along grand.

"Zane, dear," Mrs. Erickson said, a slightly pained look on her face. Did the woman not like checkers? "Why don't you give Miss Quinn a tour of the house? Cook should have supper ready by the time you've finished."

A tour of the house? The joy of the promised checkers game withered with the reminder of her assignment. Zane dutifully took her through the house, entertaining her with family tidbits and stories as they toured his mother's sitting room, the music room that doubled as a small ballroom during parties, and the office where his father worked. The office. The most likely place for Mr. Erickson to hide Mrs. Underhill's journal. Zane had no love for the place, however, and moved them out of the room before she could do more than scan the bookshelves and eye the large desk. He took her upstairs and showed her each of the five bedrooms along with the tin-lined bathroom with the biggest copper tub she ever did see. What a marvel! Even her da would be able to stretch out in it.

When they returned to the parlor, Mrs. Erickson ushered them into the dining room. Zane's father sat at the head of the table with Mrs. Erickson to his right and Zane to his left. Muriel sat next to Zane, and Grandpa Clem took the chair at the end of the table.

"Let's thank the Good Lord for our meal, shall we?" Grandpa Clem bowed his head, and Muriel quickly followed suit. "Lord, we thank thee for your abundant provision. For the delicious food we're about to eat and for the family sitting around this table. We thank you for bringing Miss Quinn to join us tonight and ask you to help her feel at home."

A grumbly sound vibrated from the head of the table, souring Muriel's pleasure over Grandpa's Clem's thoughtful words. It seemed someone wasn't all that eager to put her at ease.

"Lord, none of us deserve your grace and favor. We're all sinful, pitiful creatures in need of your redemption. May we walk through life with humility as grateful children who recognize we're nothin' without you. In the name of your holy Son, Amen." He lifted his head, grinned as if he hadn't just taken his son to task in the middle of his prayer, and picked up the bowl closest to him. "Who wants taters?"

God bless Grandpa Clem. She beamed a smile at him, and he returned it with another wink.

Dinner began well enough. Food made it onto plates. Muriel remembered not to start with the dessert fork. And Zane's mother guided the conversation in pleasant directions, urging Zane to talk about the veranda he was designing. She made a point to involve Muriel by asking her a couple questions that could be answered with a yes or no, then told a story about Zane from his childhood. This led Grandpa Clem to set his napkin aside and get into serious yarn-spinning position. The story he told about three-year-old Zane being chased by a family of frogs had to be exaggerated, but it was so hysterical, no one minded. Least of all Muriel. She found the story and the man utterly charming.

A clatter of knife on china from the head of the table killed the laughter in an instant. All eyes turned to Horace Erickson.

He braced his wrists on the table and leaned forward, his pointed glance jabbing at Muriel. "Tell me, Miss Quinn. Were you raised in Galveston?" His voice sounded polite enough, but the heat of his glare scalded.

"Father . . ." Zane's warning tone had no effect.

Mr. Erickson speared his son with an authoritative glower that brooked no opposition. "It's a yes/no question. The girl can answer for herself." He raised a brow. "Well, Miss Quinn? It's an easy enough question. Were you raised here?"

Feeling like a freshly caught fish floundering in a net, she squirmed in her seat and sent Zane a sideways glance. He nodded then reached out and clasped her hand in full view of his father. Showing his support.

She'd promised to be honest with him, and she'd not degrade his trust in her by lying now. Forcing her chin up, she looked at his father and nodded.

"Interesting. You see, I asked about your kin among my connections at the Lodge last night, and none of my contacts had ever heard of a family named Quinn owning a shipping venture operating out of our bay."

Trembling seized her limbs, but Zane tightened his hold on her hand.

"However, Mr. Roper, the chief exporter of cotton in this port, *did* recognize the name Quinn. Apparently, there's a Patrick Quinn who manages a crew of dock workers on the Central Wharf. A widowed workingman with four daughters. Is that your father?"

Muriel froze, not knowing what to say, what to do. To say yes would prove her an unsuitable match for Zane. To say no would perpetuate a lie and dishonor her da.

At her hesitation, Mr. Erickson rose from his chair and pounded a fist against the table. "Admit it! You're a gold-digging Jezebel with nothing to offer this family but a bucketful of lies!"

Chapter 17

Muriel's lips trembled, and she pressed them together in a futile effort to keep her tears at bay. A tug on her hand signaled Zane was starting to stand, but she pulled him frantically back down. She couldn't let him take the shots meant for her. She deserved his father's ire. Maybe not all of what he'd just spewed—the gold-digging Jezebel bit stung worse than lemon juice in the eye—but the rest of it was true enough. She couldn't offer anything tangible to this family. No dowry. No social connections. No political gain. Yet as she hung her head, she caught a glimpse of Grandpa Clem rising to his feet like a stately whale surfacing from the deep.

"I'm ashamed of you, Horace." He didn't raise his voice, but authority infused every syllable. "Your mama raised you better than this. Sit down."

Mr. Erickson straightened, the heat of his glare moving from Muriel to his father. "Sit down? This is *my* house. No one tells me what to do in my house. Not even you." He arrowed a furious point in Muriel's direction, and she felt the jab as if his finger had physically poked her chest. "That woman is a liar and a fraud."

"That woman is a guest in our home, deserving of hospitality, not a verbal attack by a man twice her age."

"I'm protecting my son." The words barely made it past his clenched jaw.

"You're protectin' your pocketbook and your pride. The boy's of age, Horace. He can make his own choices."

As the two men stared each other down across the length of the table, Mrs. Erickson reached a tentative hand toward her husband. "Please, Horace. Won't you sit down? Mrs. Underhill has a pristine reputation. She wouldn't have recommended Miss Quinn to us if the young lady wasn't suitable."

Mr. Erickson jerked his arm out of his wife's reach. "Octavia Underhill is a corrosive barnacle who would have sucked this family dry with her blackmailing machinations if I hadn't taken matters into my own hands. You were a fool to employ her, Sophie."

"Taken matters into your own hands?" Zane's mother retracted her arm, horror creeping across her features. "Horace. What have you done?"

"Nothing that need concern you."

He returned his narrowed gaze to Muriel. She edged closer to Zane, wishing she could hide behind him. Or perhaps disintegrate into dust so a breeze could blow her home. Never had she missed her da more than at this moment. Zane's hold on her hand was the only thing giving her the courage to keep her seat and not flee out into the night.

"Octavia probably thought to get her revenge on me by sending this little deceiver to seduce my son."

Muriel shook her head in adamant denial of the terrible claim. Not that it did any good.

"Tell your mistress I'm onto her scheme. Horace Erickson is nobody's fool."

"I ain't so sure about that." Grandpa Clem shook his head, his gaze weary and full of sorrow. "I looked into Miss Quinn, too. Not with the intent to discredit her, but to get to know the family of the little gal who saved my grandson's life and seemed well on her way to capturing his heart."

Muriel's stomach clenched. Grandpa Clem, too? It seemed she hadn't fooled anyone but herself in thinking this tawdry plan would work.

"I asked around the docks to see if anyone knew of a Mr. Quinn, and you know what I learned? Patrick Quinn might not own a shipping enterprise, but he owns his men's respect. They couldn't stop talkin' about his kindness and integrity. How he covers shifts himself when men are ill or injured so they don't have to take a cut in pay. How he mentors the young men in his crew, treating them more like sons than hired hands. Folks that don't work under him wish they did, and captains request his crew more than any other on the wharf because of his diligence. By all accounts, he's a man of deep and abidin' faith, a dedicated father, and a master of his trade. I'd be proud to welcome a man of his caliber into this family. What he's got to offer is far more valuable than an overstuffed bank account or a Masonic membership."

Muriel's heart squeezed. Tears pooled and dribbled through the gate of her lashes. What a dear, dear man. Even knowing the truth about her da, Grandpa Clem still defended her, offered friendship, and challenged her to checkers. No wonder Zane loved him so.

Releasing Zane's hand, Muriel leapt from her chair and scurried around to where Grandpa Clem stood. She threw her arms around him and hugged him tight, not caring about proper manners or social protocol or even about making a fool of herself. All that mattered was that he know how much she appreciated him.

He gently patted her back in response. "Don't think I'm gonna let you out of our checkers match," he whispered in her ear. "Zane takes after me, ya know. He won't let a little family squabble keep him from doin' what's right. Don't give up on us just yet. Ya hear?"

She leaned away from him, blinked back her tears, and nodded. Grandpa Clem smiled, the twinkle reappearing in his moist eyes. "Atta girl."

Slowly, she turned to face the table. The time for truth had come.

Zane had risen to his feet the moment Muriel stood, ready to shelter her from his father's hurtful accusations in whatever way he could. When she'd hugged his grandfather, though, something unexpected stirred inside him, banishing his rising anger with his father and transforming his affection for her into something that felt much more enduring. And when she turned to face her attacker, trembling yet holding her ground, pride surged within his heart.

"Ye're right that Mrs. Underhill misrepresented me family, Mr. Erickson, and I admit me part in the deception, but there's nothin' sordid about me motives."

"I suspected you might be Irish with that surname and flamboyant hair, but your accent—ack, there's no hiding *that*. No wonder you falsified an injury. Octavia knew I'd never welcome the daughter of a common Irish laborer into my home. I didn't spend half my life clawing my way into powerful circles only to have my son court a woman from the servant class. I'll be made a laughingstock among my peers."

Zane wagged his head and gave a disgusted and very sarcastic chuckle. "Is that all that matters to you? How *your* life is impacted? Do you care nothing about how *I* feel about the situation?"

"Of course, I care," Father blustered. "I want what's best for you. And this . . ." he gestured to Muriel as if she were an object and not a person, ". . . is not it."

Zane glanced at Muriel, praying she could see the truth of his feelings in his eyes. "I disagree." A tiny smile curled the edges of her mouth, and triumph surged through his chest as he pivoted back to face his father. "She's perfect."

"She's *Irish*!" He spat the word as if saying it defiled his tongue.

Zane shrugged. "So? Nicholas Clayton is Irish, and I'd wager he's one of the most influential citizens in this city. His buildings are defining our era."

Father sputtered for a moment before grasping another argument. "She's a liar. She admitted it herself."

"Aye, I did." Muriel jumped in before Zane could offer a defense.

She turned toward him, apology thick in her gaze. Zane gave a small nod, letting her know all was forgiven as far as he was concerned. Her chin lifted a fraction as she swung her attention back to his father.

"I misled ye with me silence and failed to correct the false picture Mrs. Underhill painted when she spoke of me da, but it has nothin' to do with money."

"Everything has to do with money," Father muttered under his breath.

"I care about Zane. We might still be gettin' acquainted, but me heart is already threaded to his." She glanced Zane's way, and his blood pulsed twice as strong and three times as fast as it had a moment ago. "Zane, I'll tell ye the whole of it, and if ye want me gone after I've said me piece, I'll not bother ye again. But if ye think what's growin' between us might be real and lastin', I ask ye to give me the chance to prove meself faithful to ye."

Zane rounded the table and took her hand in his, ignoring his father's overheated glare that was trying to burn a hole in his shoulder. "I'll give you a hundred chances, if you'll give me the same."

She straightened away from the table as if she no longer needed its support. As if holding fast to him was all she required. He moved closer and murmured softly in her ear. "We can talk in my mother's sitting room."

Muriel nodded, her eyes brimming with trust and a touch of trepidation. Whatever secret she continued to harbor weighed enough to worry her that he might yet reject her. *Nothing* would cause him to reject her. The sooner he convinced her of that fact, the sooner they could get down to the serious courtship they both desired.

She placed her hand on his arm and let him lead her away from the table.

"I won't be a party to you throwing your life away, Zane," his father growled from behind them. "Go against my wishes, and I'll cut you off."

Zane flinched, but he didn't stop walking. Not until they reached the dining room doorway and Muriel paused. She turned back to face the table, but she, too, ignored his father. Instead, she addressed herself to his mother.

"Thank ye fer the fine meal, Mrs. Erickson. I'm sorry to have caused such disruption."

Mother, who couldn't have looked more stunned if a crew of pirates had just swung through the French doors and commandeered her supper table, managed to tip her head in acknowledgment. A verbal response appeared beyond her current capabilities.

Rather ironic that a working-class Irish girl displayed better manners than either of his parents.

When they reached the sitting room, Zane closed the door halfway. He'd not risk her reputation by closing it all the way, but he wanted to give them as much privacy as possible. He led her to a pair of pale green upholstered parlor chairs situated near the small hearth on the far side of the room. Her silk skirt belled around her as she perched on the edge of the cushion. He scooted his chair closer to hers, hoping to convey the message that he wasn't going anywhere.

Zane took his seat, his knees deliciously close to hers. "I'm so sorry about my father. He was completely out of line. I wouldn't blame you if you wanted nothing to do with my family or me after that fiasco." Who would want to marry a man knowing the future held nothing but scorn from his family? His breath hitched. Maybe the true danger was of *her* wanting nothing to do with *him.* "I promise that I don't share his views," Zane hurried to add. "I respect a man who works hard to provide for his family. I'd rather have honor and integrity than a big house and expensive things. That's one of the reasons I wanted to work for Mr. Clayton. Not only have I always loved building things and been fascinated by the combination of science and art found in architecture, but I also didn't want to be one of those indolent wastrels who lived off his parents' money. I want to make my own way in the world. Even if my father doesn't cut me off, I plan to separate myself from his provision. Get my own place. Live off my own salary. I had thought to do so after completing my apprenticeship and receiving a promotion to draftsman or assistant designer. However, if the need arises sooner, I'm prepared. I've been squirreling away my earnings for the last few years. Should I . . . uh . . . find myself with a wife to provide for, I'd be able to do so. Not at this level," he said with a wave of his hand to indicate the ornate furnishings around him, "but in modest form." Heat flushed his face. "So, if you were hoping to be part of this world, you might need to brace yourself for disappointment."

"Zane." She leaned toward him, her eyes round and glimmering with sincerity. "I don't want to be part of *this* world." She, too, gestured to the well-appointed room. "I want to be part of *yer* world. Wherever ye are, that's where I want to be. Whether that be here among yer father's people, in a small house off Avenue M, or even in a different city altogether. I just want to be with ye."

Warmth infused Zane's chest. How many young women of his acquaintance would make such a proclamation? Privilege was what they knew. What they expected. He couldn't imagine any of them being content with a small house on Avenue M. Yet he could picture Muriel smiling and laughing just as much there as anywhere.

"Before we go plannin' our future, though, I have a bit more confessin' to do." Her chin dropped, as did her lashes, hiding her vibrant eyes from him. "Ye may not want any part o' me once ye learn the rest of me story."

"I very much doubt that."

Her mouth turned upward at his words, but it was a cautious smile, not one of her unfettered grins that beamed like the sun.

She lifted her reticule to her lap and played with the drawstring holding it closed. "Do ye recall yer father sayin' that he'd taken matters into his own hands regardin' Mrs. Underhill?"

Zane thought back through all the harsh things his father had said and remembered how his mother had recoiled at something he'd said along those lines when she'd tried to soothe his temper. "I think so."

"Well, Mrs. Underhill claimed that he stole a journal from her, one in which she keeps all her business records. I couldn't afford to pay her to help me find ye, so she agreed to help me if I helped her in return. I'm to find the book he stole and steal it back." She pulled a brown leather journal from her handbag. "I'm supposed to replace it with this empty one. If I don't succeed, she'll reveal the truth about who I really am, which doesn't much matter now, but she also threatened to destroy me da's reputation. To whisper lies into the ears of important men, accuse him of skimmin' cargo and conductin' underhanded dealings. Not only that, but she plans to ruin me sister's husband, too. Accuse him of stealin' from guests at the Beach Hotel and plantin' evidence to make it believable. She'll destroy me family, Zane. All because o' me. I can't let that happen." Her voice cracked and so did his heart.

"We'll find a way through this, Muriel. I promise." But would they? He wanted to help her, yet helping her meant betraying his father. His loyalty was being torn down the middle. His father or Muriel? His father had stolen a journal to protect his family. Muriel agreed to steal it back to protect hers. He'd known his father his whole life. He'd known Muriel for less than a month. Which path was the right one to take?

Chapter 18

Muriel slipped the journal back into her handbag, hoping she'd feel less vulnerable when the proof of her guilt no longer stared her in the face. A sigh slid from her lips. Zane didn't deserve to be stuck in this impossible position. 'Twas unfair to ask him to go against his da. Mr. Erickson might be an ill-tempered crab with overactive pinchers, but he was still Zane's family.

"I'm so sorry, Zane. About all of this." She hung her head and picked at the fabric of her borrowed dress.

"I'm *not* sorry," he said as he reached for her hand. "Not about *all* of it, at least." He sought out her gaze. "I'm not sorry I have the chance to court you." The roguish wiggle of his eyebrows lightened her heart and caused her belly to flip. "I'm not sorry that you speak with an utterly charming accent. I could listen to you read a grocery list and be enamored."

A small chuckle escaped. "Now ye're spoutin' blarney, ye are."

Zane held up his hand as if making a pledge. "I swear that every word I said is true."

Had the Lord e'er made a man so fine as Zane Erickson? Kind and generous to a fault. Gentle. Compassionate. Understanding. No gentleman could compare. She might have been halfway in love with him before, but she was well on her way to bein' a complete goner now.

A knock on the sitting room door drew Muriel's gaze. Mrs. Erickson stood in the opening, her expression contrite. "May I . . . May I come in?"

Muriel stiffened and tugged her hand free of Zane's gentle hold. Gracious. As if she hadn't besmirched herself enough in his mother's eyes, now here she was practically canoodling with the woman's son in her personal sitting room. All right, no actual canoodling had occurred beyond mere hand holding, but appearances often counted more than truth in these scenarios.

Zane made no move to expand the distance between himself and Muriel, however. He simply gestured for his mother to enter. "Of course."

With every step that brought Mrs. Erickson closer, the false journal in Muriel's reticule grew heavier upon her lap. Glancing down, she half expected it to have burst the seams of the bag to expose her guilt.

When his mother reached them, Zane stood from his seat and offered it to her then fetched a different chair from across the room and situated it on Muriel's other side.

"Thank you, son." Mrs. Erickson settled in the chair like a swan settling upon a lake. So graceful and elegant.

Even with years of practice, Muriel doubted she'd ever possess such poise. Living up to this woman's expectations of ladyhood would be nigh impossible. All of Mrs. Underhill's criticisms about Muriel's lack of social polish, lack of education, and lack of refinement lifted their ugly heads to chatter their accusations in her ear. She shrank in her seat, her chin dipping to her chest and her shoulders rolling forward as if she could curl into a ball and roll away. How she wished she could!

"I owe you an apology, Miss Quinn."

Shock brought Muriel's chin up and immediately set it to wagging from side to side. "Oh, nay, ma'am. 'Tis me that should be apologizin'. I'm the one who lied."

A small smile touched the woman's lips. "That's true, but I'm the one who made the deal with Mrs. Underhill that set this entire series of events in motion. My husband acted poorly this evening, and I'll make no excuses for his terrible treatment of you, but he was right about one thing. I never should have made a deal with the matchmaker, not once I learned the currency she expected for our transaction."

Zane leaned forward, a frown marring his face. "What currency? I thought you said you made payments to her each week."

She turned toward her son, a slight flush coloring her cheeks. "I do. But she insisted upon . . . insurance. To guarantee the payments won't stop if she produces a quality match before the total sum is collected."

"What kind of insurance?" Tension radiated in Zane's voice.

His mother dipped her head. "A secret. One that could ruin your father."

Muriel blinked. *Secrets?* Was that what the book held? People's secrets?

"She has a system, you see," Zane's mother explained. "The secrets remain confidential as long as the payments are made. And everyone I talked to who has used her services assured me that Mrs. Underhill never extorts more than the agreed-upon sum. Once the final payment is made, the page is removed from the book and burned. But now that I've learned that your father has interfered, I fear what might come. Mrs. Underhill is not a woman to cross. She's powerful and ruthless. Those who fail to live up to their end of the contract pay a price. A steep one. Maybe she'll be appeased if I continue making my payments. But if not . . ."

Muriel's heart throbbed in her chest as she thought of her da and her sister. Yet now it seemed the risk they faced extended to Zane's family as well. They needed to find a way out.

Empathy throbbed in Muriel's heart. Tentatively, she reached out and touched the older woman's shoulder. "I know ye have no reason to trust me, Mrs. Erickson, and I've little power in this tangled situation, but I promise I'll do all I can to protect yer family as I strive to protect me own."

Perhaps she could remove the page with Mrs. Erickson's secret before she returned the journal to Mrs. Underhill. But what about all the other people with secrets written in that unholy book? What would become of them?

"That's kind of you, Miss Quinn, but I've learned that the best way to fight deception is with truth. And while I can't reveal the truth of my husband's secret, I can certainly reveal the delightful truth of my son's courtship." Mrs. Erickson found a smile and aimed it at Muriel. "I'd like to officially launch you into Galveston society, my dear. We'll start small, of course, only inviting close friends who can be counted on to lend their support. I thought I might host a musicale here at the house. My son has told me about your beautiful singing voice." She tossed Zane a fond and rather teasing glance. "Went on and on about it those first few days after his rescue, as a matter of fact." Zane's cheeks reddened, and Muriel couldn't stop a grin from blooming in response. "How better to win over society than to charm them with your beauty and talent?"

"What about Father?" Zane's question stole the smile from his mother's face. "You can't think he'd approve of such a thing."

"Leave your father to me. I'm sure we can arrange for him to be called away on business that night." The sourness in her voice made Muriel's heart ache.

What had happened to corrupt Mr. and Mrs. Erickson's happily ever after? Marriage was designed to bring people closer, to be true partners in life, one flesh that could not be torn asunder. Yet some force had been tearing these two asunder for quite some time, and the result was heartbreaking.

Mrs. Erickson addressed her son. "Zane, I've only ever wanted your happiness, and it's becoming clear to me that Miss Quinn is the young woman most likely to make you happy. Your grandfather and I stand ready to lend you our support regardless of your father's disapproval. He'll come around eventually." She sounded more hopeful than confident in that last statement, but no one could doubt her love and commitment to her son. "Let me do this, Zane. Please."

Zane clasped his mother's hand, and his voice rasped a bit as he agreed. "Thank you, Mother."

Mrs. Erickson blinked rapidly in an effort to keep the moisture in her eyes from leaking. "Excellent. The sooner the better, to my way of thinking. We'll plan for next Tuesday evening. We'll even ask Mrs. Underhill to serve as accompanist. I happen to know she delights in showing off her musical skills to society, so perhaps we can soothe her temper even as we demonstrate her matchmaking proficiency. She'll believe her plan is working, and hopefully, we will buy ourselves some time to find a way to escape her wrath."

Muriel only knew of one way to escape Mrs. Underhill's wrath, and Zane's mother had unwittingly provided the perfect cover. Access to the Erickson home while Mr. Erickson was away. A distracted audience. Perhaps even a little help from someone with experience picking locks.

But would Zane approve? Or would it be safer to keep him in the dark until the deed be done?

Octavia paced the academy's music room, her mind traveling down one thought branch after another, searching for flaws, for inconsistencies, for traps.

When Vanessa had reported in last night after a clandestine meeting with the Ericksons' footman and informed Octavia that dinner had been a disaster, Octavia had immediately started plotting the demise of her young Irish protégé. The little fool had actually admitted to being part of a ruse and, worse, had implicated Octavia in the deception. What did it matter that the Erickson patriarchs had dug around enough to unearth the truth of her parentage? She should have kept her mouth shut and used her supposed injury to her advantage. A damsel in distress was a classic ploy for a reason. But no, she'd spoken—in that atrocious accent, no less—and brought the entire house of cards down in one fell swoop. Thankfully, she'd been smart enough not to mention the journal. The footman had not seen a book of any kind at dinner nor had he overheard any mention of one, despite the fact that Muriel had had it with her. Vanessa had seen her place it in her bag along with a couple spare hairpins.

Yet now, Miss Quinn arrived for their morning meeting and announced that she had concocted a plan to retrieve the journal. *Her.* A naïve, untried girl of nineteen with an overactive conscience who couldn't even manage to keep her mouth shut for more than a few days.

Octavia swirled around to face the infernal creature standing near the end of the piano. "Do you expect me to believe that after Sophie Erickson learned of your deception, she offered to sponsor you in society? What rot!"

Though it would be awfully convenient if it was true. But how could it be? People, especially those in lofty positions, rarely offered forgiveness so magnanimously. Especially not to outsiders who could offer them nothing substantial in return.

"Beggin' yer pardon, ma'am, but I be tellin' the truth." Muriel lifted her chin. The appendage wobbled worse than an aging soprano's vibrato, but the chit held her ground. Something few people managed to do when facing Octavia's fury. "Zane's ma loves him somethin' fierce, and she felt horrible 'bout the things her husband said at dinner. I'm thinkin' she's afeared Zane will move out and sever ties with them if she doesn't support his choice. When Zane stayed by me side after dinner, he made it clear he wasn't ready to let me go." She pushed back her shoulders and looked Octavia in the eye. "And I won't be lettin' him go, either."

Ugh. Such syrupy sweetness was nauseating. Though, it might prove useful. Love made people stupid. And easy to manipulate.

"Ye'll see it's true when ye receive an invitation."

Octavia arched a brow, immediately suspicious. Surely Sophie had pieced together Octavia's role in planting Miss Quinn in her midst. She might not know of her plan to retrieve the journal, but Octavia was not so foolish as to believe the woman's forgiveness extended to her. Desperation, on the other hand, could make a woman do all sorts of unpredictable things. Like invite an enemy into her home. Especially if the enemy in question had a reputation for ruining those who crossed her.

Yes. Sophie thought to placate her. Foolish woman. Octavia Underhill could not be placated. Diverted, perhaps. For a time, and to pursue her own agenda. But the moment she had that journal back in her possession, she'd destroy Horace Erickson, no matter how many olive branches his wife offered.

"She wishes ye to play fer me." Muriel rested her hand on the ebony piano lid, her fingertips lightly tapping the surface. "She knows no one can match yer skill, and she wishes me shown to best advantage. To impress her friends."

Octavia smoothed a hand over her indigo bodice. "I can't argue with that logic. I *am* the best pianist on the island." And it had been a dreadfully long time since she'd played for an audience outside of the academy. An audience capable of appreciating her gift.

"I thought ye might even want to play a piece or two by yerself, giving me a chance to investigate Mr. Erickson's study." Muriel nibbled on her bottom lip after making that telling statement.

Perhaps the girl wasn't a complete dolt after all. Octavia doubted her playing would be enough to keep people from noticing the guest of honor slipping out of the party, but adding an extra level of distraction could work quite nicely. And she knew just who to employ.

"Well, I suppose I'll know the truth when that invitation arrives, won't I?"

"Yes, ma'am."

Octavia swept past the girl, rounded the piano, and headed to the back of the room where a cabinet filled with vertical shelves stood. She opened the glass door and started riffling through the academy's sheet music collection.

"Well? Don't just stand there. If we are to show you off to best advantage, we'll need more than sappy Irish ballads. We have less than a week to turn you into a cultured chanteuse. Let's get to work."

Chapter 19

The following Saturday afternoon, Zane and Grandpa Clem arrived at the academy to collect Muriel. Grandpa Clem seemed a better choice of chaperone than the intrusive maid who had accompanied them before. Besides, Grandpa Clem had promised to be purposely lax in his duties.

"Zane tells me you're a swimmer." Grandpa Clem strolled down 25th Street on Muriel's right while Zane enjoyed having her left hand tucked into the crook of his arm.

Muriel smiled. "'Tis a fact. I love the sea. I've missed it over the last month. I can't remember ever goin' without swimmin' fer such a length o' time. When Zane invited me to the beach, I could hardly say yes fast enough." She swung her gaze to him, and the light radiating from her eyes had his pulse soaring like a boat in full sail. "I just wish I could get in the water."

"Why can't ya?"

Her cheeks turned a becoming shade of pink. "I don't have a proper bathin' costume. Mine is more . . . athletic in nature."

"It'd have to be. All the rigmarole fashionable ladies wear would drag you straight to the bottom if you did more than kick about in the shallows."

"'Tis why I only swim out from the hidden cove near where I first met Zane."

Kind of her not to call it the place where he got smacked in the back of the head by his own boom.

"'Tis a secret spot away from prying eyes."

He looked forward to when he could take her out in his catboat and perhaps swim with her in the Gulf. After they married. A prospect he still longed to turn into reality, once they'd cleared the impediments from their path. But right now, he needed to steer clear of imagining her in that athletic bathing costume of hers. So he turned the conversation to checkers and let Grandpa Clem crow about his winning record against his grandson.

Zane and Muriel had not had the chance to talk since that disastrous dinner two nights ago. He'd made a thorough search of his house for the stolen journal in the intervening time, however. Not that it had done him much good. Even his father's bedchamber and office had produced no fruit. None that he could access, at least. He'd found a small, locked trunk at the bottom of his father's wardrobe and a pair of locked drawers in his father's desk that he'd been unable to open. At least he'd narrowed the possibilities. Unless his father had taken the journal to his office at the Exchange. Not likely, but Zane wouldn't rule out the possibility.

"Ah, Zane. Do ye smell that?" Muriel lifted her face to the sky and inhaled deeply as a gentle breeze ruffled the loose hairs around her face. "The sea. There's no better scent."

Pure delight radiated from her, and all thoughts of journals and villains dissipated like vapor from Zane's mind under the force of her beauty.

The salty tang in the air had grown stronger as they neared the shore, but Zane had barely noticed. Until now.

"The ocean has an aroma all its own, doesn't it? Brine mixed with the fishy smell of the sargassum that washes ashore."

Her brow crinkled. "The seaweed, ye mean?" At his nod, the lines smoothed from her forehead. "Ah. Ye wouldn't think it smelled as nice if the workers at the hotel didn't rake away the old ev'ry morn. Once that stuff sits in the sun a few days it stinks to high heaven. Worse than rotten eggs." She made a face then grinned as if laughing at herself. "Me nephew Fletcher helps with the removal sometimes. When he's not in school."

Zane had never given much thought to the sargassum being removed from the tourist beaches, but it made sense that the hotel would employ workers to haul it away each day. They'd want to remove the clutter and any sulfurous stench it produced.

"Would you introduce me if we happen to see Fletcher?" He wanted to meet her family. Anyone from her world, actually. He'd only seen her in *his* world, and he longed to see her in her own. To get to know her without the veil of pretense hanging between them.

She nibbled her bottom lip then dipped her chin in agreement. "Aye. There's a good chance he'll be about."

Zane's chest warmed at the gift of her trust.

The closer they came to the shore, the more people bustled about. Carriages rolled down the thoroughfares, ladies in white dresses and parasols strolled the boardwalks accompanied by gentlemen in pale linen suits and straw hats. When they reached the Beach Hotel, they had to wait for a mule-drawn streetcar to pass on its way to collect passengers at the front of the building.

As they wound through the tourists, Muriel scooted closer and closer, her grip on her shawl tightening.

"I don't usually mingle with the fancy set," she murmured just loud enough for him to hear over the small brass ensemble playing a polka from the bandstand in front of the hotel. "Fletcher and me, we keep our distance, only combing the sand after the guests have retired to dress for dinner. I don't feel right walkin' amongst them like this."

Why had he never considered that her experience at the shore would be drastically different than his own? Perhaps taking a side street farther from the Beach Hotel would have been better. But no. He didn't want her to think he was embarrassed to be seen with her. Nothing could be less true. He felt like the verist king walking about with her on his arm. Though today wasn't about showing her off and making himself look good. Today was about learning more of her heart by seeing her in her element.

He leaned his head close to hers. "You are as elegant as any lady here, and I couldn't be prouder to have you by my side. But if you'd be more comfortable, I'd be glad to walk with you out past the Pagoda Bathhouse where there are fewer people."

"'Twould be a sight easier on me nerves."

"Then consider it done." Zane gestured to his right, away from the congestion of the hotel.

"I'm gonna grab a lemonade at the hotel and sit out on the veranda for a spell." Grandpa Clem gave a salute-style wave. "You young'uns have fun."

Muriel managed a smile for his grandfather, but the hand she'd placed in the crook of Zane's arm still felt stiff with tension.

Hoping to distract her from the self-consciousness that seemed to be inhibiting her natural zest for the seaside, Zane rambled off some random facts about the hotel that his mentor had designed.

"Did you know that the Beach Hotel is supported by three hundred cedar pilings anchored into the sand?"

"Really?" She glanced back at the sprawling four-and-a-half story building and studied it as if looking for the pilings. Then she quirked a smile at him, her natural effervescence beginning to revive. "Did *ye* know that it has two hundred rooms?"

Zane chuckled. "I forgot you have a family connection to the place. You probably know more about it than I do."

"I doubt that. Fer instance, I've no earthly idea why they'd paint the roof in red and white stripes. Seems more fittin' fer a circus tent than an elegant hotel."

"Well, it *is* a bit like a circus around here during tourist season."

Muriel's grip on his arm relaxed as she chuckled softly. "Me sister would agree with that."

Zane steered her past the rolling bathhouses that stood in a row, awaiting rental. "I believe the intent was to draw attention and make it immediately recognizable."

"'Cause someone might miss the giant, domed buildin' at the edge of the water?"

A full laugh burst from his chest at her dry remark. "It's not exactly subtle, is it?"

Her eyes danced with humor. "Not even a smidgen."

"Zane!"

Recognizing the voice, Zane drew to a halt and turned.

"I thought that was you!" Max Trimble excused himself from a group of young people that included Wilhemina Davis and a frowning Constance MacArthur. He jogged over and slapped Zane lightly on the shoulder. "I guess I know why you've been making yourself scarce lately. Why hang out with the likes of me when you have this lovely lady's company to enjoy?" He sketched a bow toward Muriel and offered one of his most charming smiles. And since this was Max, the smile was *exceedingly* charming. The rogue.

Zane managed not to roll his eyes, but only because Muriel seemed unaffected by his friend's efforts. She offered him a polite smile, but not the one that crinkled her eyes and lit her entire face.

"Max Trimble, may I present Miss Muriel Quinn? Miss Quinn, this unrepentant rogue is my good friend, Max."

Muriel inclined her head but did not speak. Was she retreating behind her wall of silence again? Did she think her accent would embarrass him?

Max displayed no such reticence. "A pleasure, Miss Quinn." He turned back to Zane. "We were about to head over to the roller rink for some skating. Why don't you and Miss Quinn join us?" He tipped his head in the direction of S.D. Flet's Roller Skating Rink on the other side of the hotel.

"Maybe another time," Zane said. "Miss Quinn and I have different plans."

"What plans are those?" Constance MacArthur sauntered over to invade the conversation and wrapped her fingers around Zane's vacant arm as if she had some claim to him. She aimed a pout in his direction. "Surely, whatever it is can wait an hour. We haven't seen you in *ages,* Zane. It's not like you to abandon your friends."

Zane could feel Muriel retreat, her hand sliding away from his elbow. He squeezed his arm against his side, trapping her hand before she could escape.

"Sorry, Constance. Not this time." Zane smiled to try to soften his answer, knowing Constance didn't take rejection well.

"Don't be silly," she insisted. "You don't mind, do you, Miss Quinn? Unless, that is, you don't know how to skate?" When Muriel gave no answer, Constance forced a laugh. "Do you know how to *talk?*"

Max frowned. "Constance, leave her be."

She waved him off. "Oh, don't be so stuffy, Max. She knows I'm teasing, don't you, Miss Quinn?"

Muriel offered a tight smile as her only response. Her eyes flashed, though, reassuring Zane that Constance wasn't succeeding in cowing her. Constance *was* succeeding in stoking his ire, however.

Zane pasted on a bland expression as he surreptitiously twisted his arm to try to break Constance's hold. Unfortunately, the woman proved as hard to shake as an attached ivy vine. What was her game? He'd never given her any reason to think he had an interest in courting her. Just because she was Wilhemina's friend and therefore made an easy fourth when Max invited Zane out didn't mean she had any claim on him. Did she suddenly feel possessive because Muriel was from outside their set?

"Have fun at the skating rink, Max." Zane shot him a pleading glance followed by a darting look to his arm where Constance's hand rested. "Stop by the house later tonight for a game of billiards."

"You got it." Max winked then took Constance's other arm. "Come on, Constance. Willie and the others are waiting on us."

Finally, the woman's fingers loosened their grip. But just as her hand slid free of Zane's coat sleeve, another player entered the scene. A freckle-faced boy of about nine or ten ran toward them, his face split in a wide grin. His trousers were rolled to just below his knees, and his legs were coated with wet sand. He waved an energetic arm above his head.

"Muriel! Muriel!"

A smile of equal width blossomed on Muriel's face as she turned to greet the youngster. "Fletcher!" She pulled her hand free of Zane's hold and jogged a few steps to meet her nephew, her arms spread wide.

The boy didn't hesitate. He flung himself into her arms, dislodging her shawl. Not that she cared. Muriel's sweet laughter filled the air as she hugged him tight and lifted him straight off the ground, heedless of the wet sand rubbing off on her aquamarine dress.

"Ah, Fletcher, but I've missed ye, me wee lad."

Zane's chest warmed at the exuberant display of affection, something that had been sadly lacking from his family for years. Except for the occasional half hugs from Grandpa Clem, his life had been rather sterile. How he longed for what the Quinns had. Open affection, demonstrative love, fierce dedication to each other instead of polite tepidness.

"Well, now we know why she's so reluctant to talk, don't we?" Constance's caustic tone scraped Zane's nerves raw. "Does your mother know you're stepping out with a common Irish tart?"

Zane jerked his face toward Constance, his glare so hot she stepped back. "There's nothing common about Miss Quinn. She's the most exceptional woman I've ever met, and anyone who dares besmirch her reputation with unfounded rumors will earn my scorn."

Constance's eyes widened for a heartbeat before they hardened. "Enjoy your summer fling with the help, Zane. Come see me when you're ready to grow up and marry a woman of standing."

"You dishonor us both with such talk," Zane said through a tight jaw. "I think it's time you rejoin Wilhemina and the others."

Constance stormed off. Zane turned to Max, who looked as shocked as he by Constance's vitriol.

"Sorry, Zane. I never meant to cause a scene. Wilhemina said something about Constance being under a lot of pressure to make a good match this summer. She must have thought she could bring you up to scratch."

Zane blew out a sigh. "You know I've never thought of her in that way." Even less now that he'd had a glimpse into her unkind spirit. His gaze drifted back to Muriel, a woman patiently exclaiming over a boy's pocketful of treasures, and he smiled.

Muriel turned a questioning glance over her shoulder then shifted her attention momentarily to Constance's retreating back. She retrieved her fallen shawl and brushed the sand from its fringe before draping it over her arm.

"Fletcher, would ye like to meet Mr. Erickson?"

The boy stuffed his shells and other miscellaneous items into his pocket and straightened his posture as he gave Zane a rather thorough inspection. "This yer fella?"

Zane tipped his hat to the boy. "I'd like to be." He strode forward a few steps and extended his hand. "It's a pleasure to meet you, Fletcher."

"Before I shake yer hand, there's somethin' I gotta ask."

Zane lowered his hand and nodded, his stomach only clenching a little at the boy's piecing gaze. "Go ahead."

"You gonna make Muriel forget her family? I've worked around this place long enough to know the fancy don't take to associatin' with our kind." He jerked his chin in the direction of where Constance had joined the others in front of the bandstand.

"Fletcher!" Muriel took the boy by the shoulder. "That's not proper, now."

"It's all right," Zane said. "I'm happy to answer." He hunkered down in front of the boy. "If your aunt does me the honor of becoming my wife one day, you and your entire family will be welcome in our home anytime. If I'm honest, I'm rather hoping to be welcome in your home as well. I can tell you are all very close. That's the kind of family I want. I'm hoping to learn a thing or two from the Quinns."

Fletcher twisted to quirk a sideways grin at Muriel. "I think he'll do."

She smiled at her nephew then turned her warm gaze on Zane, making his chest grow heavy with longing. "Aye. I think he'll do, too."

Chapter 20

Having arrived late, Muriel took a seat in one of the back pews at Grace Church then slid over to allow room for Zane and Grandpa Clem. Oh, how she'd missed this place! Worshipping the Lord with family and friends. Singing with Brother Crabtree's choir until the sermon, then taking her place in the Quinn family pew, sandwiched between Fletcher and Da. Singing songs she knew, hearing a message she could understand.

Mrs. Underhill had insisted that Muriel cease attending her home congregation while pursuing Zane. If she hoped to impress the Ericksons, she'd have to maintain the appearance of a wealthy daughter boarding at the prestigious Ursuline Academy. So she'd attended Sunday Mass with the rest of the girls the last few weeks. A service conducted completely in Latin. If she had been an actual student of the academy, she would have been trained to understand the liturgy, but since she had no experience with Latin, she'd been utterly lost. Even the music had been different. Chants, mostly. The music contained a simple beauty that her soul appreciated, but without understanding the words, all she could do was hum along and silently compose her own prayerful lyrics.

With her secret now out of the bag, Muriel saw no need to continue pretending to be someone she wasn't. In fact, she planned to ask Da after Sunday lunch if she could move back home.

She spotted his flowing white hair and broad shoulders about six rows in front of her. Her heart ached at the sight. She'd not seen or spoken to him since she'd left for the academy. How she longed for one of his enormous hugs and to see his eyes twinkling as he teased her and called her his little mermaid. Her conscience pinched. The reunion wouldn't be all joy and sunshine, though. Not with the confession she had need of making.

At least they could enjoy Sunday lunch first. Another tradition she'd sorely missed. All the Galveston Quinns crowded around Da's table, food and stories equally plentiful. A ruckus gathering to be sure. Nothing like the formal dinners at Zane's home, with all the forks and etiquette and servants. If you waited for someone to fill your plate at the Quinn house, you'd go hungry. She'd done her best to warn him, but he'd laughed and insisted he was up for the adventure.

Fletcher had promised to warn his mama that there'd be three more for supper. Muriel didn't think Alana would mind having extras at the table, though she did feel slightly guilty about not contributing to the meal. Usually, she and her sister shared the preparation duties, but with Muriel being away on her infamous husband hunt, she'd left Alana with all the cooking and clean-up. That would change today. She might not have been able to bring food, but she still remembered how to wash dishes.

Zane smiled at her as he settled into the pew, and Muriel's heart softened like butter on a windowsill. He was here. Beside her.

Accepting her despite her flaws and mistakes. Eager to meet her family. Unconcerned about their differences. Caring only about the love blooming between them. Never had she approached worship with such an abundance of gratitude streaming through her heart.

Her appreciation of grace had deepened of late. When one scampered through life without much consideration of sin, accepting grace was like accepting the swipe of a mother's damp thumb to rub away a smudge of dirt from an otherwise clean face. When one recognized the true ugliness of sin, however, how it hurt others and destroyed trust, one came to see that smudge of dirt for what it really was—an inky tattoo that no amount of scrubbing could remove. Only the miraculous gift of new skin could remove the stain. A gift only possible through Jesus, the one who makes all things new.

As the minister offered an opening prayer, Muriel added a few thoughts of her own.

I'm sorry fer all the trouble I've caused, Lord. I let selfishness guide me steps instead o' seekin' yer wisdom. Forgive me.

It wasn't the first time she'd asked, and in her heart she knew he'd already made her clean. Yet she struggled to forgive herself, especially with the threat to her family still hanging over her head.

Thank ye fer bringin' good out o' the mess I made. Evidenced by the pair of men sitting beside her and the newfound humility residing in her spirit. *And help me never again to take yer grace for granted.*

When Muriel finally lifted her head, Brother Crabtree had already risen from his place and motioned the choir to stand. He really was a dear man. So patient and encouraging. And talented. His vocals were a mere step above ordinary, but the Lord had gifted him with an ear for creating balance. The choir always sounded better with him at the helm. More harmonious. More blended. More unified. No one voice above the others. She'd taken him for granted, too. Showing up late for practice. Relying on her natural abilities to skirt by. Not respecting his time or the time of the other singers. Not respecting their gifts. And they were gifted. Their harmony reached straight into her soul and drew her heart heavenward.

The congregation joined the choir, and music lifted to the rafters. Zane held an open hymnal in front of her, sharing the music as his tenor voice rose with the chorus.

Muriel didn't need the music. Her heart knew this song. She closed her eyes and opened her mouth, ready to sing for the first time in weeks. But emotion clogged her voice, making it impossible to sustain the notes. So she dropped her volume to a mere whisper as her spirit sang for her Savior alone to hear.

> "My Jesus, I love thee, I know thou art mine;
> for thee all the follies of sin I resign;
> my gracious Redeemer, my Savior art thou;
> if ever I loved thee, my Jesus, 'tis now."

Her eyes misted, and her quiet voice trembled. *I do love ye, Jesus. So much. I'll not be pretendin' anymore. No lyin', no compromisin' me values to take the easy path. I want to make ye proud.*

> "I love thee because thou hast first loved me
> and purchased my pardon on Calvary's tree;
> I love thee for wearing the thorns on thy brow;
> If ever I loved thee, my Jesus, 'tis now."

Guilt slid from her shoulders as she visualized the cross and the man upon it. The Son of God who loved her so much that he willingly endured an agonizing physical death to spare her from a spiritual one. Grace wasn't free. Jesus had paid the price with his blood. Yet he wasn't stingy with his purchase. He lavished it upon all who would draw near enough to accept it. And oh, how she needed it.

Her lips shaped the words of the third verse, while her heart still pondered the wonder of the second. With each phrase, her voice grew a little stronger, and by the time the triumphant fourth verse arrived, her voice matched the strength of her heart. Zane's tenor swelled along with her, and even Grandpa Clem's shaky bass rose in volume, the rich harmonies stirring her soul.

"In mansions of glory and endless delight,
I'll ever adore thee in heaven so bright;
I'll sing with the glittering crown on my brow:
If ever I loved thee, my Jesus, 'tis now."

At the close of the hymn, Muriel's eyes opened and she discovered Brother Crabtree smiling over his shoulder, his gaze pinned to her. Heat rose in her cheeks when she realized her singing must have been far too loud if he had heard her over the choir. Yet there was nothing chiding in his glance, just joy and approval. As if he'd heard not her voice, but her heart.

Muriel's spirit continued to lighten through the remainder of the service. Her problems hadn't disappeared, yet they seemed less daunting after spending time focused on worship instead of worry.

After the service, the people sitting around them struck up conversations, letting her know she'd been missed and asking if she'd be singing with the choir next Sunday. Plenty of curious glances angled in Zane's direction. Never one to be deterred by a little conversatin', as he put it, Grandpa Clem shook hands and made introductions. If anyone recognized the Erickson name, they did a good job of hiding their surprise.

A shadow fell over Muriel as she spoke with Mrs. Harrell. Had a cloud swept over the sun? No cloud, only a large man blocking the light from the window across from her pew. His form was silhouetted by the sunlight behind him, but she didn't need to see the lines etched into his tanned face to recognize him.

"Da." As if she were a girl of six instead of a woman nearing twenty, she ran down the row and threw herself into his arms, never once doubting he'd welcome her embrace.

He not only welcomed her, but he lifted her feet straight off the ground as he hugged her tight. "Dear heart. How I've missed ye." He set her back on her feet, but he didn't let her go. His hands cupped her arms, and his eyes drank her in as if afraid he'd forget what she looked like. "I heard ye singin', and I thought me ears were playin' tricks. But here ye are. Me little mermaid finally swam home."

"I *am* comin' home, Da, but I'm afeared that I'm bringin' trouble with me."

Her da's eyes narrowed as he tipped his chin toward someone behind her. "Those fellas the trouble? I know a place me and the boys could toss 'em where they'd ne'er be found."

"What?" Muriel twisted to find Zane looking a tad green, while Grandpa Clem chuckled.

"I knew I'd like you." Grandpa Clem, his wiry physique looking like a twig next to the massive oak of her da, shuffled around Zane to smack Patrick Quinn on the shoulder as if they were old friends. Then he stuck out his hand. "Clem Erickson." He nodded toward Zane. "My grandson, Zane. He'll recover in a minute. He's not as used to blusterin' threats as I am."

"Ye hurt me girl, and it won't be bluster fer long." Da took the man's hand and gave it the vise treatment.

Grandpa Clem didn't so much as wince. He winked instead. "Good thing we're on the same side then, ain't it?"

Da chuckled as he released Grandpa Clem's hand, but his gaze narrowed when he turned his attention to Zane. He crossed his arms over his muscled chest. "I got a grandson of me own, and he tells me ye think to court my Muriel. That true?"

Zane stood straight and tall and closed the distance between them. "Yes, sir. If she'll have me."

Muriel's pulse throbbed as she held her breath. *Please, Da. Ye know how much he means to me.*

"If she'll have ye? Son, she left her family and completely changed who she was in order to have ye. I thought architects were supposed to be smarter than that."

Grandpa Clem hooted. "Well, the boy's still an apprentice. Quick learner, though." He aimed a warm smile at Zane then shot a challenging glance at her da. "Smart enough to care more about a gal's heart than her penchant for playactin'."

Da's nostrils flared at the less-than-favorable, yet accurate, description. After a heartbeat, he released his breath and grinned. "Well, then." He extended his hand to Zane. "I'm pleased to know ye, Zane. Ye're comin' to the house fer supper, aren't ye?"

Zane clasped Da's hand and pumped his arm, a broad smile stretching across his face. "Yes, sir. Wouldn't miss it."

"Good. I've a heap o' questions I been savin' up to ask ye."

Zane's Adam's apple bobbed, but he held her da's gaze, something many men failed to do. "I'll be happy to answer them."

How she loved being home again, squished between family around the table. Zane and Grandpa Clem joined right in, holding hands with the others as Da blessed the meal, passing around food bowls, and laughing with the same vigor as the rest of the clan. More than once, Zane met her gaze from across the table, his eyes alight with an emotion far too deep to be politeness.

The words he'd said to Fletcher on the beach yesterday rang again in her ears. How he wanted a family like the Quinns. Close. Supportive. Full of love. One that valued relationship over social status and whose riches came from time spent together instead of money earned through investments.

Perhaps she had more to offer him than she'd thought. More than just her heart.

After supper, Da challenged the menfolk to a game of pitching horseshoes in the front yard while Muriel and Alana cleared the table and cleaned the kitchen. Fletcher joined the outdoor fun, and Liam even took the wee girlies out with him to give Alana a break.

"Your Liam's a good man," Muriel said with a smile as the laughter escalated.

Alana nodded, a fond look in her eyes as she rummaged in the dishwater for the next plate to scrub. "That he is." She cast a sideways look at Muriel. "Your Zane seems mighty taken with ye. But will his family approve?"

Muriel's smile dimmed. "His da doesn't. That much we know already. His ma is kinder. She's throwin' me a party on Tuesday. Plannin' to win her friends over by showin' off me singin' voice."

Alana didn't look impressed. Her hands slowed in their washing, and she leveled a serious look at Muriel. "Ye're more than just yer voice. Ye know that, don't ye?"

Touched by her sister's thoughtfulness, Muriel nodded. "Aye. But if me voice can make things easier for Zane, I'll gladly put it to use. Bein' with me's gonna cost him a great deal, Alana. It's already cost him his da's good opinion. Could cost him his inheritance, his connections, his friends."

Though some of his friends might not be missed as much as others. Muriel wouldn't shed any tears over havin' to disassociate with the clingy Miss Constance.

"True friends will stand by him," Alana said, "no matter who he marries."

Marries. A delicious shiver ran along Muriel's nape. She'd been careful not to let her dreams jump too far ahead, but Alana's simple statement opened a floodgate of desires. Zane coming home to her every night, her making their supper, the two of them playing duets on recorders in the evening. Goodnight kisses. Good morning kisses. Good-to-see-you-any-time-of-day kisses.

Muriel fell silent, too full of daydreams to chatter while they finished the dishes. Yet, as the last plate settled atop the stack in the cupboard, the bubble of her daydreams popped. She'd postponed the unpleasant task as long as possible, but she couldn't put it off any longer.

She folded her drying towel then placed a hand on Alana's arm. "Before ye head home, I need to have a word with ye and Da. In private."

Alana searched Muriel's face for answers she'd not find until they spoke, but she nodded. "All right."

"I'll fetch Da. We can talk in his room."

Zane spotted her when she exited the house and made his way over to her. "Grandpa Clem and Fletcher are in a showdown." His eyes glowed with such joy, her heart leapt in response. He must have seen something in her gaze, though, for his expression grew serious. "What is it?"

"I need to tell them 'bout Mrs. Underhill's threats. Put them on their guard. Just in case we don't get the journal back."

Zane nodded in understanding. "Want me to come with you?"

A part of her did. Having him at her side, infusing his strength into her, would be a boon. But she shook her head. "Not this time. They don't know ye well yet, and havin' ye there might keep them from sharin' their true thoughts." Like how disappointed they were in her.

"I understand. I'll keep things lively out here. We can talk more on the way back to the academy."

He'd volunteered his family buggy to help move her things home from the academy after lunch. Not that she had more than a single bag of belongings. But any chance to spend more time with him was welcome.

"Thank ye."

"Of course." He reached for her hand and rubbed his thumb over the back of it.

Tingles danced through her belly, and her chest warmed. Da sauntered over to them, eyebrow raised. Zane dropped her hand, and Muriel would have taken her da to task for his high-handed manner had she not needed him for other purposes.

"Da? Can I talk to ye fer a minute inside?"

He shot her a penetrating look and immediately nodded. "Lead the way, love."

Da and Alana already knew about her agreement to retrieve Mrs. Underhill's stolen journal, so Muriel skipped the background and got right to the point.

"Zane's da figured out who I was, who Da was, and called me bluff at dinner a few nights ago. He demanded that Zane have nothin' to do with me, called me a gold-digging Jezebel with nothin' to offer their family but a bucketful of lies."

Da's face turned an alarming shade of red, but he held his tongue, waiting for the rest of the tale.

"Zane defended me and stayed by me side through it all, but Mrs. Underhill . . . when she found out, she threatened to ruin not only me, but the two of ye as well if I didn't find a way to get her journal. She told me of her powerful friends and how she could arrange for rumors and planted evidence to discredit both ye, Da . . ." She turned her attention to Alana. ". . . and Liam."

Muriel hung her head, shame hurting her heart. "Ye were right, Da. I never should've gotten involved with Mrs. Underhill. She's vile and vicious and doesn't care who she hurts to get what she wants. I don't care 'bout her blackenin' me name, but the thought of her harmin' either of ye . . . it tears me up inside. Zane is gonna help me find the journal, but there's a chance his da's hidden it where we won't find it. I needed to warn ye of the storm brewin'. Give ye time to batten the hatches."

"Muriel. Look at me." Her da's voice brooked no argument.

She tipped up her chin.

"I can fight me own battles, love. Ye don't need to fight 'em fer me. I can handle a few rumors. Even if this Underhill woman succeeds in ruinin' me reputation, I'll find me way. Maybe not here, but here's not the only place a man with my skills can work. I trust the Lord to provide."

"As do I," Alana said, her tone fierce. "This matchmaker wouldn't be the first snooty woman to try to blame Liam for something going missing at the hotel." She pushed up from the edge of the bed where she'd been sitting and stood like a soldier awaiting inspection. "Quinns don't cower. Nor do we throw our little sisters to the wolves to save our own skins. We stand together. Faith and family. Forever."

Da rose to his feet as well. "Aye. Faith and family." He held out his hand to Muriel. "'The Lord is on my side,'" he quoted, "'I will not fear: what can man do unto me?'"

Muriel blinked back tears as she stood and clasped first her da's hand and then her sister's. What could man—or woman—do to them? She prayed the answer would be nothing, but deep down she couldn't shake the fear that they were about to find out just how terrible the answer to that question could be.

Chapter 21

"She's left the academy."

Octavia Underhill's fingers slipped and played a discordant note on the piano in her front parlor. She had precious little time to perfect the difficult piece she intended to perform at the Ericksons' soirée on Tuesday and didn't appreciate her maid's interruption. Yet when she turned to scold Vanessa for her ill-timed pronouncement, the weighted look in the girl's eyes gave her pause.

"*Who* left the academy?"

"Miss Quinn, ma'am. She packed up her belongings not thirty minutes ago and left in Mr. Erickson's carriage. I questioned the nun on duty, and she told me that Miss Quinn has decided to return home and will no longer be boarding at the Ursuline Academy."

Why, that ungrateful little tramp. Running home to Daddy as if she didn't have other commitments to honor. Octavia rose from the piano bench and paced across the center of the room. Did she think she'd be safe from Octavia's reach just because they no longer shared a roof? Ha! She'd not escape so easily. Octavia had tentacles in all areas of business on this island. All she had to do was call in a favor . . . but wait . . .

"She left with Zane, you say?"

Vanessa's chin dipped. "Yes, ma'am."

So in all likelihood the musicale was still in play. "Go to the Ericksons and question that footman of yours. See if he's heard anything about the party on Tuesday being canceled. If not, then we will proceed as planned. Otherwise, we'll need to pivot and execute the contingency strategy."

Octavia stood behind the settee and ran her fingertips along the curved wooden trim of the sofa back, her mind busy organizing details, plot points, and variables to ensure an airtight scheme.

"What contingency is that, ma'am?"

Vanessa's voice buzzed like an irritating gnat in her ear. Hadn't the girl learned by now to leave her mistress alone when she was in the midst of a plotting session? Interruptions were vastly annoying.

"The boy," Octavia said with a wave of her hand. "The one you spotted at the beach when you followed our little chickadee on her outing. He's her weakness. One we can exploit."

"He's a . . . a child, ma'am."

Octavia spun to face the upstart who dared question her. "He's a pawn in a larger game. One your feeble brain is apparently too small to comprehend."

Vanessa's eyes widened, and she retreated in the face of Octavia's fury. As she should.

Seizing her advantage, Octavia stalked forward, the aroma of weakness feeding her craving to subjugate someone. She'd prefer that someone be Horace Erickson, or even that infuriating Irish chit who seemed bent on causing trouble, but Vanessa was handy, and she needed to be put firmly into her place. Just because Octavia had come to rely on the little maid did not mean she couldn't be replaced if she stepped out of line.

"I gave you an assignment." She enunciated each syllable with clipped precision. "I don't pay you to express your opinion. I pay you to carry out my wishes. Now do as you're told."

"Yes, ma'am." She bobbed a curtsey and fled the room.

Good riddance. Octavia paced the room, free from the weight of Vanessa's ill-hidden disapproval. As if she cared what a maid thought of her. She'd cultivated a network of influence, respect, and fear among the social elite of the wealthiest city in the south. People knew better than to cross her because her threats were never idle. And while ruining the reputations of Patrick Quinn and Liam Doherty would be more in keeping with her usual style, it was harder to successfully blacken the names of men of integrity. According to her sources, both of Muriel's kinsmen possessed pristine reputations. The blighters.

But a boy was a different story. A boy whom Miss Quinn held dear. Sentimental females with big hearts proved remarkably compliant when a beloved child was in danger. Yes, the boy would suit her purposes nicely.

She needed to send a message to the docks. Make sure everything would be ready as early as Tuesday evening. If Muriel Quinn tried to cross her, there'd be a reckoning.

Poor, unfortunate soul. She was so far out of her depth she could swim for days and never find her footing.

Octavia's throaty laugh rumbled forth like timpani rolls heralding a climactic orchestral conclusion. The thought of that syrupy sweet little songstress getting her comeuppance proved too delightful to contain her glee. And why should she? She'd earned it. Tipping back her head, Octavia let her laughter soar like a soprano's aria. Her triumph was assured.

Muriel had never experienced nerves before a performance. Singing was simply *part* of her. Yet when Zane's mother said her name and extended a hand toward her in invitation, Muriel's breath seized in her chest. Her heart pumped at an alarming rate, making her lightheaded and strangely unsteady on her feet.

Zane took her arm and leaned close to her ear. "You can do this." His assurance eased a bit of the cramping in her belly, and when she turned and saw his smile and the way his eyes lit with love, her head ceased its swimming. "Close your eyes if it helps," he said. "Pretend you're standing on that outcropping by the shore, and I'm the only one who can hear you."

Sing for Zane. The man she loved. Not for the audience of strangers politely applauding and likely growing impatient with her hesitation. Just for Zane.

Muriel smiled at him and gave him a nod. The answering brightness in his gaze filled her with enough courage to relinquish his arm and walk the handful of steps to the piano. Mrs. Underhill sat upon the bench, her fingers poised above the keys. Her lips turned upward in a smile even as her eyes speared threats through Muriel's chest.

They'd met at the academy yesterday to rehearse, and Mrs. Underhill had given her an earful about duty and contracts and promises. As if she'd needed the reminder. She'd thought of little else over the last few days.

Stay in the moment. Think o' Zane. Let the music flow.

Turning her attention away from her sinister accompanist, Muriel faced the small crowd of Zane's family and friends.

Genuine pleasure sparked in her chest as her gaze fell on a grinning Grandpa Clem standing near the mantel.

Inhaling a deep breath, she addressed the audience. "Thank ye fer yer kind welcome. I'm more accustomed to singin' in church than in front of an audience, so I have a few wee nerves dancin' around in me belly."

Polite laughter echoed softly through the parlor.

She pressed a hand to her midsection, willing the flutters to settle. Thankfully, Mrs. Erickson had cultivated her guest list with precision. Only kind gazes peered up at her from the dozen or so guests seated throughout the large music room. Well, except for Zane's scowling father. Horace Erickson had surprised them all by insisting upon attending the event. Thankfully, he stood near the back of the room and could be easily ignored. A movement closer to the piano brought her gaze back to Zane as he took a seat next to his friend Max, the friendly fella from the beach. Zane aimed a nod at her, and a few more fretful barnacles slid free of their mooring on her spirit.

"Our first selection this evening is 'The Last Rose of Summer.'" A piece that had required little practice since both she and Mrs. Underhill had gone through it together previously.

Taking a second to gather herself, she smoothed her hand down the skirt of the dark green dress that she wore only on special occasions. It seemed faded and drab compared to the fashionable silks and satins of the ladies in the audience, but she'd refused to wear another gown purloined from Mrs. Underhill's students. Besides, most of the fabric had come from one of Ma's old dresses, so wearing it was like receiving a hug from her mammy at the moment she needed it most.

With that lovely thought buoying her, she nodded to her accompanist, and rich music filled the quiet.

"'Tis the last rose of summer . . ."

A tremor beset the first few notes of the song, but she kept her gaze on Zane, and eventually the final barnacles fell away, leaving her free to sail uninhibited across the sea of music.

She followed her first selection with a newer piece, ironically entitled "Love's Old Sweet Song," then concluded her portion of the program with the ever-popular "Beautiful Dreamer." Rousing applause met her last note, and Zane shot to his feet with an enthusiastic ovation. Heat rushed to her cheeks at his display, but soon the entire audience rose to their feet as well. So stunned was she, she nearly forgot Mrs. Underhill's training for taking a bow.

Holding her skirt to the side, she dipped into a graceful curtsy, crossing one arm over her chest as she bowed her head.

Zane's mother made her way back to the piano, moisture visible in her eyes. She clasped Muriel's hand. "My dear, that was the most stirring performance I have ever heard. Absolutely beautiful." She turned to the crowd. "Truly remarkable, isn't she?"

The applause revived. Zane's friend Max even added a few whistles.

"But Miss Quinn isn't the only talented musician in the house this evening. Octavia Underhill is a classically trained pianist, and she has graciously agreed to play a few pieces for us as well. You're in for a treat."

Muriel strolled away from the piano toward the hall where a table had been set up with punch and small desserts.

Zane met her there, his face beaming. "You were amazing!"

His whispered praise set her heart aflame, but a dark-haired serving maid darting down the hall with an odd contraption in hand doused Muriel's delight with harsh reality. She wasn't finished performing tonight.

She accepted the punch Zane handed her and drank half of it in one swig. "Vanessa's here," she whispered, her head tipping toward the hall. "We need to be ready."

"I have the key to Father's office and the replacement journal you gave me." Zane patted his coat pocket. "Are you sure you can pick the lock on his desk?"

"No, but I've been practicin'. What about yer da? Should we be worried about him?"

Zane turned his attention toward the back of the music room. "He's focused on Mrs. Underhill. That's the only reason he came tonight. He doesn't trust her and is determined to keep her under surveillance. As long as she stays in the music room, he will too."

"She has some sort of distraction planned to give us a chance to slip away unnoticed. We just have to wait for the—"

A screech rent the air. Then another, followed by a dreadful banging on the piano.

"Rats!"

"No, they're squirrels."

"Horace, do something!"

Zane gaped as a pair of weasel-like creatures raced through the parlor causing havoc with every twist and turn. Muriel grabbed his arm and dragged him out into the hall.

"No time to watch. We've got to go."

"Right." He took the lead, jogging along the corridor, turning left, then left again. Muriel kept pace, thankful for the carpet runner that silenced the heels of her shoes.

Zane pulled a key from his coat pocket and pressed it into the lock on the paneled hardwood door. It turned with ease. Zane pushed the door inward and stepped inside. Muriel's heart hammered worse than it had when she'd first stepped in front of the crowd, but she followed Zane inside and closed the door quietly behind her.

Please don't let us get caught, Lord.

It was probably sacrilegious to ask God to help them break one of the commandments, but this was more of a retrieval than a theft. At least that's what Muriel told herself. God knew all the circumstances as well as their motives. Surely he would deem their cause worthy. She hoped.

"Here." Zane rounded the large desk that dominated the room and moved the chair out of the way. "This is the drawer I couldn't open." He tapped the handle on a large drawer on the left side of the desk.

Muriel reached into the pocket of her skirt and extracted a pair of bent hairpins, one with a hooked flat end to serve as the pick and the other with its U-shaped end bent into a lever. She dropped to her knees in front of the drawer and slipped the lever piece in first like Vanessa'd shown her. She slid the pick in next and tried to feel for the tumblers, but the flimsy brass of her hairpin made the task nigh impossible. She varied her angle, the pressure, her grip, anything she could think of, but time ticked by with no success.

"Please, God," she whispered.

Then all at once, something clicked. Only it wasn't the lock. It was the office door latch.

Muriel gasped as the door swung inward.

Zane's father stepped inside, a familiar leather-bound journal in his upraised hand. "Looking for this?"

Chapter 22

"Father, I can explain." Zane straightened as he turned to face his sire. His throat tightened like it used to when he'd been caught doing something naughty as a boy.

His father's scowl darkened as he strode into the office and closed the door behind him. "Explain what, Zane? Your betrayal of this family?" He crossed to the desk, his eyes blazing with barely contained fury. "I expected Octavia to try something, either on her own or with her little Irish protégée's help." He tossed a disdainful glare in Muriel's direction. "But I never considered my own flesh and blood would turn on me."

"You don't understand." Zane positioned himself in front of Muriel as he edged around the side of the desk to face his father. "Mrs. Underhill threatened to destroy Muriel's family."

"Of course she did. She's an unscrupulous blackmailer."

One with access to a secret his father apparently deemed damaging enough that he'd not been content to let Mother make the monthly payments. He'd stolen the journal to hide whatever incriminating evidence existed.

"Please." Zane extended his hand. "Give us the journal. If we return it, Muriel's family will be safe. That's what is most important."

Father's brows arched. "The well-being of *her* family is most important? What about *your* family?" He scrunched the journal into a cylindrical shape in his fist as he scoffed. "Wake up, son. She's using you. Batting her lashes and drawing you into her snare with this *damsel-in-distress* act. She's been working with that Underhill woman the entire time. Lying to you for weeks. Gaining your trust so she can manipulate you into retrieving this journal." He waved the curled edges of the slim leather notebook under Zane's nose. "The whole sob story about her family is probably a lie, too. Use your head, boy." He smacked the rolled-up journal against the side of Zane's skull. "Don't fall for her wiles."

Zane's jaw clenched. Was insulting his intelligence not enough? Did he have to swat him as if he were a disobedient puppy?

"Why'd you steal it?" Zane nodded toward the journal, his gaze challenging his father. He'd not be baited. He knew Muriel's heart. Knew she could be trusted. She'd revealed all her secrets. Unlike the man glowering at him. "What secret did you so fear getting out that you committed theft to protect it?"

His father leaned backward and sputtered. "It wasn't theft. It was a renegotiation. One I did to protect *you*. You and your mother."

"From what?" Zane pressed. "From what might happen if the truth came out about your business practices? Mother told me about the secret. About how it would ruin you." She'd given him no specifics, but he'd imagined several possible scenarios. Manipulating the market to ensure greater profit. Falsification of records. Forged receipts. Dishonest weighing of cotton shipments. A broker in a position of power could engage in any or all of those practices with few repercussions. Unless someone produced evidence of his guilt. "Sounds to me like you were protecting yourself."

"Easy to sit in judgment when the chair's cushioned and comfortable." Father raised a single brow, his scorn palpable. "Who do you think gave you this comfortable life?" He thumped his chest with the journal. "I did. Your education, your exposure to the architecture of Europe, even your apprenticeship with Nicholas Clayton—none of it would have happened without my provision. Black and white might work for your ink drawings, but the business world operates in shades of gray. Right and wrong is a matter of perspective."

Zane shook his head. "Calling wrong right doesn't make it so."

Though learning of past wrongs tainted the right he'd enjoyed. He'd profited from his father's dishonesty. The house he lived in, the schools he attended, the connections that led to his apprenticeship. All fruit from a rotted tree. Zane prayed the Lord would redeem his ill-gotten gains and use them for good. He'd have to be cut away and grafted into a new tree, though. One with godly roots.

Muriel's hand slipped around Zane's arm, and a bit of sunshine returned to banish the gloom brought on by his father's cold-heartedness.

"Please, Mr. Erickson," she said. "I need that journal. If I don't return it to Mrs. Underhill, she's gonna hurt me da and me sister. Ye can remove the pages pertainin' to yer own situation. I have no desire to see anyone in yer family suffer, either."

Father grunted. "How generous of you. But what about the other families? Do you wish to see them suffer?" He looked back to Zane. "The Trimbles are in here. Did you know that? Is the blackmail of Max's parents acceptable to you?"

"Of course not." Now Zane was the one sputtering.

Max? He'd mentioned something about his mother seeking a matchmaker for him, but Zane had failed to put two and two together.

"Where's your black and white morality now? Is aiding an extortionist acceptable if it helps one person and hurts dozens of others?"

"It's not the same." It wasn't, was it? "Those people surrendered their secrets willingly, knowing the consequences. Muriel's family did nothing to earn Mrs. Underhill's retribution."

Father smiled, and Zane's stomach soured.

"Your little lady friend there made an agreement with Mrs. Underhill, though, didn't she? In order to get her hooks into you. So she's as guilty as anyone else in this book. Why help her and not the others?"

No answer jumped to Zane's mind.

His father's smile grew. "Gray areas. Maybe you're more like me than either of us thought."

Muriel moved out from behind Zane. "The agreement I made with Mrs. Underhill only entailed her revealin' me true background and shamin' meself if I failed to return her journal. It had nothin' to do with framin' me da or me sister's husband for crimes they didn't commit. That's what be different, Mr. Erickson. She changed the deal and is threatenin' folks with no connection to her at all. If the consequences would only fall on me, I'd take them as me due. But it's not right for me da and brother-in-law to pay a price they ne'er agreed to."

Father clicked his tongue as he wagged his head. "So naïve. You didn't really expect to swim with a shark and not get bitten, did you? At least I had a plan. First, I ensured all evidence of our family secrets were burned to ash, then I hedged my bets by rigging the game. A little financial inducement bought the cooperation of her butler and ensured the journal ended up in my hands. Finally, I gave Mrs. Underhill a taste of her own medicine. Find my son a suitable bride or I'd expose her schemes and release her clients from their financial responsibilities. And since you are completely *un*suitable," he said with a disdainful glance at Muriel that made Zane grind his molars, "it seems it's time to hold up my end of the bargain. I think the *Galveston Daily News* will find this little book quite interesting, don't you? They might even pay a tidy fee to purchase it from me."

"So all that talk about protecting the secrets of the people in that book was just a . . . a ruse? You plan to *sell* them?" Unbelievable! He'd known his father could be a ruthless businessman, but had his conscience really become so hardened that he would choose profit over human decency?

He smiled. Actually smiled. As if he were proud of himself. "Anonymously, of course. I'll broker the deal through a third party. No need for anyone to learn how the journal came to be discovered." The smile flattened and his eyes narrowed. "That woman never should have involved herself in my affairs."

Zane fell back a step, nausea stirring his stomach. "You're as much a villain as she is," he murmured.

Father shrugged, making no effort to deny the charge.

The horrifying truth brought new clarity to Zane's mind. He'd never take a cent from his father again. He'd move out of this house at once, live off his apprentice salary. It would mean forgoing the finer things, but he'd never cared much for fancy clothes or expensive furnishings anyway. He did like having a cook, but maybe Muriel would take pity on him and invite him to supper a few times a week. If she still allowed him to court her.

"There's no reason for the coming scandal to touch you, son." Father waved dismissively at Muriel. "Let her sort her own problems. She's lied and manipulated you from the beginning. You owe her nothing."

"I owe her my life. Or did you forget where and how this relationship began? She pulled me from the Gulf and manipulated my lungs into breathing again." Zane trudged around the desk and put his face an inch from his father's. "From the beginning, Muriel has revealed herself to be a caring and courageous woman. Her only misstep came in heeding the advice of a sea snake. I'll not make the same mistake by heeding yours. Now give me that journal, and let us be done with this."

Zane clasped the edge of the leather cover, but his father jerked it away and backed toward the door. He pointed the rolled-up notebook at Zane like a wagging finger.

"You marry that girl, and you're done with this family. I'll cut you off. You'll not see a penny of my money."

Was the man so blind, he thought money was their only connection? A pang hit Zane's heart. Maybe it was.

"Now that I know how you make your money," Zane said, "I'm going to cut myself off. I'll live on what I make working for Mr. Clayton."

"Fool!" Father spat. "You think she'll have you without my money? That's all a woman like her cares about."

"Ye're wrong." Muriel came to Zane's side and slid her hand around his arm. Zane instantly felt a foot taller. "I never wanted Zane fer his money. I only ever wanted *him*. Ye're the fool if ye cut him out of yer life. He's yer son. There's no greater treasure than family."

"Ha! Even now she's scheming. Hoping I'll change my mind. Well, I won't. Stick with him, sweetheart, and you'll end up with nothing."

"Nay." Her fingers tightened on Zane's arm, and he turned to see her eyes upon him, their hazel depths glowing with love. "I'll end up with everything."

"Not everything!" Father waved the journal then yanked open the door.

Zane lurched forward, intending to chase his father down, but Muriel held tight to his arm. "Let him go. He'll not be giving it up."

He glanced back at her. "But what about your family?"

Her shoulders slumped. "I'll plead fer mercy, I suppose, though I doubt she'll give any. 'Tis in God's hands now. I pray his mercy outweighs Mrs. Underhill's ruthlessness."

Zane cupped her cheek. "I'm sorry, Muriel. Father . . . he . . ."

What excuse could he give? None existed. His father had proven to be selfish, pitiless, and corrupted by greed. Zane's hand fell from her face, and he looked away, too shamed to meet her gaze.

Muriel took his face in hand and brought his chin around. "I'm the one who's sorry, Zane. Sorry to come between yer father and yerself. For the wounds he inflicted upon ye. I pray he sees the truth before it's too late. That his relationship with ye can be mended."

He leaned into her touch, thankful to have her by his side. To have her affection. Her support. Perhaps even her love.

"I'll pray for that, too. But I meant what I said. I'll be leaving his house. This week, if I can find a place to live."

She smiled. "Finally, I've got connections that can be of use to ye. We'll find ye a place. Don't ye fret."

His heart rate kicked up a level. "Would you . . . help me pick it out? After all, I'm . . . ah . . . hoping it will eventually be your home, too."

Pink flushed her cheeks, but her smile widened. "Zane Erickson. That wouldn't be a proposal, now, would it?"

Now he was the one with overheated cheeks. "Let's . . . ah . . . call it a declaration of intent. I'll need time to get my affairs in order and have a conversation with your father before I can make it official. But I love you, Muriel, and I want you to be part of my world. Wherever that world might be."

Her thumb stroked the edge of his jaw, and the shivers it produced drove his thoughts straight to her lips.

"Those're the sweetest words I've e'er heard." Her whispery voice set him ablaze. "And I declare me own intent . . . I intend to be yer wife, Zane Erickson. To love ye all my livelong days and let nothin' but death separate us."

As if she'd just said the vow before a preacher, Zane drew her against his chest, more than ready to kiss his future bride. But as he lowered his mouth toward hers, the sound of running footsteps in the hall restored his sanity. He lifted his head and backed away, regretfully losing the connection of her hand on his face as his arm uncoiled from her waist.

Vanessa, Mrs. Underhill's intrusive maid, ducked her head into the office. After spying them, she ducked her entire self inside and closed the door behind her.

"Did you get the journal?" The young woman was out of breath and wielding none of the condescending confidence that usually exuded from her countenance.

Muriel shook her head. "Nay. Zane's father has it still. He's made it clear he'll not be givin' it up. I'll find Mrs. Underhill and tell her."

"No!" Vanessa ran forward and grabbed Muriel's arm. "You can't. You have to give her the journal. Tonight."

"But I don't have it."

"Then pretend you do." The maid waved her hand in a jerky fashion. "Use the . . . the replacement journal."

Zane frowned as he reached into his coat pocket and fingered the leather of the blank notebook he carried. "What good will that do? The moment Muriel hands it over, Mrs. Underhill will open it and see that it's a fake. A stunt like that will only earn her ire."

"You don't understand." She didn't spare Zane more than a glance. Instead, she took hold of Muriel's other arm and gave her a little shake. "She'll probably ruin me for telling you, but I got brothers of my own, and I'll not be able to live with myself if something happens to him."

The color leaked from Muriel's face. "Happens to who, Vanessa?"

"Your nephew. Octavia's got him stashed on a boat anchored offshore about a half-mile west of the Beach Hotel. If you don't hand over the journal, she'll signal the smuggler she hired, and the boy will suffer an *accident* at sea."

Muriel reached for the desk behind her, her agonized gaze piercing Zane's heart. "God preserve us. She's got Fletcher."

Chapter 23

The wooden edge of the desktop dug into Muriel's hands, the pain only a fraction of the torment slashing her heart.

Fletcher. Dear, sweet Fletcher. A boy who combed the beaches after a storm to rescue starfish and return them to the sea. The most innocent of them all had been caught in a net meant for Muriel. She had to cut him free before any harm befell him.

Instinct told her to fall at Octavia Underhill's feet and beg for mercy. To offer herself in Fletcher's place. Perhaps Mrs. Underhill would still find value in her singing voice. She could take Muriel on tour and keep all the proceeds. Muriel would gladly forfeit her own freedom to secure Fletcher's. But even as she lurched away from the desk to run from the room, an unearthly calm settled over her. Jumbled, panicked thoughts clicked into order, and a plan crystalized.

"Vanessa." Muriel cast a quick glance at the clock on the shelf across from the desk. "Find Mrs. Underhill. Tell her that Zane be trackin' down the journal and will meet her at the dunes west of the hotel at eight-thirty."

"Yes, miss."

Thankfully, the young maid responded to the instruction without question and hurried from the office to carry out her assigned task. Mrs. Underhill would likely wonder why Muriel was sending Zane to hand over the journal instead of seeing to the task herself, but Vanessa would be able to answer honestly that she didn't know.

Zane's hand came to rest on Muriel's back, and she pivoted to face him. Emotion surged, and she had to fight off the temptation to collapse against his chest and let him hold her. But she couldn't afford the luxury of basking in his comfort right now. Time was ticking, and every moment counted.

"I need ye to go after yer da. Tell him what's happened. Beg him to give ye the journal. Everything will be easier if he does, but I'll not be puttin' all me eggs in that basket. Mrs. Underhill can't be trusted to uphold her end of the bargain."

Zane searched Muriel's face, and his brow crinkled. "I'll do everything I can to convince him to help. But there's no guarantee he'll surrender, even to help a child. What should we do if I don't get it?"

Bless him for listening instead of arguing. She didn't have the mental strength to fight him *and* Mrs. Underhill tonight.

"Do what Vanessa suggested—use the replacement journal. Stall as long ye can, refuse to hand it over until Fletcher is safely on shore. Whatever ye can think to do. If she's workin' with smugglers, though, there's a good chance she'll have hired men to take the journal from ye by force. So be careful."

"Where will you be?"

Muriel set her jaw. "Rescuin' Fletcher."

Zane reared back. "What? How?"

She paced to the bookcase, plotting her course aloud more to settle it in her mind than to explain it to him. "The sun will be settin' soon. If ye lend me yer carriage, I can make a stop by me house to grab me suit then get to the hotel and scout out the location of the boat anchored offshore. The fishin' boats will all be in by now, so there's likely to be only the one. It'll be dusk by then, but that'll play in our favor. They won't see me comin'. I'll slip into the water slightly to the east and use the longshore currents to guide me west. Fletcher's a grand swimmer, so if I can signal him, he might be able to slip overboard without the smugglers noticin'. If they have him tied, I'll have to climb aboard to free him, but they'll be watchin' the shore, not the sea, so I should be able to climb aboard without anyone bein' the wiser."

"That's too dangerous, Muriel." Zane ran a hand down his face, his eyes tortured. "What if they see you? They could . . ." His voice choked, and he tore his gaze away from her. "You'll barely be dressed, and . . . well . . . smugglers are rough men. It could go very badly."

Muriel clasped his arm. "I *have* to go, Zane. I'm the only one who can make that swim. But you can send in reinforcements. Go and get Grandpa Clem and me da. If Fletcher's missin', Liam and Da will be huntin' fer him. Probably at the docks and rail yard. Find them, if ye have time, but don't miss yer appointment with Mrs. Underhill. If she signals the boat before I can get to Fletcher, we might lose him."

Unwanted tears rose in her eyes, but she ruthlessly batted them away.

"I'll not let her hurt him, Zane. I *won't*."

He held her gaze, his jaw working as if arguments were beating on the back of his teeth, ready to pour out. He swallowed them, though, and gave a quick nod. "I won't either."

His vow strengthened her spirit and dried her eyes.

Then he raised a brow. "You better swim home to me, Muriel Quinn. I don't aim to live my life without you."

"I will. I promise." She'd come too far to lose him now.

He leaned down and pressed a firm kiss to her forehead. "I love you."

Her eyes slid closed for just a heartbeat. "I love ye, too," she whispered. Then she grabbed his hand and pulled him toward the door. "Come on."

Zane led Muriel to the carriage house and found the family carriage already hitched and ready to go. He sent a prayer of thanks heavenward, but it was cut short by the groom who protested when Zane handed Muriel into the equipage.

"Sorry, sir. Your father asked me to ready the carriage and drive him to the lodge. I expect him any minute. I can hitch up the grays to the other buggy, though, so you can drive your lady home."

Zane shook his head. "There's no time for that. A boy's life is in danger." He finished handing Muriel into the carriage then closed the door. "I need you to stay with Miss Quinn. Drive her wherever she asks to go, no matter how unconventional the request might seem. It's imperative, Eddie. Please."

The young groom shifted from foot to foot. "But Mr. Zane, your daddy pays my salary. I can't just ignore his orders."

"I'll deal with my father and take full responsibility. You have my word." Knowing his father was coming to the carriage house saved him the time of tracking him down.

When Eddie made no move to climb into the driver's seat, Zane touched the man's shoulder. "Please, Eddie. We just learned Miss Quinn's nephew has been kidnapped."

The groom's eyes rounded. "Kidnapped?"

Zane nodded. "Yes. He's only ten. *Please*. We have a plan to retrieve him, but time is of the essence."

"God help him." Eddie swallowed hard then met Zane's gaze with determination. "I'll take her, sir. And I'll not spare the horses."

Zane clapped him on the back. "Good man. Thank you."

Eddie scampered up into the driver's box and took up the reins. With a click of his tongue and a snap of the lines, Eddie set the horses in motion.

"What the devil?" Father jumped out of the way, narrowly avoiding being clipped by the moving carriage. "Get back here, you fool! That's *my* transport."

"Not anymore." Zane hurried to intercept him. "I commandeered the vehicle for Muriel."

"Bah." Father shoved past him. "That girl is a plague."

Zane snagged his father's arm and twirled him around, ignoring the scowl of disbelief on his sire's face. "That girl is going to be my wife. And if you will cease defaming her for a moment, I'll explain what is happening."

Father jerked his arm away from Zane's hold and tugged his coat sleeve back into its proper place. "I see what is happening plainly enough. You've chosen that gold-digging Jezebel over your own flesh and blood. I should write you out of my will this very night."

"Do it!" Zane's veins throbbed in his neck. "I don't want your money. I want to save a young boy's life. That's what's at stake here. Or is a child's life less important than your date at the lodge?"

Father's scowl tightened. "What nonsense are you spewing now?"

"Muriel's nephew has been abducted. Mrs. Underhill is using him as leverage to ensure we hand over that journal you stole."

His father scoffed. "Please. You're far too gullible. Can't you see that girl's still manipulating you? It's all about that stupid book. She doesn't care about you at all."

A roar of frustration swelled in Zane's throat, begging for release. "For pity's sake. Can you set your suspicions aside for two seconds? Muriel wasn't the one who told me. Mrs. Underhill's maid told us. Right after you left your office. Mrs. Underhill has hired a group of smugglers to do her dirty work. They have Fletcher stowed away on a boat anchored offshore. If I don't hand over her journal, the boy will be dumped at sea."

"It's a bluff." Father's eyes didn't quite match his casual, unconcerned tone. They dodged side-to-side as if he were calculating the odds at a high-stakes poker game. "Octavia might have paid to have a boat weigh anchor offshore to lend credence to her story, but she'd not harm a child. She's a woman. Women don't have the stomach for things like that."

"What if you're wrong?" Zane pressed. "Can you live with a child's blood on your hands? I can't. I'm going to that meeting whether you give me the journal or not."

"Don't be a fool. This isn't your problem. Let Miss Quinn and that mountain of a father of hers handle it. There's no reason for you to get involved."

"No reason?" Zane's hands slapped against his sides in exasperation. "What about common decency? Honor? I gave my word to Muriel that I'd help her, and I aim to do just that."

Zane huffed out a disgusted breath and strode for the exit. He needed to find Grandpa Clem.

"Zane. Wait." His father chased him down and took hold of his arm. "It could be dangerous, son. If you show up empty-handed, Octavia could take her anger out on you. On this family."

Zane spun on his father. "By telling your secrets, you mean? Do you never stop thinking of yourself? A ten-year-old boy's life is hanging in the balance, and all you care about is your own position."

"Hang my position," Father growled. "I care about *you*. If that woman hired smugglers, they'll not balk at taking their pound of flesh. We nearly lost you after that boating accident. I won't allow you to place yourself in danger again."

"You have no say in the matter. I'm going whether you approve or not." Zane turned to leave.

"You can't show up without the journal, Zane."

He halted and turned to face his father. "Then give it to me." He extended his hand. "Please."

Father rubbed a hand over his face and paced a few steps away. "But if this is all a ruse, I'll be forfeiting my advantage for nothing."

"Then come with me," Zane dared. "See for yourself if the boy is in trouble. Decide if I'm worthy of making the sacrifice."

"Fine! But the journal is staying with me."

Of course it was. Zane gestured toward the house. "Go fetch it from whatever lockbox you stashed it in. I'll find Grandpa Clem and meet you back here. We have to find Patrick Quinn and send him after Muriel as quickly as possible. Otherwise she'll be facing down a boat full of smugglers on her own."

Chapter 24

As soon as Zane's carriage slowed in front of her house, Muriel threw open the door and jumped out, not waiting for assistance.

"Keep yer seat, Eddie. I'll just be a minute."

The Ericksons' driver had navigated the streets with skill, speed, and a smidgeon of reckless abandon. Muriel couldn't have asked for a better blend. She attacked her task with the same daring, having half of the hooks running down her bodice undone before she made it through the house and to her room. Heedless of crushing the fabric, she unfastened the skirt closure and let it fall to the floor while she shrugged out of the open bodice and tossed it onto her bed. Her fingers untied the front laces of her corset with practiced efficiency. She tore off her petticoats, chemise, and drawers, then sat on the edge of her bed to remove her shoes and stockings.

Muriel tugged open the dresser drawer that had been closed to her for far too long. The sight of the navy-blue swimming suit brought a momentary rush of joy before thoughts of Fletcher banished everything but urgency. She yanked the masculine bathing costume from the drawer, gathering the one-piece knitted wool garment in her hands. She stepped into the attached drawers that reached nearly to her knees then wiggled and tugged to get the short-sleeved tunic over her hips. Stretching the wool up over her chest, she slid her arms into the sleeves then tied closed the small opening at the front. She knotted it twice to ensure it didn't come open while she swam. After throwing a loose-fitting housedress over the ensemble, she shoved her feet into the special ankle-high bathing shoes her da insisted she wear to protect her from the shells and stones that lined the sea floor. The thin leather soles wouldn't hold up long to regular use, but she didn't want to take the time to change her shoes once she reached the shore. Besides, she had Zane's carriage to take her most of the way.

She needed to take her hair down and fashion it into a tight plait for swimming, but she'd do that on the way. Every minute saved increased her chances of reaching Fletcher before the deadline. So she grabbed her hairbrush and a ribbon then ran outside.

"To the Beach Hotel, Eddie," she called as she yanked open the carriage door. "And use the west side entrance."

"Yes, miss."

As soon as she clicked the door shut, he set the horses in motion. Muriel tore the pins from her hair with a ruthlessness that left her scalp stinging, then yanked her brush through her tresses until the tangles pulled free.

The carriage bumped over ruts and teetered around corners, sliding Muriel about on the seat and making fashioning a plait tight enough for swimming quite a challenge. Thankful to have a task to focus on that kept the worry at bay, she worked the braid over her left shoulder then fastened the end with a dark blue ribbon.

Once finished, Muriel peered out the lowered carriage window into a dusk rapidly transitioning into night.

Merciful Father, please keep Fletcher safe. She bit her lip. *It's me own fault he's in this mess. So if you deem a price needs to be paid, let me be the one to pay it.*

The salty tang of the sea filtered in through the open window, a smell that had always stirred her heart with cheer. Her mouth set in a determined line as the ocean's aroma settled into her bones. Tonight she swam not for pleasure but for purpose. Doubts niggled, reminding her that she hadn't swum since Zane's accident, and that had been no significant distance. Without her regular exercise routine, would she tire before she reached the boat?

Grant me the endurance and speed I need to save Fletcher. Freshen me muscles and stretch me lungs 'till I be fit fer the journey. I need ye, Lord. Relyin' on me own strength is what tied me to Mrs. Underhill in the first place. I'll not be makin' that same mistake again.

A hymn filtered through her mind at that moment, deepening her prayer.

I need Thee, O I need Thee;
ev'ry hour I need Thee;
O bless me now, my Savior,
I come to Thee.

The Beach Hotel loomed ahead, and Muriel's chest began to throb. Alana must be frightened out of her mind. How Muriel dreaded telling her sister why her son was in danger, but there was no time for tender-footin' around with long explanations. Muriel would just have to spit out the truth and take whatever stinging lashes Alana flung. Her heart could bear the cuts as long as her arms and legs remained whole.

When the carriage rolled to a halt, Muriel climbed down without assistance and marched toward the door that led to Alana and Liam's personal quarters. Bracing herself as if she were about to swim through a swarm of jellyfish, she reached for the door handle and let herself inside.

"Liam? Is that you?" Alana rushed from the girls' room carrying eighteen-month-old Colleen clutched to her chest. Four-year-old Shannon trailed behind. "Did ye find . . . Muriel?" Tears sprang to her sister's eyes as she rushed forward. "Did Da send ye? Praise be! I was about to lose me mind with the waitin'. Fletcher went to pay a call on Laraline Seward and didn't make it home fer supper. Liam went after him, but he's been gone fer over an hour. Somethin's happened to me boy. I know it." Her words broke off on a quiet sob as she reached for Muriel's hand.

Muriel took it and squeezed, her heart brimming with sorrow and sympathy. "I know where he is, Alana. And I aim to get him back fer ye."

Tension speared through Alana's fingers a moment before she tugged her hand free. "What do ye mean, ye know where he is?"

Regret tore a hole through Muriel's chest. "Mrs. Underhill hired smugglers to take him in order to force me hand. She's an evil woman desperate to get what she wants. So desperate, she'll use a wee one as leverage."

Alana paled and stumbled backward. She reached a trembling hand down to cup Shannon's head where the girl had buried her face in her mam's skirt. "Fletcher's been taken by smugglers? God help us." Color suddenly rushed to Alana's waxy cheeks. She advanced on Muriel like an avenging angel. "I told ye not to get involved with that woman! But ye always have to do things yer own way, don't ye? Never thinkin' of the trouble it might bring to others. Now my babe is in the hand of smugglers because of ye! Get out o' me house! Out!"

Muriel bore up under the accusations, knowing her sister's fear for Fletcher fueled the barbed shouts, yet tears still pooled in her eyes. Nevertheless, she held firm.

"Alana, ye have every right to yer anger, but getting to Fletcher is more important than flailing me hide right now. He's on a boat anchored offshore. I'm gonna swim out to him under the cover of twilight while Zane meets with Mrs. Underhill. If I can get to him before eight-thirty, there's a good chance I can rescue him before she can signal the smugglers. Even if Zane hands over the real ledger, I don't trust her to keep her word about not harmin' Fletcher. He'll be safer with me."

"In the water?" Alana's voice rose in pitch. "Are ye mad? We need to alert the city police. Have her arrested."

"Fer what? She doesn't have Fletcher. He's out on a boat. We've got no proof that she ordered the kidnapping outside of her maid's say-so, and ye know how the serving class is treated. No one will believe Vanessa over her well-connected mistress. Fer all we know, Mrs. Underhill has the constable in her pocket, too. The woman seems to have blackmailing tentacles stretching across the entire island. Besides, we've no time. I'll barely have time to swim out to the schooner once I spot it."

"Ye don't even know where it is?" Alana reached for the bench of the hall tree positioned near the front door and lowered herself onto the seat. "Saints above."

"I know 'tis west o' the hotel. Zane'll meet Mrs. Underhill in the dunes, and the boat will be near enough to signal." Muriel strode past her sister and turned into the kitchen. "Do ye still keep yer keys in the top drawer?"

She yanked open the nearest cabinet and found what she sought. Brass keys jangled as she clasped their ring and pulled it from the drawer. She spun back toward the hall only to find that her niece had followed her and stood in the doorway.

"Shannon, fetch yer da's spyglass fer me, would ye?"

The little girl stared at Muriel with wide eyes then turned toward Alana. "Ma?"

"'Tis all right, Shannon. Do as yer auntie says." Alana rose from the bench. Holding Colleen tight against her chest, she approached Muriel and took her husband's ring of hotel keys. "The center dome is the highest point of the hotel. 'Twill give ye the best view of the Gulf." She held out a short, stubby key. "This 'un will get you into the attic space beneath the dome. There's dormer windows facing each direction, so ye can scout west as well as south. Take the service stairway at the back."

Muriel grabbed the key. "Thank ye." She met her sister's worried gaze. "I'll get him back, Alana. I swear it."

Something deeper than fear entered Alana's eyes as her desperate grip closed around Muriel's hand. "I know ye love him nearly as much as I do, Muri, but I beg ye not to do anythin' foolish. I couldn't bear to lose two pieces of me family in one night."

Muriel blinked back tears and nodded. After clearing her throat, she tipped her head toward the door. "There's a carriage outside. The driver's name is Eddie. Tell him ye're me sister. Bring out some towels and a set of dry clothes for Fletcher. I'll meet ye there when I get down from the dome."

Shannon returned and held out the small, telescoping spyglass Liam kept with his collection of nautical tools.

Muriel smiled and bent down to accept it. "Thank ye, dear heart." She straightened and returned her attention to her sister. "Zane is lookin' fer Da and Liam. If they miss each other, tell Da to row out west of the anchored schooner. When I get Fletcher, the currents will pull us that direction. We'll look for his light and head for the boat."

Alana gave a sharp nod, renewed energy evident in her straight posture. "I'll have the hotel's caretaker ready the water taxi."

"Good. That'll save time." The hotel's Whitehall rowboat would be fast, especially with Da at the oars.

Muriel took the keys and made her way up to the fourth floor of the hotel. Hurrying up three flights of stairs winded but didn't tire her. Too much urgency flowed through her muscles to let a few stairs slow her down. It took a minute to wind her way through the odd collection of items stored in the hotel attic, but after banging her shin on an iron bedstead turned on its side, she made it to the round window that overlooked the Gulf.

She polished the glass with her sleeve then peered out into the sea, angling her line of sight to the west as she searched for a mast. A shadowy shape caught her eye, but the fading light played tricks on her vision. Muriel pulled the collapsed spyglass from her skirt pocket and extended it to its maximum length. It took a few attempts to locate the ship through the spyglass, but once she did, her heart gave a triumphant thump. A schooner with sails snugged down. A dark line trailed down the bow—likely the anchor cable. She scanned the rest of the area and found no other ships. She had her target.

"I'm comin', Fletcher."

Muriel darted back through the attic and down the stairs. Finding Alana at the carriage, she handed off the keys then directed Eddie to take her as far west into the dunes as the carriage could go. The undeveloped area of the island boasted no roads and only a few rutted paths, so he wouldn't be able to take her the entire way, but any distance would help.

"I found the boat," she told Alana. "Looks to be less than a mile offshore. Once I get past the breakers, I should be able to reach the vessel in thirty minutes or so."

Alana pulled a watch from her skirt pocket. "'Tis twenty to eight now."

"I'll make it." It'd be tighter than she'd hoped with the time required to travel into the dunes, but she'd make it work. She had to.

Alana touched her shoulder. "I know ye will." She pulled Muriel into a one-arm hug, squishing wee Colleen between them.

Forgiveness flowed in that embrace, and Muriel drank it in, drawing strength from it.

"Take care, Muri," Alana said as she released her hold. "I love ye."

Muriel blinked back the mist forming in her eyes. "I love ye, too."

Alana gave Muriel a little push toward the carriage's open door. "Now go get me boy."

Eddie took the horses farther into the dunes than Muriel expected. He risked miring the wheels in the sand but seemed to realize that getting to the shore was more important than getting home afterward.

"Sorry, miss. The carriage is too heavy to go farther." He climbed down from the seat and looked at her as if waiting for more instructions.

She handed him the spyglass. "See that ship there?" She pointed at the schooner anchored slightly to the west of their position.

Eddie turned to face the sea and held the glass to his eye. "Yes. That where they're holdin' the boy?"

"Aye. Keep watch on the boat. Ye might also turn that spyglass on the dunes. See if ye spot Zane and an older woman. That'd be Mrs. Underhill. Any witness ye can bear against her would be helpful. Oh, and if ye see a large man with a flowin' white beard comin' through here, tell him ye're with me. Might spare ye some trouble." She winked at him. "That'll be me da. He can be a tad intimidatin' when he's riled."

Eddie swallowed. "I'll keep that in mind."

Muriel smiled then headed for the shore.

Eddie jogged after her. "Miss! Wait! Where are you going? It'll be dark soon. It's not safe."

Sweet man. Muriel slowed long enough to look over her shoulder. "Don't fret, Eddie. I'm just goin' fer a swim."

"A . . . swim?" His horror-stricken eyes stirred laughter in her chest as she turned and resumed her hurried trek over the sandy dunes to the shore.

Let him be scandalized. She had a nephew to fetch.

Once she hit the wet sand, she spurred herself into a jog, running parallel with the sea to cover the most ground possible before she entered the water. When she deemed her position close enough, she looked around for a place to leave her clothes. Spotting a large piece of sun-dried driftwood far enough from the waves to avoid being taken by the tide, she hurried to it, pulled off her dress, and draped the garment over the log.

Feeling exposed without her cove, Muriel ran toward the water and immediately waded out until she stood waist-deep in the Gulf. She eyed the schooner in the distance and took a series of slow, deep breaths. She timed the rolling waves, feeling the ocean's rhythm.

Don't swim too fast. Ye don't want to burn out before ye get there. Controlled strokes. Steady pace.

Her heart had been in a constant, yet interrupted, state of prayer since she left Zane's house, but she took a moment to focus her thoughts heavenward.

I've felt ye with me, Lord. Showin' me a path to Fletcher. Be with me now. Give me strength, a calm spirit, and clarity of mind. I can't do this without ye.

As a low wave rolled in, she dove headfirst and stroked underwater to get past the first line of waves. Came up for air, then dove again until she made it past the breaker line. The water was cooler in the evening than during her daytime swims, but the surface had soaked up enough summer heat during the day to keep her shivers at bay.

Once past the breakers, she came up for air and sighted the ship. Time for the most important swim of her life.

Chapter 25

By the time Zane saw Muriel off in the family carriage, most of the guests had scattered into their own conveyances to make their way home after the fiasco of rampant rodents. Mother had taken up residence on the fainting couch in the main parlor while Catherine Trimble sat dutifully at her side, patting her hand and assuring her that her reputation as a hostess was not utterly ruined.

"There you are." Max scuttled up to him, a teasing grin stretching his face. "I haven't had this much fun in ages. I think all musicales should end in a ferret finale."

Zane kept walking, scanning the room for Grandpa Clem. "Ferrets?" he asked absently.

"Yeah. I nearly caught one of the things before it bit my thumb and ran under Mrs. Underhill's skirts." Max kept pace with him. "That woman has a stronger constitution than I expected. She didn't let out a single squeal. Just swept out of the room with that furball clinging to her garters as if nothing were amiss."

"Everything's amiss," Zane muttered as he pushed through the door that led to the dining room.

"What?" Max's voice lost its jocularity, but Zane paid him little heed since he'd found Grandpa Clem, elbow deep in the almond macarons.

His grandfather waggled his eyebrows. "I thought I better guard the food from those wily critters." When Zane failed to smile, his own expression sobered. "What's wrong, son?"

He'd not told his grandpa much about Muriel's agreement with Mrs. Underhill since it wasn't his secret to tell, but Grandpa Clem had been at the dinner where everything came to a head with his father, so he'd probably filled in some of the blanks himself.

Mindful of Max's presence, Zane kept the details to a minimum. "Muriel's nephew has been abducted."

"What?" Max's vocabulary seemed to have shrunk to that single word, though his volume had increased rather dramatically.

Zane shot him a warning look, and Max covered his mouth with his hand.

"I don't have time to go into the details. I need help searching for Muriel's father and brother-in-law. She thinks they'll likely be scouring the rail yards and wharves for the boy."

Grandpa Clem nodded. "That's where most young men get taken and pressed into service on outbound ships. How old is he?"

"Only ten."

Grandpa Clem shook his head. "Lord, have mercy."

"I pray he will," Zane said. "Muriel's gone after him."

"On her own?" Grandpa Clem's eyebrows arched in shock.

Zane knew what his grandpa was thinking. What kind of man let his woman go after smugglers on her own?

The desperate kind.

"She has a lead on the boat and plans to swim out to where it's anchored while I make the exchange with the villain responsible for the abduction."

Max groped for the wall. "Whoa. What exchange? I feel like I came into the theatre during the third act and have no idea what's going on."

Zane clapped him on the shoulder. "You don't need to get involved, Max. It's likely dangerous. I'm sure your mother would prefer you take her home."

He straightened away from the wall, a scowl on his face. "Our driver can see Mama home. I'm not about to abandon my best friend in his time of need." He waved off the rebuttal that Zane tried to give. "You can explain things to me later. Just tell me what I can do to help."

The tension radiating through Zane's neck eased a bit, and he slapped his friend's back. "I can use more eyes searching for Muriel's kin."

"You got it."

Thank you, Lord.

"Grandpa Clem and I have both met them, so we'll split up. You and Grandpa Clem take the rail yard, and I'll search the wharves with my father."

Grandpa Clem's eyebrows shot up again. "Horace is comin'?"

Zane's mouth tightened. "Reluctantly, but yes, he's coming."

"'Bout time that boy of mine did somethin' worthwhile," Grandpa Clem muttered beneath his breath.

"We need to hurry." Zane headed for the door. "If they're going to help Muriel, we need to find them before eight o'clock."

Grandpa Clem checked his watch. "Best take the horses, then. Max can borrow your mama's mare."

Zane nodded. "Father should be heading to the stables now."

"I'll make our excuses to our mothers and meet you there," Max said before dipping out of the room.

Grandpa Clem's gaze narrowed. "Think I'll grab my old revolver. Best to be prepared so the worst don't get the upper hand."

A shiver ran over Zane's skin. Bullets were the last thing this night needed, but he wasn't so naïve as to assume the other side would act with honor. He gave his grandpa a nod and headed to the stables.

The search took less time than Zane expected. It seemed Patrick Quinn had mobilized his entire crew along the docks. Dozens of men were out looking for Fletcher, and they all pointed Zane in the same direction—Labadies Wharf. Smaller, darker, farther west. More likely to boast criminal types after dark. A place no father or grandfather would ever wish to hunt for their child.

As Zane came around a warehouse, he spotted a large, well-muscled man with flowing white hair holding a thin man with a bottle in his hand up against the wall of a cargo shed. The thin man's feet dangled at least a foot above the dock.

"Mr. Quinn!" Zane nudged his mount into a trot and left his father by the warehouse. The horse's hooves made hollow-sounding clops on the timber beams extending over the bay.

Patrick Quinn turned toward Zane, his expression frightful. "He heard a pair of smugglers talkin' 'bout me grandson. I need to jar his memories loose."

Zane dismounted and touched the man's wide shoulder. "Muriel knows where Fletcher is. She's going after him now."

"Alone?" He roared the word and tossed the inebriated sailor to the side then spun to face Zane, grabbing him by the arms. "Ye let her go after smugglers alone?" The force of his grip felt as if he might snap Zane's arms like twigs.

"She needs me to meet Mrs. Underhill," Zane ground out. "I'm to keep the woman busy so Muriel can swim out to the smuggler's ship anchored offshore, west of the hotel. Muriel sent me to find you so you could row out to meet her. She intends to rescue Fletcher, but she needs our help."

All at once, the pressure on Zane's arms released and blood began flowing into his forearms and fingers again.

"The smugglers are on the other side of the island?" Quinn's tortured gaze matched the tightness in Zane's heart.

"Yes." Zane held out his reins. "Take my horse. I'll ride double with my father. If Liam was searching the train yard, Grandpa Clem should have found him by now and given him the news. I'll do everything I can to stall Mrs. Underhill and buy you time to help Muriel."

Quinn took the reins and pierced Zane with a deep look. "Ye love her, don't ye?"

"I do. And it's killing me that she's putting herself in danger. But she's the stronger swimmer. And I wouldn't want her facing Mrs. Underhill and her hired thugs anyway. She's safer in the water." Zane swallowed hard. "She blames herself for Fletcher's kidnapping. I worry she'll take risks to rescue him. Get to her fast, sir. Keep her safe."

"Only the Lord can keep that one safe," her father said, fondness softening his features for a moment. "But the Almighty gave me these arms fer a reason, and I aim to use 'em."

He placed his foot in the stirrup and hauled himself into the saddle with an awkwardness that proved he was more at home on the water than on a horse, but the determined set of his mouth ensured no animal would get the best of him this night.

"Watch yer back, Erickson," he said. "If that woman would steal a child, she'll not hesitate to send ye to the undertaker."

Zane nodded, well aware of the danger that awaited him.

"I see the viper brought a couple friends." Zane's father's voice sounded as if it had been squeezed from a lemon. "Seems my despisal of the woman has not been misplaced. I still can't believe she actually arranged that child's abduction."

Zane lowered the spyglass he'd borrowed from Eddie after finding the carriage parked in the dunes. No matter how hard he squinted through the lens, he couldn't see Muriel anywhere in the water. He could see the boat well enough, even in the rapidly fading light, but the darkness of twilight hid all evidence of a slender swimmer making her way across the surface of the waves.

He prayed she was still on the surface. The sea was calm, but the same darkness that hid her hid other dangers.

Don't go down that road. Trust her to know her abilities. Trust God to watch over her. And her father.

Zane might not have spotted Muriel, but he *had* spotted the white planking of a large rowboat hitting the water west of the hotel. Patrick Quinn and Liam Doherty were on their way to assist. Two fathers rowing to save their children. They would make it. They had to.

And he had to deal with Mrs. Underhill. God help him.

"Did you hear me, Zane?" His father rounded the back of the carriage and smacked Zane's arm. "She's here."

"I know." His pulse had kicked from a jog into a full-blown sprint when the distant jangling of harness had met his ears a moment ago.

He lifted the spyglass to his eye again and aimed it inland. Octavia Underhill strolled across the dunes. A pair of rough-looking fellows assisted her, one at each elbow. The men also carried lanterns. Smugglers' lanterns. The type used to signal ships from shore.

Heaven help me. What do I know of clandestine meetings and bargaining with men of the criminal class? I'm an architect's apprentice, for pity's sake.

But there'd be no drawing himself out of this situation. Geometric calculations and ruled edges carried no weight with those who operated outside the lines of morality. Yet Muriel was counting on him. What if he failed her?

"Bury those thoughts, son." His father's clipped voice carried no derision, only instruction. "Doubts are deadly with this crowd. If they sense your fear, your feelings of inadequacy, they'll go for the jugular."

Zane lowered the spyglass and turned to his father, the tightness in his gut loosening just a little.

Horace Erickson lifted his chin and held his son's gaze with a penetrating stare. "Hold yourself as if you hold all the cards. As if Octavia and her minions are the ones in need of *your* approval. *You* are in control, and they are lucky you even agreed to this meet."

"I don't think I can."

Father narrowed his eyes. "Of course you can. You're an Erickson." He sighed. "Look, Zane. I know you don't approve of my business practices, and to be honest, after seeing all the ramifications of this journal debacle, I'm starting to question a few things myself. But you've got to trust me. I know how that Underhill woman thinks. How she operates. Perception of power is everything. She's desperate. Use that against her. Plus, she doesn't know about the stunt your woman is pulling. That means *you* have the upper hand. Don't give it away by letting her smell your fear."

As much as Zane hated to admit it, his father might be right. He certainly had experience dealing with power-hungry businessmen and crafty cotton buyers and coming out on top. "I guess I can pretend to be you."

Father chuckled and slapped Zane's back. "That's the spirit."

Zane checked his watch. Three minutes 'til the designated meeting time. He snapped the lid closed and tucked the timepiece into his trouser pocket then extended his palm toward his father. "I'll take the journal now. It's time for me to keep my appointment."

Father quirked a sly grin. "Not a chance, son. I'm going with you."

A protest rose to Zane's lips, but then he saw it. A flash of fear in his old man's eyes. For his son or his reputation? As cynical as his opinion of his father had turned lately, Zane knew in his heart that at this moment, his sire cared more for his son than his business. If there was to be any hope of salvaging their relationship moving forward, he couldn't push him away now.

So he nodded, handed the spyglass to Eddie, then headed off across the dunes, his father at his side.

Chapter 26

Octavia smiled as the two Erickson men approached. Her stomach had lurched slightly when she'd first identified Horace Erickson's features from several yards away in the dying light. Dealing with an inexperienced pup would've been far easier than scrapping with a full-grown bulldog with all his teeth and a battle-tested stubbornness. But the fact that Horace was here told her something very important—he cared more about his son than about keeping her ledger. So what if he'd bested her once before? She outnumbered the Ericksons three to two, and both of her accomplices carried weapons. Horace didn't strike her as the type to be proficient with guns. Money and position were his weapons of choice. Neither of which would do him much good out here on the dunes.

"Horace," she purred. "I'm surprised to see you. My business is with your son."

The man raised a brow. "Your business became my business the moment you planted that female imposter in my son's life and attempted to turn him against me. I told you what you had to do to earn your precious journal back, yet you insisted on playing games. You gambled and lost, my dear. Time to end the charade."

The jackal. Depict her as the villain, would he? Well, two could paint with that brush.

Narrowing her gaze, she took a step forward. "I find it quite ironic that you accuse me of playing games, sir, when we both know that you are the master of cheating the system. You come to my house under false pretenses, lie to me about paying off your wife's account, bribe my butler into betraying me, then steal *my* belongings. *You* are the one who set this series of events in motion, Horace. Until you interfered, I was simply a businesswoman using my social connections to form advantageous marriages."

The younger Erickson winced a bit at her recounting. So he *didn't* know the full story. Well, she was happy to expose his father's duplicity. She'd already recognized cracks in their relationship. Creating a few more could only help her cause.

"Let's not whitewash your business practices, Octavia. You deal in blackmail, pure and simple."

"Nonsense." She turned to Zane. "Men like your father are too small-minded to admit that a woman can possess just as much business acumen as any of the gents hobnobbing at the Lodge. If a man operates in the gray areas of what is legal and ethical, he's considered shrewd. A woman, however, is considered a schemer. Just look at your father." She gestured to Horace with a flourish. "He actively manipulates the cotton market, making himself and his cronies richer while stealing money from hardworking farmers." The edge of Zane's mouth tightened. Excellent. She batted her eyes with manufactured innocence. "Wasn't your grandfather a cotton farmer? I can't imagine he'd be too happy to learn of his son's machinations. And just think of your poor mother's shame if the story made it into the papers. The Erickson name is so respected in these parts."

Oh, the boy was riled. Just look at the tension radiating through him. He'd gone utterly rigid at the news of his father's unethical dealings. How delightful. Octavia swallowed a cackle.

Dirk Grossman, one of the men she'd hired for this evening's work, cleared his throat. "Night's a-fallin', ma'am. Best be gettin' on with your business."

Instead of snapping at the underling for interrupting her, as he deserved, Octavia pasted a smile on her face and waved her hands as if to clear the air.

"Quite right, Mr. Grossman. As much as I'm enjoying our little tête-à-tête, we have a transaction to conduct." She held her palm out to Horace. "My journal, Mr. Erickson."

Zane stepped forward, jostling her hand. "Not until Fletcher Doherty is returned to us. Have him brought ashore. We won't return the journal until we see that he is unharmed."

The pup had teeth after all.

Well, so did she. "You're in no position to make demands." She gave him her most disdainful glare. "Is he, boys?"

On cue, two pistols cocked. Such a lovely sound. The sound of power. So nice that her hirelings' reputations for being adept at coercion had not been exaggerated.

Horace raised his hands. "Hold on, now," he said. "No need for violence."

The coward.

A laugh escaped her. She couldn't help it. "There is if it speeds your compliance." She scoured all amusement from her voice. "Now hand over my journal."

Motion to her left drew her gaze to Zane as he reached for his coat pocket. "I'll retrieve it if you tell your men to hold their fire."

"Zane, no." An actual wobble modulated Horace's tone.

He was afraid. Afraid that if his son gave up their leverage, Dirk and Gunther would rid her of the evidence of this encounter. Which they would. Couldn't have them carrying tales back to town, after all. That little guttersnipe Muriel might make a stink, but a few rumors of a gold-digging young woman seeking revenge after being rejected by the man she'd targeted should blacken her name sufficiently. Octavia could even arrange for the police to find the murder weapon in the young lady's home. It would be easy enough to plant.

Zane ignored his father, however. Kept his gaze locked on Octavia as he worked his jaw and waited.

"Very well," she said. "Hold your fire, gentlemen. Let him retrieve my property."

He reached into his pocket and pulled out the journal. Octavia's pulse leapt at the sight of the familiar brown leather.

"What are you doing?" Horace rasped.

"She's won, Pops," Zane said. "This game of horseshoes is over. We got close, but she scored the ringer."

She *had* won. And they'd soon learn there'd be no second place.

"I'm not letting you forfeit just yet." Horace pulled something from inside his coat. Another journal.

Wait. Octavia looked from one to the other. Which one was the right one? The poor lighting made it impossible to tell.

She edged toward Horace. Logic dictated he'd have the real one.

"Now!" Zane yelled the word, and all at once, both journals flew through the air.

Octavia gasped and moved to chase the book Horace threw. Horace lunged forward and tackled her directly into Gunther.

She screamed and flailed until Gunther tossed her aside. That's when she spotted Dirk writhing in the sand with Zane Erickson atop him throwing a punch to the smuggler's jaw.

Dirk roared and bucked. He'd make quick work of the pup, she had no doubt, but she had bigger things to worry about at the moment.

"Signal the boat," she cried, not caring which man carried out her order. "Signal the boat!"

All she'd done so far was ask a man to return her personal property. She could talk her way out of that. Dirk and Gunther would sail away with the tide, leaving nothing beyond the Ericksons' word that any abduction had taken place. No proof. As long as the boy was gone.

She crawled through the sand and beach grasses as the men fought behind her. Gunther had dropped both his gun and his lantern when Horace felled him. Seizing the lantern, Octavia pushed to her feet and climbed to the top of the dune nearest her. A dull thumping sound had her glancing over her shoulder. A third man on a horse approached. The sand beneath her feet shifted as if it were falling through a nearly empty hourglass. Turning back toward the sea, she held the lantern aloft and slid back the metal shutter to expose the light. Moving the shutter back and forth, she flashed the prearranged signal.

Boat in sight, Muriel pushed through the last few yards of water to reach the hull. She pressed her palm against the wooden planks at the waterline, and relief coursed through her. She'd made it! But getting here was only half the battle. Her muscles ached from the exertion, but energy thrummed through her as her attention immediately shifted to the next stage—getting onboard without being seen.

Gentle waves slapped against the hull. Rigging creaked. Edges of the canvas sail not fully secured flapped lightly in the breeze. All sounds that could mask her arrival.

Feeling along the edge of the boat, she made her way to the rear. The crew would be looking for a signal from shore, so they would likely be in the bow of the boat. No one should be prowling the stern.

Recalling all the times as a child when she'd swum around her da's work skiff and climbed in using the rudder as a stepstool, she grabbed hold of the vertical sternpost that served as the backbone of the schooner and sunk her legs down into the water to feel for the rudder. The schooner was a good deal larger than her da's skiff, but she was a good deal taller now than she'd been as a young sprite. She found the upper curve of the rudder blade with one foot and shifted until she secured a steady position. After bringing in her second foot, she pushed upward slowly, so as not to make a splash. Her shoulders rose out of the water, and her hands adjusted to a higher position on the sternpost. Keeping her weight inward, she clung to the hull as she straightened. Her hips and waist hit the night air, sending shivers through her as the water released its grip. She reached for the rail edge and peeked into the boat before straightening to her full height. Coils of rope sat on the decking nearby, along with a barrel and a pile of rigging she couldn't identify. She spied no sailors, however. Praise the Lord.

Muriel stretched to her full height, looped her right arm over the railing then strained to hook her leg over as well. Gritting her teeth, she leveraged her hips upward until she rolled over the side and onto the deck. She lay atop the coiled rope she'd fallen upon for several seconds, listening intently for any clue that she'd been spotted.

A pair of male voices echoed from the front of the ship, about fifty feet away. She prayed no others were wandering about. Darting glances from side-to-side, she bent into a low crouch and used the aft deckhouse cabin as cover while she picked her way on silent feet to the middle of the ship, searching for Fletcher.

Deep shadows covered the schooner, hiding her, but also hiding her nephew.

"Fletcher," she whispered. "Where are ye?"

A muffled sound accompanied by the scrape of what could be a shoe on wood echoed a few feet ahead. Feeling exposed, she scurried forward and darted behind the main mast near the center of the schooner. When she peeked around the large beam, familiar wide eyes stared back at her above a dark-colored gag.

Fletcher!

After casting a quick glance ahead to ensure she'd drawn no one's notice, she rounded the mast, held a finger to her lips, then tugged the gag down past Fletcher's chin.

"Muriel? Ye gotta help me. They mean to throw me overboard while I'm trussed like a chicken." He sat on the deck, his back against the mast, his wrists bound in front of him, and a rope binding his ankles.

To ensure he couldn't swim. The vile pirates!

"I'll not let anythin' happen to ye. I promise." But she needed to find something sharp to cut his ropes. "I saw a hatchet hangin' from a peg on the cabin wall. I'll go fetch it."

Thank heaven for sailors needing to be ready to cut fouled rigging. She snatched the small axe from the wall and made her way back to Fletcher. She couldn't afford to draw attention with the loud thump brought on by a chop, and his ankles were too close together anyway. So she knelt in front of her nephew, stretched his feet an inch or two apart, and started sawing through the hemp.

"Did you see that?" One of the men from the front of the boat had turned, his voice carrying in their direction.

Muriel froze, her heart pounding.

"I'm gonna check on the boy."

"Wait," the second man said. "I think I see something on shore. Is that the signal?"

Muriel sawed with a frenzy. "If I can't get ye free in time, remember to float." She glanced up and met Fletcher's gaze. "Don't panic when ye hit the water. Just be still and float. I'll get to ye. I promise."

Fletcher pressed his lips together and nodded.

"Yep. That's the signal. I'll fetch the boy."

Muriel jumped to her feet and held the hatchet up. "Spread yer feet," she urged.

The frayed rope created slack, and Fletcher pulled a couple inches. Muriel bent down and chopped through the rope. His legs sprang apart.

"Hey!" Thundering footsteps.

Muriel yanked the hatchet from the decking and looked desperately for another rope to chop. Fletcher's hands were tied in front of him. She couldn't get to that rope without injuring him. Her only chance was to sever the leash tied around the mast above his head.

The deck vibrated as the smuggler bore down on them.

She swung at the rope where it was lashed to the mast. The hemp snapped. Fletcher scrambled to his feet.

His hands were still bound, but they had no time.

"Jump!" she yelled as she yanked the hatchet free.

She turned and threw it at the advancing smuggler then ran for the side of the ship. The sound of the hatchet clanking harmlessly to the ground echoed behind her. Fletcher struggled to get over the railing, so she hoisted him by the elbow and tossed him over. She moved to follow him, but a meaty hand grabbed her ankle.

"Not so fa—"

Desperate to get to Fletcher before he drowned, she acted on instinct. Twisting to face her attacker and ignoring the resulting pain in her knee, she used the railing for leverage and smashed her other foot into his face. The instant his fingers loosened, she flipped backward over the side of the boat to be swallowed by the sea.

243

Chapter 27

A fist slammed into Zane's jaw, jerking his head to the side and grinding his skull into the sand. His advantage over the smuggler had been short lived, and now he couldn't help but wonder if *he* would be short-lived. The burly fellow had managed to get a leg between them and flipped Zane onto his back with a bone-jarring thud then pounced and pummeled with the skill of a man accustomed to brawls. Unlike Zane, whose only recent brawling experience was with a catboat mast. He'd lost that one, too.

He fought back as best he could, blocking blows with arms bent over his face and looking for an opening. Only . . . no opening came. Only blow after blow.

Until a gunshot cracked the night air.

"Get off my grandson, or the next bullet is goin' straight through your skull."

Grandpa Clem?

Grossman ceased punching and raised his hands. "Easy, old man. Your kid jumped me. I was just defendin' myself."

The moment the blows stopped, Zane scuttled backward across the sand like a soft-shell crab desperate to escape a snapping seagull. Gaze still locked on the smuggler as he retreated, Zane caught the glance the man darted to the left. A dark object lay in the white sand. Zane bounded to his feet and snatched up the gun.

"You all right, Zane?"

"Yep." He hurt all over, actually, but that didn't matter. Muriel was waging a war of her own, and he needed to finish here and find her.

"Good." Grandpa Clem stayed atop his horse, spouting orders like a general. "Go give your daddy a hand." He twisted his head toward their driver. "Eddie! Get in here and tie this feller up. I sent Max after the police. They'll be here soon."

At that news, Grossman pivoted toward the beach and started running. Grandpa Clem nudged his horse into action and cut him off like a professional cowboy. Assured Grossman would be no trouble, Zane aimed his pilfered weapon at the second fellow. Grandpa Clem had taken him hunting and taught him to shoot, but he'd never aimed at a person before.

"Let him go!"

Neither man seemed to hear him. They were too busy fighting over something. As they tussled, Zane spotted the pistol clamped between them. His gut clenched. If it went off . . .

Zane lowered the hammer of his own revolver, tucked it into his belt, then hurried forward. He had to stop them somehow. Before someone ended up dead.

What could he do to stop the fight without endangering his father? The two were so embroiled, it was hard to tell where one stopped and the other started.

Help me.

A gust of wind kicked sand into Zane's face, making him jerk his head and rub at his watering eyes.

Not helpful, Lord.

Or was it?

Zane's pulse leapt as he dropped to the ground and scooped up a double handful of sand. Then just as the two men rolled toward him, he flung the sand into both their faces. They flinched and sputtered. Zane pounced. He kicked the smuggler in the head and snatched the pistol from the two men's loosened grips. The smuggler cursed and flailed, but Zane dodged easily.

The sand wouldn't blind him for long, though. So as the man struggled to his feet, Zane circled behind him and felled him with a boot to the back of his knee. He cried out as he tumbled forward, and Zane shoved his shoulders, ensuring he sprawled face-first in the sand. Zane quickly straddled him and kept him pinned with a knee to his back.

"Eddie! I need a binding."

His driver hurried over, a strip of leather in his hand that looked like one of the horse's lead lines. Together, they wrestled the smuggler's hands behind his back and secured his wrists with a wrap job to rival any sailor's rigging.

"Water!" His father's cry brought Zane's head around. "My eyes are burning."

Grandpa Clem reached him before Zane could. "Here, son. Let me." He brushed away Horace's sand-covered hands that were likely making things worse, and gently rubbed the grains from his face with a handkerchief. "The tears God gave you will wash the sand away in a minute."

Zane left the two bound smugglers in Eddie's care and hobbled over to where his father crouched, wishing there was something he could do.

A shadowy movement to his right brought his head around, just in time to see Octavia Underhill dart close enough to grab something out of the sand.

The journal.

"Hey!" Zane shot to his feet.

Octavia bolted. But sand dunes weren't made for older women in long, fashionable skirts and impractical shoes. She'd barely run ten yards toward her carriage before her ankle twisted and she went down. Zane caught up to her with ease.

Taking hold of her elbow, he hoisted her to her feet.

"Let go of me, you fiend!"

He tightened his grip. "Not a chance. You have a date with the police."

Her white hair had come loose from its pins during her mad dash around the dunes, and it hung about her face in wild disarray. Her hard eyes glittered as she jutted her chin. "You pathetic whelp. You have nothing on me. By the time I get done with the police, they'll be arresting your father and giving me a medal."

"Not after they see this." Father limped over to them holding up the other journal. He turned it toward her and fanned the pages. Pages filled with ink. He grinned. "You grabbed the decoy, Octavia. I'll enjoy roasting you on your own spit. Extortion. Kidnapping. Attempted murder."

She shot daggers at him. "The only thing I'm guilty of is running a successful business. *You* extorted *me*, stole from me, and fabricated false charges against me."

Zane's jaw clenched. "They aren't false, and you know it. You abducted a ten-year-old boy and used him as a pawn to get what you wanted."

"I would never harm a child. The very idea is absurd."

Sickened by her callous deceit and self-serving twisting of the truth, Zane leaned his face close to hers and jabbed some *untwisted* words her way. "*You* brought us out here. *You* hired thugs to intimidate and likely kill us."

"I hired protection, nothing more sinister than that."

"*You* signaled the boat," Zane countered. "Everything was on *your* orders."

"That's preposterous! You have no proof of any of these outlandish claims!"

"That's where you're wrong." Zane smiled. "We have the boy." Her eyes widened ever so slightly. "Did you not wonder why Muriel sent me to hand over the journal?" Octavia swallowed, her gaze darting from Zane to his father and back again. "She's a swimmer. A world-class swimmer. One who could reach a boat anchored offshore with no one ever noticing. By now, she's rescued her nephew and is rendezvousing with her father. We've got proof, Mrs. Underhill. Enough to keep you locked up for years."

"That's . . . that's impossible." She tossed her hair back as if to show her unconcern, but her face glowed pale in the twilight.

"Time will tell." Zane released his hold on her and turned his face toward the sea, praying his bold words proved true.

"Where'd they go? Do you see 'em?"

"They went over the port side."

Muriel ignored the calls of the sailors above, her focus locked on a struggling Fletcher kicking in the water about ten feet from her.

I told ye to float, Fletcher, not swim.

But the boy was terrified. Of course he'd try to get away. He swam on his back, his bound arms on his chest as his legs kicked. He remained afloat for the moment, but he'd tire quickly, especially with his shoes and wet clothes adding weight. Even now, his face bobbed barely above the surface.

"There! I see the boy."

"What about the girl?"

"Don't matter. Our job was the boy. I'm taking a shot."

Muriel immediately did a surface dive, but instead of folding cleanly into the water, she angled her body to slap against the surface and kicked her legs to spray water into the boat. She prayed the commotion would distract the smugglers and perhaps even draw their fire. She'd be a harder target to hit. Once under water, she stroked long and hard, determined to get to her nephew. A muffled *clap* sounded behind her, and the water shuddered with the impact of a bullet. Something stung her calf, making her flinch and draw her knees to her chest. But only for a heartbeat. Fletcher was sinking.

Uncoiling, Muriel stroked and lunged through the water to get to Fletcher. Another shot echoed from above, more muted, as if from a greater distance. And this time, no pressure-filled vibrations punched the water around her. Kicking toward the surface, she came up beneath her nephew, and at the last minute, rolled over so that his back bumped against her chest. Hugging him to her with one arm, she propelled them toward the surface with the other. As their heads broke through, they both sucked in air.

"I got ye, Fletcher. Rest easy, lad."

Tension drained from his body as he relaxed against her. Until another shot cracked through the night air. He flinched. As did Muriel.

"'Tis all right," she murmured. "It came from behind us." Turning them in the water, she spotted a bright light aimed at the smuggler's ship. "Someone's helpin' us."

"Revenue cutters!" One of the smugglers shouted.

"Weigh anchor!" the other answered. "If they stop to help the boy, we can outrun 'em. Make sail!"

Thanking the Lord that the smugglers were no longer shooting, she swam Fletcher toward the light as the ship behind them groaned and clanked with the retrieval of the anchor. A beam of light from a reflector lantern swept the sea slowly. Then she heard it. Her name. In Da's deep bellow. Praise the Lord!

"Here!" She stopped swimming and waved her free arm above the waves. "We're here!"

The light panned over, making her squint against the brightness. Fletcher added his shouts to hers.

Oars slapped water as Liam's voice called out, "I'm comin', Fletcher. Hold on, son."

"Da!" Fletcher's voice choked on a relieved sob, and Muriel's heart throbbed in response.

Minutes later, Da had the rowboat positioned alongside them. Liam hauled his son out of the water and hugged the boy to his chest.

"Praise be. I thought I'd lost ye."

"Muriel saved me, Da. She saved me." Tears from both Fletcher *and* Liam overtook his explanation.

Muriel held onto the side of the boat with one hand as she watched the reunion, her soul so overflowing with gratitude, she couldn't think past that moment.

"Give me yer hand, dear heart."

Da. Muriel turned her attention away from Fletcher to find her father leaning toward her, arm extended. His eyes glistened with moisture and his white hair glowed in the moonlight. Her own guardian angel. She reached for him. He clasped her arm and drew her from the water and straight into his arms.

"Ye're safe now." His arms encircled her, forming a cocoon against the night air as the heat from his body warmed her skin. He cupped her head to his chest and leaned his jaw against her wet hair. The comforting beat of his heart echoed in her ear. "Thank the Lord Almighty. Ye both are safe."

"Muriel, yer bleedin'!" Fletcher pointed at Muriel's leg.

"Am I?" She leaned away from her da and examined her left calf. A stream of blood trickled down her leg. And because she was looking at it, the ornery thing decided to start stingin' again. She winced. "Ah. One of the bullets nicked me. It's not deep. I'll be fine."

"What ye'll be is wrapped in that blanket and sittin' down so I can row ye to shore and have a doctor tend ye." Da gave a look that forbade her to argue, not that she planned to do so. His plan suited her just fine. Except for one part.

"Aye. But I need to see Zane before the doctor, Da." Liam draped a blanket over her shoulders from behind, and she clasped it closed around her as shivers set her to trembling. "I need to know he's all right."

"Fine, but ye'll bandage that leg and put on a proper dress first."

Muriel smiled at his gruffness. "Yes, Da."

After setting aside the rifle he'd used to scare off the smugglers, he resumed his seat at the oars, turned the Whitehall toward shore, and rowed for home. His gaze returned to her again and again, as if to reassure himself that she was indeed whole and well.

Her own gaze darted to the shore, her heart longing for the same reassurance regarding the fate of another man she loved.

Chapter 28

Liam directed the reflector light toward the dunes as they rowed parallel to the breakers. Since Fletcher had dry clothes waiting for him in Zane's carriage and Muriel's dress had been stashed nearby on the beach, Liam searched for the conveyance on shore.

"There!" Muriel pointed to a shadowy lump that looked somewhat carriage-like.

When her brother-in-law focused the beam that direction, her heart gave a leap. Another shadowy form materialized nearby. A man-shaped form with arms waving above his head.

Zane? She grabbed the edge of the boat and leaned toward shore, half-tempted to jump overboard and start swimming.

Lord, please let it be Zane. Or someone else who can tell me he's all right. I need him to be all right.

"This is the place, Da. Take us in."

He maneuvered the oars to aim the bow at the shore then timed his rows to move with the waves. The instant Muriel felt the scrape of the sand on the hull, she scrambled over the side of the boat and waded to the shore, not caring that the hem of her blanket dragged through the water.

"Muriel." Da's voice grated a warning. "Ye'll get yer bandage wet."

Da had cut away the tail of his shirt for her to wrap around her calf. Her leg throbbed a bit, but it wasn't going to slow her down.

"I'll be grand, Da," she called over her shoulder, ignoring the sting of the saltwater splashing against the scratches and scrapes she'd accumulated during her adventure. "We can sort it out when we get to the hotel."

"Don't forget yer dress," he growled.

"I haven't." She'd already spotted the piece of driftwood that held her clothes a few yards to the left.

Leaving the men to drag the boat ashore, she ran to where she'd left her dress, limping only slightly. She dropped her blanket, hastily pulled the housedress over her head, and did up the front buttons. Her still-moist swimming costume clung to her skin in a particularly clammy fashion, but she had bigger things to worry about than damp fabric and a lack of proper undergarments. She needed to find Zane.

Zane ran toward the beach, the search lantern his beacon. He'd watched that bobbing light for the last thirty minutes as it had grown brighter and closer, praying with every breath that it signaled Muriel's return.

Max had shown up ten minutes ago with the police. The officers had taken the smugglers into custody with no qualms, but they'd been hesitant to arrest Mrs. Underhill, thanks to her damselesque dramatics. Weeping. Protesting her innocence. Claiming to be the victim. Until she went a tad too far and implied that the smugglers had brought her out to the dunes against her will. Grossman and his companion couldn't turn on her fast enough. And when Father handed over the journal and explained that the true victim was a ten-year-old boy, the officers changed their tune. They did ask that the boy and his parents come to the station to make a statement on the morrow, but that was to be expected.

What hadn't been expected was how easily Father surrendered the journal. Or the apology he offered Zane privately for contributing to the entire fiasco by stealing it in the first place. Facing his own mortality had apparently made an impact on him—one Zane hoped would set him on a more faithful path moving forward.

As Zane crested the last dune between him and the beach, he angled his approach to try to see around the lantern shining so brightly from the bow. A man stood ankle-deep in the surf to the right of the boat, arms outstretched to a blanket-wrapped boy standing on one of the seats.

Fletcher. Thank heaven, the boy was safe.

He hurried forward, craning his neck as he sought a glimpse of Muriel. Patrick Quinn was lifting the oars from the oarlocks and bringing them inboard, his wide shoulders blocking Zane's view of the rear of the boat. Was she back there? Injured? He stumbled on the wet sand, a pain jabbing his chest. Was she . . . dead?

"Muriel?" His voice cracked. He cleared his throat and asked again. Louder. "Where's Muriel?

Her father stood in the boat and turned. Zane searched behind him, but the rear of the craft was empty.

Dear God. Had she been lost at sea? He reached for the bow of the boat, his legs suddenly incapable of holding him up without assistance.

"Is she . . . ?" He couldn't say it.

"Easy, lad." Patrick Quinn hopped down from the boat and clapped a hand to Zane's shoulder. "She's fine. A little banged up, but in better shape than ye." His gaze scoured Zane's face. "Been practicin' yer boxin' skills, have ye?"

"What few I possess." He started to turn, intending to search the beach for Muriel, but her father grabbed hold of Zane's shoulders and forced him to face east.

"Hold up, lad." Mr. Quinn's gaze lifted over Zane's head. "She ain't decent yet."

Zane twisted his neck, his need to verify she was alive overriding his sense of propriety.

Mr. Quinn sighed. "All right. Guess she's close enough." He released Zane's shoulders.

Zane immediately turned, spotted her a few dozen yards up the beach, and called her name as his heart surged to life. "Muriel!"

With reinvigorated legs, he took off at a run.

Her head came up at his call, and her face lit. "Zane? Oh, Zane!" She jumped over the discarded blanket at her feet and hurried toward him, her gait uneven in the sand.

As they closed the distance between them, Zane's heart inflated to a painful degree. She was here. Alive. And smiling at him as if his heart wasn't the only one pulling apart at the seams.

Her steps slowed as she drew near, but his didn't. He scooped her straight off the ground and into his arms. Her laughter rang into the night with such joyful purity that his eyes misted.

"Thank God," he murmured as he drank in her beautiful face, her smile, her glistening eyes. "Thank God you're all right."

"I am now." She cupped his face, her smile dimming as she took in his swollen eye and bruised countenance. "I feared fer ye somethin' awful. And now I see it wasn't fer nothin'." She wagged her head. "Yer poor face. I'm so sorry I put ye in harm's way."

He lowered her feet to the sand but spread his palms across her back to keep her snug against his chest. "I put *myself* in harm's way. And I'd do it again. With no regrets. I love you, Muriel."

Tears pooled in her eyes, but her smile beamed brighter than the search lantern. "Ah, Zane. I love ye, too. With me whole heart." She flung her arms about him and hugged him tight, pressing her face against his chest.

His heart sighed at her words, releasing some of the pent-up pressure and leaking warmth throughout his entire body. He ran his hands in circles over her back then moved to caress her arms. A shiver coursed through her. From the night air? Or from his touch? Heaven knew his entire body hummed at her nearness.

She leaned back slightly and lifted her chin, her hazel eyes gleaming and . . . inviting. An invitation he wasn't about to refuse, not when he longed for her like a sailor longed for the sea. Yet she deserved care. Delicacy. Especially after all she'd been through this night. His fingers trembled as he stroked the edge of her face. Her lashes fluttered closed, and her breath hitched softly. His gut tightened as he lowered his mouth to hers, his own breathing growing ragged. Their lips pressed together gently at first, tentative and testing. He'd never kissed a woman before, yet love had a way of guiding and inspiring. Instinct, desire, and deep-seated gratitude urged him to deepen the connection, to celebrate the lives that could have been lost but weren't, the love that could have been destroyed but was instead intensified into something that would endure forever.

He cupped her head and slanted his mouth over hers, letting her feel a bit of his hunger, his ardency. Her hands found their way to his shoulders and clung to him as if she needed his support. She had it. For all of their days.

She raised up on her toes and kissed him back with equal zest, and his pulse ratcheted. She tasted of sea salt and sweetness. A heady mix. A sigh-like moan vibrated at the back of his throat, and he knew he better stop before the fog of desire completely obliterated his sense.

He pulled back and watched her lashes slowly lift. A smile blossomed across her face at the same time, a smile he'd never tire of seeing. Especially when formed with kiss-plumped lips.

How he loved her. Her courage. Her big heart. Her dedication to family. He wanted to spend the next fifty years listening to her sing and hearing her profess her love in that charming Irish lilt.

"Will you marry me, Muriel?" The words popped out without any forethought, but he had no desire to take them back. "I know our future has more questions than certainties at the moment, but I'm sure that I want to spend it with you at my side. As my wife. If you'll have me."

He hadn't thought it possible for her smile to widen any farther, but she proved him wrong. "Of course I'll marry ye. There's nothin' in the world I want more."

Zane pressed a kiss to her forehead then clasped her to his chest and marveled at how the worst night of his life had turned into the best.

"All right, you two." Patrick Quinn called out from a distance not all that far away.

Zane's face heated as he relaxed his hold on Muriel.

"Liam and Fletcher are packed away in the carriage. We're ready to set off. Alana's surely worried herself into a tizzy by now."

Muriel released her hold on Zane's shoulders and stepped to the side. "We're comin', Da."

It didn't take long to bundle Muriel up into the carriage next to her father. Liam planned to send a crew from the hotel to fetch the rowboat in the morning, so they left it moored on the beach above the tide line. Thankfully, the police had carted the smugglers and Mrs. Underhill away in her carriage already, so Muriel didn't have to face the dreadful woman. Zane, Grandpa Clem, Max, and Zane's father rode their mounts behind the carriage as Eddie drove, ready to lend a hand should the wheels become mired in the sand. Liam invited everyone to stop at the hotel for coffee and medical attention before heading out, and Max insisted on being informed of all the happenings, since he'd missed the action while fetching the law.

Alana Doherty must have been watching for them at the window, for the moment the carriage turned down the service drive, she darted from her home, leaving the door wide open. She said nothing, just waited, the edge of her apron crushed in her fisted hands.

As soon as Eddie halted the team, the carriage door swung open, and Liam scrambled out.

"Liam?" Alana walked toward her husband with short, shaky steps. "Is he . . ."

Liam reached back inside, plucked his son from the seat, and set him on the ground.

"Mammy!" Fletcher ran for her, arms wide.

Alana burst into tears. "Fletcher!" She stumbled forward then hunkered down so she could wrap her arms around her son. "Ah, me boy. Me sweet, beautiful boy." Her sobs were the most joyful sound Zane had ever heard. "Ye're home. Thank God, ye're home."

Zane dismounted and handed his reins to Grandpa Clem so he could be near Muriel. Her father helped her out of the carriage, and she hobbled toward her sister. Zane frowned. Had she hurt her leg? He'd been too wrapped up in her being alive to notice if she'd been favoring it.

Fletcher, like most boys, could only take so much motherly affection before squirming. As Alana rose to her feet, she kept a hand on his shoulder but allowed him to twist and face the rest of the group.

"She saved me, Mammy." Fletcher grinned in Muriel's direction. "Auntie Muriel saved me."

Alana stepped toward her sister and clasped Muriel's hand. A look passed between them that carried both gratitude and forgiveness. "She most certainly did. A right hero, she is." Alana lifted her gaze to the men standing around. "As are all of ye. I can't thank ye enough for what ye did tonight. For bringing me boy home." She released Muriel's hand and gestured for the group to follow her. "Come on inside with ye, then. I've got coffee and tea and a big pot o' soup if any of ye are hungry."

Muriel skittered away to Alana's room to change into some dry undergarments and one of her sister's dresses. Da stopped in long enough to tend her wound and wrap it in a proper bandage before returning to the front room and all the regaling going on. Zane had promised not to tell what'd happened with Mrs. Underhill until Muriel returned, but she still felt the need to hurry to make sure she didn't miss anything. She toweled her hair, brushed it, and rebraided it, too tired to bother with pinning it up, even though she'd be in mixed company. They were all family now. Or would be soon. The thought brought a smile to her heart as she left the room and found her way to the parlor.

Da had baby Colleen crooked in one arm and Shannon snugged upon his knee, the young girl's eyes wide as she took in the boisterous group of strangers in her home. Alana sat in the rocker, Fletcher in her lap, his feet dangling nearly to the floor. Muriel imagined her sister was glad for shortage of seating since it provided the perfect excuse for holding her son a little longer.

A small space remained open beside Zane on the sofa, and Muriel slipped in next to him, her heart doing a little flip as he smiled. Never had she been more thankful for close quarters. The warmth emanating from his side flowed into her, welcoming her to lean against him. Which she did. Gladly.

It took more than an hour for all the tales to be told. Smugglers with guns, fistfights, daring grandpas on horseback. Long swims, daring rescues, and ordinary men pretending to be revenue cutters. Heroism was applauded and laughter released tensions.

After hearing everything that happened on the beach while she'd been in the water, Muriel sent several prayers heavenward in thanks. God must have been watching over them. Nothing else could explain their success.

Max leaned forward in his chair and aimed a wagging head at Zane and his father, who sat next to him on the other side of the sofa. "I can't believe the two of you rushed a pair of gun-toting smugglers. How could you have possibly known what Zane was planning, Mr. Erickson?"

Zane's father chuckled. It was the first time she could recall hearing a happy sound come from the man. "He called me *Pops*."

"Pops?" Grandpa Clem's brow crinkled. "That's what *you* call *me*. And only when you're exasperated."

"Exactly." Mr. Erickson patted Zane's knee. "My boy's got a keen wit. Thinks quickly under pressure. Just like his old man."

"Like his grandpa, you mean," Grandpa Clem teased.

Zane shared a private smile with Muriel, and her insides warmed even more.

"As soon as he called me Pops," Zane's father continued, "I knew something was up. Then he mentioned playing horseshoes, and all I could think about was the way Pops taught Zane to arch those shoes high and far when we visited the old farm. It was just the distraction we needed to get the upper hand."

Grandpa Clem winked at Muriel. "Always knew those lessons would come in handy one day."

Da rose from his chair, one sleeping granddaughter in each arm. "I'm gonna put these wee ones to bed."

"I'll give ye a hand," Liam said.

Grandpa Clem stood next. "We oughta be gettin' back, too. Sophie will want to know what's happened." He shot his son a telling glance.

Horace Erickson let out a breath. "If she's even speaking to me. She practically skewered me when I told her I was leaving after the party fiasco."

Grandpa Clem clapped Horace's shoulder. "Nothing some honesty and a heartfelt apology can't fix."

"We'll see." He turned back to look at Zane. "You coming, son?"

"In a minute."

Max followed the older Ericksons outside, and Alana accompanied Fletcher to his room after giving Muriel a secret, sisterly grin.

Zane helped Muriel to her feet, walked with her to the door, then pivoted to face the recently emptied parlor. "Something miraculous happened tonight."

"I know," Muriel said, slipping her hand into his. "God's hand must've been upon us for everythin' to work out as it did."

Zane turned to her. "I'm not just talking about the rescue. Something's changed with my father. The caustic shell that constantly surrounds him has cracked. I don't know if it was the realization that he might not survive the night or that I might not, but he's different."

"I noticed, too." She leaned her head against his shoulder. "I pray the Lord will continue softenin' his heart, Zane. Fer ye and yer ma." She raised her head to look at him. "Perhaps there need not be a rift between ye after all."

"I'd like that." His jaw tightened. "I still aim to make my own way financially, but watching your father with Alana's kids made me think about the children *we* might have someday. I'd like them to know *both* their grandfathers."

"They will." Her mind instantly filled with images of Zane snuggling their babe in his arms. His proud smile and love-filled eyes. "If I've learned anything from these last weeks, 'tis that God can redeem anythin'. Even yer da."

Zane lifted their clasped hands and placed a kiss on her knuckles. "You're a generous woman, Muriel Quinn."

"'Tis easy to be generous when I have everything I ever wanted. You."

His smile tipped up at one corner, and his gaze heated in a way that brought memories of their kiss scorching back through her memory. Was it too soon to ask for another? Apparently not, for his head was even now bending toward hers. Shivers danced along her nape as she tilted her head back to ease his approach.

"You're stuck with me now." The low rumble of his voice vibrated through her like a low chord from an organ that one felt more than heard. "I'm going to be part of your world forever."

Sounded like heaven. And she would have told him so had the touch of his lips not stolen every last thought from her brain.

All save one. Her happily ever after had just begun.

Author Note

As a historical author, I love incorporating real pieces of history into my fictional works. When I decided to give a western spin to *The Little Mermaid*, I knew at once that I would set the story in Galveston, since that is one of the few places in Texas with significant ties to the sea. However, I did *not* expect to find an Ursula waiting for me there.

While studying an old map of the Galveston area, I discovered the Ursuline Academy for young ladies on Avenue N, also known as St. Ursula's by the Sea. According to the *Galveston Monthly*, The Order of St. Ursula was instituted in the 1500s for the purpose of educating girls and caring for the ill and needy. The Ursuline Order of nuns became the first female educators to cross the Atlantic and settle in North America. The Convent of New Orleans, founded in 1727, was considered a pioneering establishment for the education of youth in what would become the United States.

In 1847, a group of seven nuns left New Orleans and traveled across the Gulf of Mexico to Galveston to start a small convent there. They opened the first Catholic school for girls in Texas and soon gained a stellar reputation across the entire state. They expanded to accepting boarders and thrived despite being beset by fires, yellow fever, and civil war. Discovering this academy gave me goosebumps of the best kind. I knew I needed to incorporate the Ursuline Sisters into my story.

As I dug deeper into the research, I found records of a particular young nun who was buried in the Ursuline Academy cemetery in 1894. Sister Mary Vincent Niemeyer had been born in 1860 and would have been twenty-six at the time of my story. She seemed like the perfect gentle soul to befriend Muriel during her stay at the academy. Tragically, Sister Mary Vincent died in 1894, but I'm sure she made an impact on many young girls' lives, just as she did for Muriel in this story.

In 1891, the Ursuline nuns hired famed Galveston architect Nicholas J. Clayton to construct a larger building for their growing academy. Completed in 1895, it became one of the grandest examples of High Victorian Gothic architecture in the country. According to the Rosenberg Library Museum, the Ursuline Academy is considered Clayton's most impressive work. With its massive walls, towers, turrets, lofty roofs, and flying buttresses, it was a visual masterpiece. It even managed to withstand the devastating hurricane of 1900 and served as a refuge for an estimated 1,500 people who had lost their homes. Since my hero is an assistant architect to the great Nicholas Clayton, I like to imagine that Zane was part of the team that created such an amazing structural work of art.

About the Author

For those who love to smile as they read, bestselling author Karen Witemeyer offers warmhearted historical romance with a flair for humor, feisty heroines, and swoon-worthy Texas heroes. Voted #1 Readers' Favorite Christian Historical Author by *Family Fiction Magazine*, Karen is a multiple award-winning author and a firm believer in the power of happy endings. She is an avid cross-stitcher, tea drinker, and gospel hymn singer who makes her home in Abilene, Texas, with her heroic husband who vanquishes laundry dragons and dirty-dish villains whenever she's on deadline.

To learn more about Karen's books and to sign up for her free newsletter featuring special giveaways and behind-the-scenes information, visit her website at karenwitemeyer.com.

Review Request

If you enjoyed *Part of Your World,* please consider writing a quick review. Leaving a positive review is one of the best ways a reader can show their appreciation to the author. Reviews are also a gift to fellow readers as they search for stories they are likely to enjoy. Thank you!

Once Upon a Time in Texas Series

To Love a Beast – A beauty invades the home of a scarred recluse to save her family's bookbinding business, but more than books bind these two when a fearsome hunter attempts to write their ending.

Part of Your World – A young architect has no interest in the marriage his mother wishes to arrange—until the mysterious woman who saved his life reappears as a potential match. Will trusting this silent beauty endanger more than his heart?

More Texas Fairy Tales

Fairest of Heart – Beauty has been nothing but a curse to Penelope Snow, and this time it nearly kills her. Rescued by a Texas Ranger and seven retired drovers, she is given a chance at a fresh start. Too bad the honorable Ranger she fancies suspects her of being a jewel thief.

If the Boot Fits – What's a girl to do when the most interesting man at her matrimonial ball isn't one of the bachelors on her father's guest list? Hunt him down, of course, using the only clue at her disposal—the boot he left behind.

Cloaked in Beauty – A Pinkerton detective on a secret assignment. A missing heiress with a pet wolf. A dragon of a man hunting them all. Keeping her out of harm's way may be just as impossible as keeping her out of his heart. Little Red Riding Hood and Sleeping Beauty entwine for a romantic fairy tale adventure.